Paddington at Large

Paddington at Large

REVISED EDITION

by Michael Bond

with drawings by Peggy Fortnum

Houghton Mifflin Company
BOSTON

www.houghtonmifflinbooks.com

RNF ISBN 0-395-91294-6   PAP ISBN 0-618-19678-1
Library of Congress Catalog Card Number: 63-14525

Printed in the United States of America
QUM 10 9 8 7 6 5 4 3 2 1

Contents

Paddington
at Large

CHAPTER ONE

Paddington Breaks the Peace

"I KNOW I KEEP ON saying it," exclaimed Mrs. Brown as she placed an extremely large vegetable marrow on the kitchen scales, "but I'm sure Paddington must have been born with green paws. Have you seen this one? He's beaten his best by over half a pound."

"Hmm," said Mrs. Bird. "Well, I'll grant you one thing, green paws are better than idle ones, and at least gardening keeps him busy. We haven't had an upset for weeks now."

The Browns' housekeeper hastily touched wood as her eyes followed the progress of a small brown figure clad in a shapeless hat and an equally disreputable-looking duffle coat as it made its way down the garden path before disappearing into a potting shed behind the raspberry canes.

Mrs. Bird was never very happy about any of Paddington's activities that took him out of her sight for too long at a time, and Paddington's interest in gardening had lasted much too long for her peace of mind.

All the same, even Mrs. Bird had to admit that for some time past things had been remarkably peaceful at Number Thirty-two Windsor Gardens.

It had all started when Paddington arrived home from the market one day carrying a giant packet of assorted seeds, which he'd bought for the bargain price of tenpence. At the time it had seemed such good value for money that Mr. Brown had been only too pleased to let him have a corner of the garden, and for several evenings afterwards Paddington had been kept very busy counting the seeds, making sure none of them were stuck to his paws as he sorted them into separate piles in order of size before he planted them.

Only Mrs. Bird had been full of forebodings. "Woe betide the man in the shop if they don't all come up,"

she remarked when she noticed that the seed packet had been marked down. "I can see there'll be some nasty scenes."

But despite Mrs. Bird's misgivings, within a week or two the first of the seeds began to sprout, and in no time at all Paddington's Patch was such a blaze of color it soon put the rest of the garden to shame.

From that moment on Paddington spent most of his spare time out-of-doors, and when he began supplying the household with vegetables as well as flowers, everyone had to agree with Mrs. Brown that he must have been born with green paws.

"I must say the garden is a picture at the moment," she continued, as she turned to help Mrs. Bird with the washing-up. "Even Mr. Curry called out this morning and said how nice it looks."

"If I know Mr. Curry," said Mrs. Bird darkly, "he was probably after something. He doesn't say things like that without a very good reason."

"Perhaps he wants some cheap vegetables," said Mrs. Brown. "You know how mean he is."

"He'll be lucky with that bear," replied Mrs. Bird. "And quite right too, seeing the state his own garden's in. It's a disgrace."

Mr. Curry's lawn was very overgrown with weeds, and Mrs. Bird held strong views about the way the seeds blew over the fence whenever there was a strong wind.

"Funnily enough," said Mrs. Brown, "I think he was just getting his lawnmower out when he spoke to me. Perhaps he's going to make a start."

"Not before time," snorted Mrs. Bird. "And I shall believe it when I see it. He's much more likely to give the job to some poor boy looking for odd jobs than do it himself."

Mrs. Bird gave the washing-up several nasty jabs

with her sponge, but if she had been able to see Mr. Curry as she spoke she would probably have snorted even louder, for at that moment the Browns' neighbor was peering over the fence at Paddington with a very cunning expression on his face.

Unaware of the danger he was in, Paddington was sitting on a patch of ground behind the raspberry canes, busy with his accounts. Mrs. Bird paid him strict market rates for all his vegetables, and although she kept a careful note of all his sales, Paddington wasn't the sort of bear to take chances and he liked to make doubly sure by keeping his own record. He had just finished entering the words *marrows-verry large-one* in his notebook when Mr. Curry's voice shattered the morning air.

"Bear!" he roared. "What are you doing, bear? Resting on your laurels?"

Paddington jumped up in alarm at the sound of Mr. Curry's voice. "Oh, no, Mr. Curry," he exclaimed when he had recovered from the shock. "I was only sitting on my begonias."

Mr. Curry looked at him suspiciously, but Paddington returned his gaze very earnestly.

The cunning expression returned to Mr. Curry's face as he looked round Paddington's garden. "I'm glad to see you're all up to date, bear," he said. "I was wondering if you would like to earn yourself some extra bun money if you've a few moments to spare."

"Er... yes, please, Mr. Curry," said Paddington doubtfully. From past experience he felt sure that any job for which Mr. Curry was willing to pay good bun money would take far longer than a few minutes, but he was much too polite to say so.

"Are you any good at climbing trees?" asked Mr. Curry.

"Oh, yes," said Paddington importantly. "Bears are good at climbing things."

"That's good," said Mr. Curry, waving a hand in the direction of a large tree near his house. "In that case, perhaps you'd like to pick a few apples for me."

"Thank you very much, Mr. Curry," said Paddington, looking most surprised at the thought of being paid just for picking a few apples.

"Oh, and while you're up there," said Mr. Curry casually, "there's a dangerous branch that needs cutting down. I'm afraid I have to go out, but it's very kind of you to offer, bear. Very kind indeed."

Before Paddington had time to open his mouth, Mr. Curry produced a saw and a length of rope from behind his back and pointed to the branch in question.

"Now don't forget," he said as he handed the bits and pieces over the fence, "you tie one end of this rope to the branch, then you loop the other end over the top of the tree and tie it back down to something heavy on the ground. That's most important—otherwise the branch might fall down too quickly and cause a nasty accident. I don't want to come back and find any broken windows.

"And if you finish before I get back," continued Mr. Curry, "perhaps you'd like to cut my grass. I've put the mower all ready, and if you make a good job of it there might even be some more money."

With that Mr. Curry turned on his heels and disappeared in the direction of the house, leaving Paddington anxiously holding the rope between his paws. He felt sure he hadn't said anything to Mr. Curry about cutting down his branches, let alone uttered a word about mowing the grass. But the Browns' neighbor had a way of twisting things so that other people were never quite sure what they had said.

If it had simply been a matter of cutting the grass, Paddington might have pretended that he'd got something stuck in his ear by mistake and hadn't heard properly. But as he studied Mr. Curry's tree he began to look more and more thoughtful.

A few moments later he jumped up and began hurrying around as he made his preparations. Paddington liked climbing trees, and he was also very keen on sawing. To be able to do both at the same time seemed a very good idea indeed, especially when it was in someone else's garden.

All the same, as he looked around for something heavy to tie the rope to, he soon decided that it was easier said than done. The nearest object was Mr. Curry's fence, and that was so rickety a piece of it came away in his paw when he tested it with one of his special knots.

In the end Paddington settled on Mr. Curry's lawn-mower, which looked much more solid, and after making a double knot round the handle to be on the safe side, he began to climb the apple tree, armed with the saw and a jar of his favorite marmalade.

Mr. Curry's tree was rather old and Paddington

didn't like the way it creaked, but at long last he settled himself near the branch that had to be cut down, and after making sure the other end of the rope was properly tied, he dipped his paw in the marmalade jar and got ready for the big moment.

Paddington was a great believer in marmalade. He'd often used it for all sorts of things besides eating, and now that he took a closer look at Mr. Curry's saw he felt sure it might come in very useful for greasing the blade in an emergency. There weren't many teeth left, but of those that were still intact most were rusty, and the rest stuck out at some very odd angles.

Taking a final look round to make sure everything was as it should be, Paddington gripped the saw with both paws, closed his eyes, and began jumping up and down as he pushed it back and forth across the branch.

In the past he'd usually found any kind of sawing hard work, but for once everything seemed to go smoothly. If anything, Mr. Curry's tree was in an even worse state than his saw, and within a few minutes of starting work there came a loud crack, followed almost immediately afterwards by a splintering noise as the branch broke away from the tree.

When the shaking stopped Paddington opened his eyes and peered down at the ground. To his delight the branch was lying almost exactly where he had planned it to be, and he felt very relieved as he scrambled back down the tree to view the result of his labors. It wasn't often that any jobs he did for Mr. Curry went right the first time, and he spent some moments sitting on the sawn-off branch with a pleased expression on his face while he got his breath back.

Turning his attention to the lawn, Paddington began to wish more than ever that he hadn't heard Mr. Curry's remark about cutting it. Apart from the fact that there seemed to be an awful lot, the grass itself was so long it came up almost to his knees, and even when he stood up it was a job to see where the lawn finished and the rest of the garden began.

It was as he looked round for the mower in order to make some kind of a start that Paddington received his first big shock of the day. For although there was a long trail leading down through the grass from the shed, and although there were two deep wheel marks to show where it had been left standing, Mr. Curry's lawnmower was no longer anywhere in sight.

Paddington's shocks never came singly, and as he nearly fell over backwards with surprise at the first one, he promptly received his second.

Rubbing his eyes, he peered upwards again in the hope that it had all been part of a bad dream, but everything was exactly as it had been a few seconds before. If anything, it was worse, for having rubbed his eyes he was able to make out even more clearly the awful fact that far from having disappeared into thin air, Mr. Curry's lawnmower was hanging as large as life from a branch high above his head.

Paddington tried pulling on the rope several times, but it was much too tight to budge, and after a few more halfhearted tugs he sat down again with his chin between his paws and a very disconsolate look on his face as he considered the matter.

Thinking it over, he couldn't for the life of him see a way out of the problem. In fact, the more he thought about it, the worse it seemed, because now that Mr. Curry's lawnmower was up the tree he couldn't even make amends by cutting the grass for him. Mr. Curry wasn't very understanding at the best of times, and from whatever angle Paddington looked at the tree, even he had to admit that it was one of the worst times he could remember.

*

"Paddington's very quiet this morning," said Mrs. Brown. "I hope he's all right."

"He was poking around in Mr. Brown's garage about an hour ago," said Mrs. Bird, "looking for some shears. But I haven't seen him since. If you ask me, there's something going on. I met him coming up the garden path just now with a wrench in his paw and he gave me a very guilty look."

"A wrench?" said Mrs. Brown. "What on earth does he want with a wrench in the garden?"

"I don't know," said Mrs. Bird grimly. "But I've a nasty feeling he's got one of his ideas coming on. I know the signs."

Almost before the words were out of Mrs. Bird's mouth there came a series of loud explosions from somewhere outside. "Gracious me!" she cried as she rushed to the French windows. "There's a lot of smoke behind the raspberry canes."

"And that looks like Paddington's hat," exclaimed Mrs. Brown as a shapeless-looking object suddenly began bobbing up and down like a jack-in-the-box. "Perhaps he's having a bonfire. He looks as if he's trodden on something hot."

"Hmm," said Mrs. Bird. "If that's a bonfire, I'm a Dutchman."

Mrs. Bird had had a great deal of practice at putting two and two together as far as Paddington was concerned, but before she could put her thoughts into words the banging became a roar and Paddington's hat, which had disappeared for a few seconds, suddenly shot up in the air, only to hurtle along behind the top of the canes at great speed.

Any doubts in Mrs. Bird's mind as to what was going on were quickly settled as Mr. Brown's power mower suddenly came into view at the end of the raspberry canes, carrying with it the familiar figure of Paddington as he held onto the handle with one paw and clutched at his hat with the other.

The mower hit Mr. Curry's fence with a loud crash and then disappeared again as quickly as it had come, leaving behind it a large hole and a cloud of blue smoke.

If Mrs. Brown and Mrs. Bird were astonished at the strange turn of events in the garden, Paddington was even more surprised. In fact, so many things had happened in such a short space of time he would have been hard put to explain matters even to himself.

Mr. Brown's power mower was old and rather large, and although Paddington had often watched from a safe distance when Mr. Brown started it up, he had never actually tried his paw at it himself.

It had all been much more difficult than he had expected, and after several false starts he had almost given up hope of ever getting it to go, when suddenly the engine had burst into life. One moment he'd been bending over it pulling levers and striking matches as he peered hopefully at the engine; the next moment there had been a loud explosion, and with no warning at all the mower had moved away of its own accord.

The next few minutes seemed like a particularly nasty nightmare. Paddington remembered going through Mr. Curry's fence, and he remembered going round the lawn several times as the mower gathered speed. He also remembered feeling very pleased that Mr. Curry had left his side gate open as he shot through the opening and out into the road, but after

that things became so confused he just shut his eyes
and hoped for the best.

There seemed to be a lot of shouting coming from
all sides, together with the sound of running feet.
Once or twice Paddington thought he recognized the
voices of Mrs. Brown and Mrs. Bird in the distance,
but when he opened his eyes it was only to see a large
policeman looming up ahead.

The policeman's eyes were bulging and he had his
hand up to stop the traffic. Paddington just had time
to raise his hat as he shot past and then he found
himself being whisked round a corner in the direction
of the Portobello market, with the sound of a heavy

pair of boots adding itself to the general hubbub.

He tried pulling on several of the levers, but the more he pulled, the faster he seemed to go, and in no time at all the noise of his pursuers became fainter and fainter.

It felt as if he had been running for hours when suddenly, for no apparent reason, the engine began to splutter and slow down. As the power mower came to a stop, Paddington opened one eye cautiously and found to his surprise that he was standing in the middle of the Portobello Road, only a few yards away from the antique shop belonging to his friend Mr. Gruber.

"Whatever's going on, Mr. Brown?" cried Mr. Gruber as he came running out of his shop and joined the group of street traders surrounding Paddington.

"I think I must have pulled the wrong lever by mistake, Mr. Gruber," said Paddington sadly.

"Good thing for you your hat fell over the carburetor," said one of the traders who knew Paddington by sight. "Otherwise there's no knowing where you'd have ended up. It must have stopped the air getting in."

"What!" exclaimed Paddington anxiously. "My hat's fallen over the carburetor?" Paddington's hat was an old and very rare one which had been given to him by his uncle shortly before he left Peru, and he felt very relieved when he saw that apart from a few extra oil stains there was no sign of damage.

"If I were you," said someone in the crowd, nodding in the direction of a group of people who had just entered the market, "I should make yourself scarce. The law's on its way."

With great presence of mind Mr. Gruber pushed the power mower onto the pavement by his shop. "Quick, Mr. Brown," he cried, pointing to the machine's hopper. "Jump in here!"

Mr. Gruber barely had time to cover Paddington with a sack and chalk "Today's Bargain" on the outside of the hopper before there was a commotion in the crowd and the policeman elbowed his way through.

"Well," he demanded, as he withdrew a notebook from his tunic pocket and surveyed Mr. Gruber, "where is he?"

"Where is he?" repeated Mr. Gruber innocently.

"The young bear that was seen driving a power mower down the Queen's Highway a moment ago," said the policeman ponderously. "Out of control he was, and heading this way."

"A young bear?" said Mr. Gruber, carefully placing himself between the policeman and Mr. Brown's mower. "*Driving a power mower*. What sort of bear?"

"Dressed in a duffle coat that's seen better days," replied the policeman. "And wearing a funny kind of hat. I've seen him around before."

Mr. Gruber looked about him. "I can't see anyone answering to that description," he said gravely.

The policeman stared long and hard at Mr. Gruber and then at the other traders, all of whom carefully avoided catching his eye.

"I'm going for a short walk," he said at last, with the suspicion of a twinkle in his eye. "And when I get back, if I see a certain 'bargain' still outside a certain person's shop, I shall make it my duty to look into the matter a bit further."

As the crowd parted to let the policeman through, Mr. Gruber mopped his brow. "That was a narrow squeak, Mr. Brown," he whispered. "I hope I did the right thing. Not knowing the facts, I didn't know quite what to say."

"That's all right, Mr. Gruber," said Paddington as he peered out from under the sack. "I'm not very sure of them myself."

Mr. Gruber and the other traders listened carefully while Paddington went through the morning's events for their benefit. It took him some time to relate all that had taken place, and when he'd finished, Mr. Gruber rubbed his chin thoughtfully.

"First things first, Mr. Brown," he said briskly as he

locked the door to his shop. "It sounds as though you'll need a hand getting Mr. Curry's lawnmower down from his tree before he gets home, so I think I'd better push you back to Windsor Gardens as quickly as possible. Unless, of course, you'd rather walk?"

Paddington sat up in the hopper for a moment while he considered the matter. "I think if you don't mind, Mr. Gruber," he announced gratefully as he pulled the sack back over his head, "I'd much rather ride."

Apart from not wishing to see Mr. Curry or the policeman again that morning, Paddington had a nasty feeling that Mrs. Brown and Mrs. Bird must be somewhere around, and he didn't want to delay matters any further by going all through his explanations once again before he'd had time to think them out properly.

In fact, all in all, Paddington was only too pleased to have the chance of a comfortable ride home in the dark and the safety of a hopper full of grass clippings, especially as he'd just discovered the remains of a marmalade sandwich that he'd fastened to the inside of his hat with a piece of Scotch tape for just such an emergency.

CHAPTER TWO

Mr. Gruber's Outing

MOST MORNINGS WHEN he wasn't busy in the garden, Paddington visited his friend Mr. Gruber, and the day after his adventure with the power mower he made his way in the direction of the Portobello Road even earlier than usual.

He was particularly anxious not to see Mr. Curry for a few days, and he agreed with Mrs. Bird when she said at breakfast that it was better to let sleeping dogs lie.

Not that Mr. Curry showed much sign of sleeping.

From quite an early hour he'd been on the prowl, alternately peering at the hole in his fence and glaring across at the Browns' house, and Paddington cast several anxious glances over his shoulder as he hurried down Windsor Gardens, pushing his shopping basket on wheels. He heaved a sigh of relief when he at last found himself safely inside Mr. Gruber's shop among all the familiar antiques and copper pots and pans.

Apart from a few grass clippings stuck to his fur, Paddington was none the worse for his adventure, and while Mr. Gruber made the cocoa for their elevenses he sat on the horsehair sofa at the back of the shop and sorted through the morning supply of buns.

Mr. Gruber chuckled as they went over the previous day's happenings together while they sipped their cocoa. "Hearing about other people's adventures always makes me restless, Mr. Brown," he said as he looked out of his window at the bright morning sun. "Particularly when it's a nice day. I've a good mind to shut up shop after lunch and take the afternoon off."

Mr. Gruber coughed. "I wonder if you would care to accompany me, Mr. Brown," he said. "We could go for a stroll in the park and look at some of the sights."

"Ooh, yes, please, Mr. Gruber," exclaimed Paddington. "I should like that very much." Paddington enjoyed going out with Mr. Gruber, for he knew a great deal about London and he always made things seem interesting.

"We could take Jonathan and Judy," said Mr. Gruber, "and make a picnic of it."

Mr. Gruber became more and more enthusiastic as he thought the matter over. "All work and no play never did anyone any good, Mr. Brown," he said. "And it's a long time since I had an outing."

With that he began to bustle round his shop tidying things up, and he even announced that he wouldn't be putting his knickknack table outside that day, which was most unusual, for Mr. Gruber always had a table on the pavement outside his shop laden with curios of all kinds at bargain prices.

While Mr. Gruber busied himself at the back of the shop, Paddington spent the time drawing a special notice in red ink to hang on the shop door while they were away. It said:

IMMPORTANT AN-OUNCEMENT
THIS SHOP WILL BE CLOSED FOR THE ANNULE
STAFF OUTING THIS AFTERNOON ! ! ! !

After underlining the words with the remains of the cocoa lumps, Paddington carefully wiped his paws and then waved goodbye to Mr. Gruber before hurrying off to finish the morning shopping.

When she heard the news of the forthcoming outing, Mrs. Bird quickly entered into the spirit of things and made a great pile of sandwiches—ham and two kinds of jam for Mr. Gruber, Jonathan, and Judy, and some special marmalade ones for Paddington.

These, together with a box of freshly made cookies and some bottles of lemonade, filled Jonathan's rucksack to the brim.

"Sooner Mr. Gruber than me," said Mrs. Bird after lunch as she watched the heavily laden party set off up the road, led by Mr. Gruber carrying a large guidebook and Paddington with his suitcase, opera glasses, and a pile of maps.

"Paddington did say they're going to the park, didn't he?" asked Mrs. Brown. "It looks rather as if they're off to the North Pole."

"Knowing Paddington," said Mrs. Bird darkly, "perhaps it's as well they're prepared for any emergency!"

In Mrs. Bird's experience, an outing with Paddington was more likely than not to end up in some kind of disaster, and she wasn't sorry to be out of the way for a change.

All the same, Mrs. Bird would have been hard put to find fault with the orderly procession that neared the park some while later, and even the policeman on duty nodded approvingly when Mr. Gruber signaled that they wanted to cross the road. He at once held up the traffic with one hand and touched his helmet with the other when Paddington raised his hat as they went by.

It had taken them quite a long time to reach the park, for there had been a great many shop windows to look in on the way, and Mr. Gruber had stopped

several times in order to point out some interesting sights he didn't want them to miss.

Although Paddington had been in a number of parks before, it was the first time in his life he had ever seen a really big one, and as Mr. Gruber led the way through the big iron gates he decided he was going to enjoy himself. Apart from the grass and trees there were fountains, swings, and deck chairs, and in the distance he could even see a lake shimmering in the afternoon sun. In fact there was so much to see he had to blink several times in order to make sure he was still in London.

Mr. Gruber beamed with pleasure at the look on Paddington's face. "It might be an idea to go and sit by the lake first of all, Mr. Brown," he said. "Then you can dip your paws in the water to cool off while we have our sandwiches."

"Thank you very much, Mr. Gruber," said Paddington gratefully. The hot pavements always made his feet tired, and being able to cool them and have a marmalade sandwich at the same time seemed a very good idea.

For the next few minutes Mr. Gruber's party was very quiet indeed, and the only sound apart from the distant roar of the traffic was an occasional splash as Paddington dipped his paws in the water and the clink of a marmalade jar as he made some extra sandwiches to be on the safe side.

When they had finished their picnic, Mr. Gruber led the way towards a small enclosure where the swings and slides were kept, and he stood back while Paddington, Jonathan, and Judy hurried inside to see what they could find. Paddington in particular was very keen on slides, and he was anxious to test a large one that he had seen from a distance.

It was when the excitement was at its height that Mr. Gruber suddenly cupped one hand to his ear and called for quiet.

"I do believe there's a band playing somewhere," he said.

Sure enough, as the others listened they could definitely hear strains of music floating across the park. It seemed to be coming from behind a clump of trees, and as Mr. Gruber led the way across the park it gradually got louder and louder.

Then, as they rounded a corner, another large enclosure came into view. At one end of it was a bandstand, and in front of that were rows and rows of seats filled with people listening to the music.

Mr. Gruber pointed excitedly at the bandstand. "We're in luck, Mr. Brown," he exclaimed. "It's the Guards!"

While Mr. Gruber went on to explain that the Guards were a very famous regiment of soldiers who kept watch over Buckingham Palace and other important places, Paddington peered through the fence at the men on the platform. They all wore brightly colored uniforms with very tall black hats made of fur, and their instruments were so highly polished they sparkled in the sun like balls of fire.

"It's a good many years since I went to a band concert in the park, Mr. Brown," said Mr. Gruber.

"I've *never* been to one, Mr. Gruber," said Paddington.

"That settles it then," replied Mr. Gruber. And as the tune came to an end and the audience applauded, he led the way to the entrance and asked for four ten-

penny tickets. They just managed to squeeze themselves into some seats near the back before the conductor, a very imposing man with a large mustache, raised his baton for the next piece.

Paddington settled himself comfortably in his seat. They had done so much walking that day he wasn't at all sorry to be able to sit down and rest his paws for a while, and he applauded dutifully and cheered several times when, with a flourish, the conductor at last brought the music to an end and turned to salute the audience.

Judy nudged Paddington. "You can see what they're going to play next," she whispered, pointing towards the bandstand. "It's written on that board up there."

Paddington took out his opera glasses and leaned out into the aisle as he peered at the board with interest. There were several items called "Selections" that he didn't immediately recognize. These were followed by a number of regimental marches, one of which had just been played. After that came another selection, from something called a "Surprise Symphony," which sounded very good value.

But it was as he peered at the last item that a strange expression suddenly came over Paddington's face. He breathed heavily on his glasses several times, polished them with a piece of rag that he got from his suitcase, and then looked through them again at the board.

"That's a selection from Schubert's Unfinished Symphony," explained Judy in a whisper as the music started up again.

"What!" exclaimed Paddington hotly as his worst suspicions were confirmed. "Mr. Gruber's paid tenpence each for our tickets and they haven't even finished it!"

"Schubert died a long time ago," whispered Judy, "and they never found the rest of it."

"Tenpence each!" exclaimed Paddington bitterly, not listening to Judy's words. "That's two buns worth!"

"Ssh!" said someone in the row behind.

Paddington sank back into his seat and spent the next few minutes giving the conductor some hard stares through his opera glasses.

Gradually, as the music reached a quiet passage, everyone closed their eyes and began to sink lower and lower in their seats, until within a matter of moments the only movement came from somewhere near the back of the audience as a small brown figure got up from its seat by the aisle and crept towards the exit.

Paddington felt very upset about the matter of the

Unfinished Symphony, particularly as it was Mr. Gruber's treat, and he was determined to investigate the matter.

" 'ere," said the man at the entrance. "If you goes out, you won't be allowed in again. It's against the rules and regulations."

Paddington raised his hat. "I'd like to see Mr. Schubert, please," he explained.

"Sherbet?" repeated the man. He cupped one hand to his ear. The band had reached a loud passage and it was difficult to hear what Paddington was saying. "You'd better try over there," he exclaimed, pointing to a small kiosk. "I believe they 'as some ice cream."

"Ice cream?" exclaimed Paddington, looking most surprised.

"That's right," said the man. "But you'll 'ave to be quick," he called as Paddington hurried across the grass with an anxious expression on his face. "Otherwise I shall have to charge you for another ticket."

The lady in the kiosk looked rather startled when Paddington tapped on the side. "Oh, dear," she said, as she peered over the counter. "One of them soldiers has dropped his busby."

"I'm not a busby!" exclaimed Paddington hotly. "I'm a bear and I've come to see Mr. Schubert."

"Mr. *Schu*bert?" repeated the lady, recovering from her shock. "I don't know anyone of that name, dear. There's a Bert what sees to the deck chairs, but it's his day off today."

She turned to another lady at the back. "Do you know a Mr. Schubert, Glad?" she queried. "There's a young bear gentleman asking after him."

"Sounds like one of them musicians," said the second lady doubtfully. "They usually 'as fancy names."

"He wrote a symphony," explained Paddington. "And he forgot to finish it."

"Oh, dear," said the first lady. "Well, if I were you, I'd go and wait under the bandstand. You're bound to catch them when they come off. There's a door at the back," she added helpfully. "If you wait in there, it'll save disturbing all the people in the audience."

After thanking the ladies for all their help, Paddington hurried back across the grass towards some steps that led down to a small door marked STRICTLY PRIVATE at the rear of the bandstand.

Paddington liked anything new, and he'd never been inside a bandstand before. It sounded most interesting and he was looking forward to investigating the matter.

The door opened easily when he put his paw against

it, but it was when he closed it behind him that he made the first of several nasty discoveries, for it shut with an ominous click, and try as he might, he couldn't pull it open again.

After poking at it for several minutes with an old broom handle which he found on the floor, Paddington groped around until he found an upturned box, and then he sat down in order to consider the matter.

Apart from the fact that it was dark inside the bandstand, it was also very dusty, and every time the band played a loud passage a shower of dust floated down and landed on his whiskers, making him sneeze. In fact, the more Paddington thought about things, the less he liked the look of them, and the less he liked the look of things, the more he thought something would have to be done.

*

"Oh, dear," groaned Judy. "I've never known such a bear for disappearing."

Mr. Gruber, Jonathan, and Judy had opened their eyes at the end of the piece of music only to discover that Paddington's chair was empty and he was nowhere in sight.

"He's left his cookies behind," said Jonathan, "so he can't have gone far."

Mr. Gruber looked worried. "They're just about to play the Surprise Symphony," he said. "I do hope he's back in time for that." Mr. Gruber knew how keen Paddington was on surprises, and he felt sure he would enjoy the music.

But before they had time to discuss the matter any further, the conductor brought the band to attention with a wave of his baton and quiet descended on the audience once again.

It was when the band had been playing for about five minutes that a puzzled look gradually came over Mr. Gruber's face. "It seems a very unusual version,"

he whispered to Jonathan and Judy. "I've never heard it played like this before."

Now that Mr. Gruber mentioned it, there did seem to be something odd about the music. Other people in the audience were beginning to notice it as well, and even the conductor was twirling his mustache with a worried expression on his face. It wasn't so much the way the music was being played as a strange thumping noise that seemed to be coming from the bandstand itself and also seemed to be getting louder every minute.

Several times the conductor glared at the man who was playing the drums, until at last, looking most upset, the man raised his sticks in the air to show that he had nothing to do with the matter.

At that moment an even stranger thing happened. One moment the conductor was standing in front of the band glaring at the musicians; the next moment there was a splintering noise, and before everyone's astonished gaze he appeared to rise several inches into the air before he toppled over, clutching at the rail behind him.

"Crikey!" exclaimed Jonathan as a loud sneeze broke the silence that followed. "I'd know that sneeze anywhere!"

Mr. Gruber, Jonathan, and Judy watched with

growing alarm as a board in the floor of the bandstand gradually rose higher and higher and after some more splintering noises a broom handle came into view and waved about in the air. A few seconds later the broom handle was followed by a familiar-looking hat and some even more familiar-looking whiskers.

"Excuse me," said Paddington, raising his hat politely to the conductor. "I'm looking for Mr. Schubert."

"Bears in my bandstand!" spluttered the conductor. "Thirty years I've been conducting and never once fallen off my podium, let alone been knocked off by a bear!"

Whatever else the conductor had been about to say was drowned in a burst of applause. First one person started to clap, then another, until finally the whole audience was on its feet applauding. Several people shouted "Bravo!" and a number of others echoed it with cries of "Encore!"

"They call it the Surprise Symphony," said a man sitting next to Mr. Gruber, "but I don't think I've ever been more surprised in my life than when that young bear came up through the floor."

"Very good value for tenpence," said someone else. "What will they think of next?"

It was some while before the applause died down,

and by that time the conductor had recovered himself and even began to look quite pleased at the way the audience was clapping.

"Very good timing, bear," he said gruffly as he returned Paddington to his seat and gave him a smart military salute. "It would have done credit to a Guardsman."

"All the same," said Jonathan some while later as they were strolling home through the park, "it's a jolly good thing someone started clapping or there's no knowing what might have happened. I wonder who it was?"

Judy looked at Mr. Gruber, but he appeared to be examining one of the nearby trees, and if there was a twinkle in his eye it was hard to see. In any case, before they had time to discuss the matter any further the quiet of the afternoon was broken by the sound of music and marching feet.

"It must be the band on their way back to the barracks," said Mr. Gruber. "If we hurry, we may be in time to see them." So saying, he quickly led the way in the direction of the music until they reached the side of the road just as a long line of soldiers came swinging into view, led by the officer in charge.

"I'm glad you've seen the Guards marching, Mr. Brown," said Mr. Gruber some moments later, as the

music died away and the last of the soldiers disappeared from view. "It's a lovely sight."

Paddington nodded his agreement as he replaced his hat. He'd been most impressed, and although when they'd passed by the soldiers had all been staring very smartly straight ahead, he was almost sure the man in charge had turned his eyes in their direction for a fraction of a second.

"I had a feeling he did too, Mr. Brown," said Mr. Gruber when Paddington mentioned it. "And I should certainly make a note of it in your scrapbook. I don't suppose it'll ever happen again, and it's a very good way to round off a most enjoyable day."

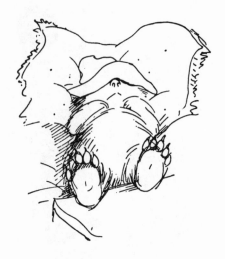

CHAPTER THREE

Goings-On at Number Thirty-two

PADDINGTON WOKE WITH a start and then sat up in bed rubbing his eyes. For a moment or two he wasn't quite sure where he was, but gradually, as a number of familiar objects swam into view, he realized with surprise that he was in his own room.

The afternoon sun was streaming in through the window, and after blinking several times he lay back again with his paws behind his head and a thoughtful expression on his face.

Although he wasn't quite sure what had disturbed

38

him, he felt very glad he'd woken when he did, for he had been in the middle of a particularly nasty dream about a large jar of his special marmalade from the cut-price grocer in the market.

In the dream something had gone wrong with the lid, and no matter how much he'd tried, nothing would budge it. Mrs. Bird's best tin opener had broken off at the handle, and when he'd tried squeezing it in a doorjamb the door had fallen off. Even Mr. Brown's hammer and chisel had made no impression at all, and after several bangs the head had flown off the hammer and broken the dining room window. In fact, if he hadn't woken at that moment, there was no knowing what other awful things might have happened.

Paddington heaved a sigh of relief, and after dipping a paw into an open jar of marmalade by his bed in order to make sure everything really was all right, he closed his eyes again.

The Brown household was unusually quiet and peaceful that afternoon, for Paddington had the house to himself. In the morning the postman had brought Jonathan and Judy a surprise invitation to a tea party, and by the same delivery a letter had arrived asking Mrs. Brown and Mrs. Bird to visit an old aunt who lived on the other side of London.

Even Paddington should have been out, for Mr. Brown had given him several books to take back to the public library, together with a long list of things he wanted him to look up in the reference department.

It was Mr. Brown's list that had proved to be Paddington's undoing, for he had taken it upstairs to his room after lunch in order to study it, and before he knew where he was he had nodded off.

Thinking the matter over, Paddington wasn't quite sure whether it was the result of an extra large lunch, with two helpings of apple pie and ice cream, or the hot afternoon sun, or even a mixture of both, but whatever the reason, he must have been asleep for over an hour, for in the distance he could hear a clock striking three.

It was as the last of the chimes died away that Paddington suddenly sat bolt upright in his bed and stared with wide-open eyes at the ceiling. Unless he was dreaming again, there was a strange scraping noise coming from somewhere directly overhead. It began by the door, then passed across the room in the direction of the window and paused for a moment before coming all the way back again.

Paddington's eyes got larger and larger as he listened to the sound, and they nearly popped out altogether a few moments later when a noise remarkably like that of a hammer and chisel broke the silence that followed the scraping.

After pinching himself several times to make sure it had nothing to do with his dream, Paddington jumped out of bed and hurried across the room in order to investigate the matter.

As he flung open the window, an even stranger thing happened, and he jumped back into the room as if he had been shot, for just as he peered outside a long black snakelike object came into view and hung there twisting and turning for several seconds before it finally disappeared from view below the ledge.

Paddington backed across the room and, after making a grab for his hat and suitcase, rushed out onto the landing, banging the door behind him.

Although after the dream and the strange events that had followed he was prepared for almost anything, Paddington certainly wasn't expecting the sight that met his eyes on the landing, and he almost wished he'd stayed in his room.

Only a few yards away, between his door and the top of the stairs, there was a ladder that definitely hadn't been there after lunch. It was leaning against the trap door in the ceiling, and worse still, the trap door itself was wide open.

Paddington was a brave bear at heart, but even so it

took him several moments to pluck up his courage again. After pulling his hat well down over his head and carefully placing his suitcase at the top of the stairs in case of an emergency, he began climbing slowly up the ladder.

It was when he reached the top rung and peered over the edge into the loft that Paddington's worst suspicions were realized. For there, tiptoeing across the rafters with a flashlight in one hand and what looked like a long knife in the other, was a man in a cap and blue overalls.

Holding his breath, Paddington considered the matter for several seconds before coming to a decision. As quietly as possible, he stretched his paw into the darkness until he felt the edge of the trap door, and then he flung it back into place and pushed the bolt home as hard as he could before scrambling down the ladder onto the landing and safety.

All at once there was a commotion in the roof as someone started to shout and several bumps were followed by the sound of banging on the other side of the trap door. But by that time Paddington was much too far away to hear what was going on. The sound of the Browns' front door slamming had added itself to the general hubbub, and he was halfway down Windsor Gardens, hurrying along the pavement with a very determined expression on his face indeed. All in all, he decided that bad though his dream had been, things had been even worse since he'd woken up, and it was definitely time to call for help.

After rounding several corners Paddington at last reached the place he had been looking for. It was a large, old-fashioned stone building that stood slightly apart from the rest on a corner site. Most of the windows had bars across them, and at the top of some steps leading up to the entrance there was a blue lamp with the word POLICE written across it in white letters.

Paddington hurried up the steps and then paused at the entrance. Leading from the hall were a number of doors, and it was difficult to decide which was the best one. In the end he picked on a large brown door on his right. It looked more important than any of the others, and Paddington was a firm believer in going to the top whenever he had an emergency.

After knocking several times, he waited with his ear against the keyhole until he heard a gruff voice call out, "Come in," and then he pushed the door open with his paw.

The only person in the room was a man sitting behind a desk near the window, and he looked rather cross when he saw Paddington. "You've come to the wrong place," he said. "Undesirables are supposed to report round the back."

"*Undesirables!*" exclaimed Paddington hotly, giving the man a hard stare. "I'm not an undesirable. I'm a bear!"

The man jumped up from behind his desk. "I beg your pardon," he said. "The light's none too good, and I thought for a moment you were Hairy Harry."

"*Hairy Harry?*" repeated Paddington, hardly able to believe his ears.

"He's what we call the Portobello Prowler," the man added confidentially, "and he's been giving us a lot of trouble lately. He's only small and he slips in through pantry windows when no one's looking."

His voice trailed away as Paddington's stare got harder and harder. "Er... what can we do for you?" he asked.

"I'd like to see Sid, please," said Paddington, putting down his suitcase.

"Sid?" repeated the man, looking most surprised. "I don't think we have any Sids here. We've several Alfs and a Bert, but I don't recall any Sids offhand."

"It says on the notice outside you've got one," said Paddington firmly. "It's written on the door."

The man looked puzzled for a moment, and then his

face cleared. "You don't mean *Sid*—you mean CID. That's quite a different matter," he explained. "CID stands for Criminal Investigation Department."

"Well, there's a criminal in Mr. Brown's roof," said Paddington, not to be outdone. "And I think he needs investigating."

"A criminal in Mr. Brown's roof?" repeated the man, taking a notepad and pencil as he listened while Paddington went on to explain all that had taken place.

"Good work, bear," he exclaimed when Paddington had finished talking. "We don't often catch anyone red-handed. I'll send out an alert at once."

With that he pressed a button on the side of his desk, and in a matter of seconds the police station became a hive of activity. In fact, Paddington hardly had time to adjust his hat and pick up his suitcase before he found himself being led by several policemen into a yard at the back of the building, where he was bundled into the back seat of a large black car.

Paddington felt most important as the car shot down the road in the direction of Windsor Gardens. He had never been inside a police car before, and it was all very interesting. He didn't remember ever having traveled quite as fast either, and he was most

impressed when a policeman on traffic duty held up all the other cars and waved them across some lights that were red.

"Right, bear," said the CID man as the car screeched to a halt outside the Browns' house, "lead the way. Only watch out—if he's got a knife he may be dangerous."

Paddington thought for a moment and then raised his hat. "After you," he said politely. Taking things all round, Paddington felt he'd had his share of adventures for one day, and apart from that he was anxious to make sure his store of marmalade was safe before anything else happened.

*

"Do you mean to say," exclaimed the policeman as he looked down at the man in the blue overalls, "you were putting up a television aerial all the time?"

"That's right, officer," said the man. "And I've got a letter from Mr. Brown to prove it. Gave me the key for the house, he did. Said there would be no one else here as he was getting rid of them for the day and I was to let myself in on account of it being a special surprise for the rest of the family and he didn't want them to know about it."

The man in the overalls paused for breath and then handed a card to the policeman. "Higgins is the name. Tip Top Tellys. If you ever want a job done, just give me a ring."

"Tip Top Tellys?" repeated the CID man, looking distastefully at the card. He turned to Paddington. "I thought you said he had a knife, bear?"

"That wasn't a knife," said Mr. Higgins. "That was my tweeker."

"Your *tweeker!*" exclaimed Paddington, looking most upset.

"That's right," said Mr. Higgins cheerfully as he held up a long screwdriver. "Always carry one of these on account of having to give the old tellys a tweek when they want adjusting.

"Tell you what," he added, waving his hand in the direction of a large cabinet that stood in one corner of the dining room, "I'm nearly ready to switch it on. Just got to connect the aerial. With this young bear's permission, I vote we take five minutes off and brew up a cup of tea. There's nothing like a nice cup of tea for cooling things down."

Mr. Higgins gave Paddington a broad wink. "If there's a detective play on, we might even pick up a few hints!"

As a spluttering noise came from one of the policemen, Paddington disappeared hurriedly in the direction of the kitchen. The CID man's face seemed to have gone a rather nasty shade of red, and he didn't like the look of it at all.

All the same, when he returned a few minutes later staggering under the weight of a tray full of cups and saucers and a large plate of buns, even the policemen began to look more cheerful, and in no time at all the living room began to echo with the sound of laughter as everyone recounted his part in the afternoon's adventure.

In between explaining all about the various knobs on the television and making some last-minute adjustments, Mr. Higgins kept them all amused with tales of other adventures he'd had in the trade. In fact, the time passed so quickly everyone seemed sorry when at last it was time to leave.

"I've just sold two more television sets," whispered Mr. Higgins, nodding towards the policemen as he paused at the door. "So if I can ever do you a favor, just let me know. One good turn deserves another."

"Thank you very much, Mr. Higgins," said Paddington gratefully.

Having waved goodbye to everyone, Paddington shut the front door and hurried back into the living room. Although he was pleased that the mystery of the bumps in the roof had been solved, he was anxious to test Mr. Brown's new television set before the others arrived home, and he quickly drew the curtains before settling himself comfortably in one of the armchairs.

In the past he had often watched television in a shop window in the Portobello Road, but the manager had several times come out to complain about his breathing heavily on the windows during the cowboy films, and Paddington was sure it would be much nicer to be able to sit at home and watch in comfort.

But when he had seen a cartoon, some cricket, two musical shows, and a program on bird watching, Paddington's interest began to flag, and after helping himself to another bun he turned his attention to a small booklet that Mr. Higgins had left behind.

The book was called "How to Get the Best out of Your Television," and it was full of pictures and diagrams—rather like maps of the Underground—showing the inside of the set. There was even a chapter showing how to adjust the various knobs in order to get the best picture, and Paddington spent some time sitting in front of the set turning the brightness up and down and making unusual patterns on the screen.

There were so many different knobs to turn and so many different things it was possible to do with the picture that he soon lost all account of the time, and he was most surprised when the living room clock suddenly struck six.

It was while he was hurriedly turning all the knobs back to where they'd been to start with that something very unexpected and alarming happened.

One moment a cowboy on a white horse was dashing across the screen in hot pursuit of a man with a black mustache and side whiskers; the next moment there was a click, and before Paddington's astonished gaze the picture shrank in size until there was nothing left but a small white dot.

He spent some moments peering hopefully at the screen through his opera glasses, but the longer he looked, the smaller the dot became, and even striking a match didn't help matters, for by the time he had been in the kitchen to fetch the box the spot had disappeared completely.

Paddington stood in front of the silent television set with a mournful expression on his face. Although Mr. Brown had gone to a lot of trouble in order to surprise the family, it was quite certain he wouldn't be at all pleased if they received that much of a surprise and arrived home to find it wasn't even working.

Paddington heaved a deep sigh. "Oh, dear," he said as he addressed the world in general. "I'm in trouble again."

*

"I can't understand it," said Mr. Brown as he came out of the living room. "Mr. Higgins promised faithfully it would be all ready by the time we got home."

"Never mind, Henry," said Mrs. Brown as the rest of the family crowded round the doorway. "It *was* a surprise, and I'm sure he'll be able to get it working soon."

"Crikey!" exclaimed Jonathan. "He must have been having a lot of trouble. Look at all the pieces."

"Don't bother to draw the curtains. We'll eat in the kitchen," said Mrs. Brown as she took in the scene. There were bits and pieces everywhere, not to mention a large number of valves and a cathode ray tube on the settee.

Mrs. Bird looked puzzled. "I thought you said it wasn't working," she remarked.

"I don't see how it could be," replied Mr. Brown.

"Well, there's something there," said Mrs. Bird, pointing to the screen. "I saw it move."

The Brown family peered through the gloom at the television set. Although it didn't seem possible Mrs. Bird could be right, now that they looked, there was definitely some kind of movement on the glass.

"It looks rather furry," said Mrs. Brown. "Perhaps it's one of those animal programs. They do have a lot on television."

Jonathan was nearest to the screen, and he suddenly clutched Judy's arm. "Crumbs!" he whispered as his eyes grew accustomed to the dark and he caught sight of a familiar-looking nose pressed against the glass. "It isn't a program. It's Paddington. He must be stuck inside!"

"This is most interesting," said Mr. Brown, taking

out his glasses. "Switch on the light, someone. I'd like a closer look."

As a muffled exclamation came from somewhere inside the television, Jonathan and Judy hurriedly placed themselves between Mr. Brown and the screen.

"Don't you think you ought to ring Mr. Higgins, Dad?" asked Judy. "He'll know what to do."

"We'll go down and fetch him if you like," said Jonathan eagerly. "It won't take a minute."

"Yes, come along, Henry," said Mrs. Brown. "I should leave things just as they are. There's no knowing what might happen if you touch them."

Rather reluctantly, Mr. Brown allowed himself to be shepherded out of the room, closely followed by Jonathan and Judy.

Mrs. Bird was the last one to leave, and before she closed the door she took one last look round the room. "There are some rather nasty marmalade stains on that television cabinet," she said in a loud voice. "If I were a young bear, I'd make sure they're wiped off by the time Mr. Higgins gets here... otherwise certain people may put two and two together."

Although Mrs. Bird kept a firm hand on goings-on in the Brown household, she was a great believer in the proverb "Least said, soonest mended," especially when it had to do with anything as complicated as television.

If Mr. Higgins was surprised at having to repay Paddington's good turn so soon, he didn't show it by so much as the flicker of an eyelid. All the same, after Mrs. Bird had spoken to him, he took Paddington on one side and they had a long chat together while he explained how dangerous it was to take the back off a television set if you didn't know what you were doing.

"It's a good thing bears' paws are well insulated, Mr. Brown," he said as he bade goodbye to Paddington. "Otherwise you might not be here to tell the tale.

"That's all right," he said cheerfully as Paddington thanked him for all his trouble. "Got a bit of marmalade on my tweeker, but otherwise there's no harm done. And I daresay it'll wash off."

"It usually does," said Mrs. Bird with the voice of experience, as she showed him to the door.

As the Browns trooped into the living room for their first evening's viewing, it was noticeable that one member of the family settled himself as far away from the screen as possible. Although Mr. Higgins had screwed the back on the television as tightly as his tweeker would allow, Paddington wasn't taking any more chances than he could help.

"Mind you," said Mr. Brown later that evening, when Mrs. Bird came in with the bedtime snack, "I still can't understand what it was we saw on the screen. It was very strange."

"It was probably some kind of interference," said Mrs. Bird gravely. "I don't suppose it'll happen again, do you, Paddington?"

As she spoke, several pairs of eyes turned in Paddington's direction, but most of his face was carefully hidden behind a large mug, and very wisely he only nodded his agreement. Not that he was having to pretend he felt tired, for in fact it was only the cocoa steam that was keeping his eyelids open at all. Nevertheless, there was something about the way his whiskers were poking out on either side of the mug that suggested Mrs. Bird had hit the nail on the head. As far as the Brown family was concerned, there was one kind of interference they weren't likely to get on their television again in a hurry.

CHAPTER FOUR

Paddington Hits the Jackpot

"LUCKY FOR SOME?" exclaimed Mr. Brown. "Don't tell me we've got to sit and watch that awful thing. Isn't there anything better on the other channel?"

The rest of the family exchanged uneasy glances. "Paddington did ask if we could have it on," said Mrs. Brown. "It's his favorite program and he seemed particularly anxious we shouldn't miss it tonight."

"In that case," said Mr. Brown, "why isn't he here?"

"I expect he's popped out somewhere," said Mrs.

Brown soothingly. "He'll probably be back in a minute."

Mr. Brown sank back into his seat with a grunt and stared distastefully at the television screen as a fanfare of trumpets heralded the start of *Lucky for Some* and the master of ceremonies, Ronnie Playfair, came bounding onto the stage, rubbing his hands with glee.

"I wouldn't mind," said Mr. Brown, "if he asked sensible questions. But to give all that money away for the sort of things he asks is ridiculous."

The living room curtains were drawn, and the Brown family, with the exception of Paddington, who had been unaccountably missing since shortly after tea, were settled in a small half-circle facing the television set in preparation for their evening's viewing.

Over the past few weeks a change had come over the routine at Number Thirty-two Windsor Gardens. Normally the Browns were the sort of family who entertained themselves quite happily, but since the arrival of the television set, practically every evening had been spent in semidarkness as they sat with their eyes glued to the screen.

All the same, although Mr. Brown was the first to admit it out loud, the nine days' wonder of having pictures in their own home was beginning to wear thin, and there were several signs of restlessness as yet another fanfare of trumpets burst from the loud-speaker.

"I do hope nothing's happened to Paddington," whispered Mrs. Brown. "It's not like him to miss any of the programs, especially a quiz. He's very keen on them."

"That bear's been acting strangely all the week," said Mrs. Bird. "Ever since he got that letter. I've a nasty feeling it may have something to do with it."

"Well, it can't be anything bad," said Mrs. Brown. "He seems to have spent all his time with his whiskers buried in those encyclopedias of Mr. Gruber's. He even missed his second helping at lunch today."

"That's just it," said Mrs. Bird ominously. "It's much too good to be true."

While Ronnie Playfair's face grew larger and larger on the screen as he explained the program to the studio audience and the viewers at home, the Browns began to discuss Paddington's strange behavior over the past week.

As Mrs. Bird said, it had all begun when he'd received an important-looking letter by the first post one morning. At the time no one had paid it a great deal of attention, for he often sent away for catalogues or any free samples that he saw being advertised in the newspapers.

But a little later that same morning he had arrived home pushing Mr. Gruber's encyclopedias in his basket on wheels, and the next day, after borrowing Mr. Brown's library cards, another pile of books had added themselves to the already large one at his bedside.

"He's been asking the oddest questions too," said Mrs. Brown. "I don't know where he gets them from."

"Well, wherever it is," said Mr. Brown as he looked up from his evening paper, "I hope he gets back soon."

Mr. Brown liked plays, and he had just discovered there was a particularly good one about to start on the other channel.

"Crikey!" exclaimed Jonathan suddenly, jumping up from his seat and pointing at the television screen. "No wonder he isn't here! Look!"

"Gracious me!" exclaimed Mrs. Bird as she followed his gaze. "It can't be!"

Mr. Brown adjusted his glasses. "It jolly well is," he said. "It's Paddington and Mr. Gruber."

While the Browns had been talking, Ronnie Playfair had finished describing the workings of the program. Waving his hand cheerily to the studio audience, he stepped down off the stage in the beam of a large spotlight and announced that the first contestant of the evening was a Mr. Brown of London.

As he made his way up the aisle the camera followed him, and eventually it came to rest on two familiar faces at the end of one of the rows of seats. Mr. Gruber's look of embarrassment was tinged with a faint air of guilt as he caught sight of his own face on a nearby screen. Although Paddington had assured him that the Browns liked surprises, he wasn't at all sure they would be keen on this particular one.

But Mr. Gruber was soon lost from view as a small brown figure sitting next to him raised a battered hat to the camera and hurried up the aisle after the master of ceremonies.

If the Browns were overcome at the sight of Paddington climbing onto the stage, Ronnie Playfair was equally at a loss for words, which was most unusual.

"Are you sure you're the right Mr. Brown?" he asked nervously, as Paddington dumped his suitcase on the stage and raised his hat to the audience.

"Yes, Mr. Playfair," said Paddington, waving a piece of paper importantly in the air. "I've got your letter asking me to come."

"I... er... I didn't know there were any bears in Notting Hill Gate," said Ronnie Playfair.

"I *come* from Peru," said Paddington. "But I *live* in Windsor Gardens."

"Oh, well," said Ronnie Playfair, recovering himself

slightly, "we won't ask you to peruve that, but I suppose we must expect the *bear* facts tonight. *Peruve* that," he repeated, laughing at his own joke in a rather high voice. "*Bear* facts." His voice died away as he caught Paddington's eye. Paddington didn't think much of Ronnie Playfair's jokes, and he was giving him a particularly hard stare.

"Er... perhaps you'd like to step forward and send a message home," said the master of ceremonies hurriedly. "We always ask our contestants to send a message home—it makes them feel at ease."

Paddington bent down and took a piece of paper out of his suitcase. "Thank you very much, Mr. Playfair," he exclaimed as he began advancing on the camera.

The Browns watched in dumb fascination as Paddington loomed larger on their screen. "Hullo all at Number Thirty-two," said a familiar voice. "I hope I shan't be late, Mrs. Bird. Mr. Gruber promised to bring me straight home and —"

Whatever else Paddington had been about to say was lost as there came a loud crash and the picture disappeared from the screen.

"Oh, no," cried Judy. "Don't say it's broken down. Not tonight of all nights."

"It's all right," said Jonathan. "Look—they've got another camera on."

As he spoke another picture flashed onto the screen. It wasn't quite such a nice one as the closeup of Paddington had been. Until just before the end, when it had suddenly gone soft and muzzy, that one had shown almost every whisker, whereas the new picture was looking towards the audience and there appeared to be some confusion. One of the cameramen was sitting on the floor surrounded by wires and cables, rubbing his head, and Ronnie Playfair seemed to be having some kind of an argument with a man wearing headphones.

"He wasn't on his marks," cried the cameraman. "He kept following me. You can't take proper closeups if people don't stay on their marks."

Paddington peered at the floor. "My marks?" he repeated hotly. "But I had a bath before I came out."

"He doesn't mean *dirt* marks," said Ronnie Playfair, pointing to a yellow chalk line. "He means that sort. You're supposed to stay where I put you—otherwise the cameras can't get their shots."

"You did ask me to step forward," said Paddington, looking most upset.

"I said *step* forward," said Ronnie Playfair crossly. "Not go for a walk."

Ronnie Playfair had been master of ceremonies on *Lucky for Some* for several years with never a word out of place, let alone an upset like the one that had just occurred, and there was a strained look on his face as he picked his way back across the cables, closely followed by Paddington, who was peering anxiously at the floor in case he lost sight of his chalk mark again.

"Now," he said as they reached the center of the stage and stood facing the other cameras, "what would you like to be questioned on?" He waved his hand in the direction of four barrels which stood in a row on a nearby table. "You can have history, geography, mathematics, or general knowledge."

Paddington thought for a moment. "I think I'd like to try my paw at mathematics, please," he announced amid applause from the audience.

"Crikey!" exclaimed Jonathan. "Fancy choosing math!"

"Knowing the way Paddington does the shopping," said Mrs. Bird, "I think it's a very wise choice."

Paddington had a reputation among the street traders in the Portobello market for striking a hard bargain, and it was generally acknowledged that you had to get up very early in the morning indeed in order to get the better of him.

"I must say he always keeps his accounts very

neatly," said Mrs. Brown. "I'm sure it's the right choice."

"Mathematics?" repeated Ronnie Playfair. "Well, we'd better look for the first question." He put his hand into one of the barrels and withdrew a piece of paper. "A nice easy one to start with," he announced approvingly, "and a very good question for a bear. If you get it right there's a prize of five pounds."

After a short roll of drums Ronnie Playfair raised his hand for silence. "For a prize of five pounds," he announced. "How many buns equal five?

"I must warn you," he added, winking at the audience, "think carefully. It may be a trick question. How many buns equal five?"

Paddington thought for a moment. "Two and a half," he replied.

Ronnie Playfair's jaw dropped slightly. "Two and a half?" he repeated. "Are you sure you won't change your mind?"

"Two and a half," said Paddington firmly.

"Poor old Paddington," said Jonathan. "Fancy getting the first one wrong."

"I am surprised," said Mrs. Bird. "It's not like him at all. Unless he's got something up his paw."

"Oh, dear," said the master of ceremonies as he picked up a hammer and struck a large gong by his side. "I'm afraid you're out of the contest. The answer is five."

"I don't think it is, Mr. Playfair," said Paddington. "It's two and a half. I always share my buns with Mr. Gruber when we have our elevenses and I break them in half."

Ronnie Playfair's jaw dropped even further and the smile froze on his face. "You share your buns with Mr. Gruber?" he repeated.

"Give him the money!" cried someone in the audience as the applause died down.

"You said it might be a trick question," cried someone else amid laughter. "Now you've got a trick answer."

Ronnie Playfair fingered his collar nervously, and a strange look came over his face as he received a signal from the man wearing headphones to give Paddington the money.

"Are you going to stop now, bear?" he asked hopefully as he handed Paddington five crisp one-pound notes, "or do you want to go on for the next prize of fifty pounds?"

"I'd like to go on please, Mr. Playfair," said Paddington eagerly as he hurriedly locked the money away in his suitcase.

"I shouldn't do that," said Ronnie Playfair as he

dipped his hand into the barrel and withdrew another piece of paper. "If you get this question wrong, I shall want the five pounds back."

"Oh, dear," said Mrs. Brown. "I feel all turned over inside. I hope Paddington doesn't do anything silly and lose his five pounds. He'll be so upset we shall never hear the last of it."

"Right!" said Ronnie Playfair, holding up his hand once again for silence. "For fifty pounds, here is question number two, and it's a two-part question. Listen carefully.

"If," he said, "you had a piece of wood eight feet long and you cut it in half, and if you cut the two pieces you then have into half, and if you then cut all the pieces into half again, how many pieces would you have?"

"Eight," said Paddington promptly.

"Very good, bear," said Ronnie Playfair approvingly. "Now," he continued, pointing to a large clock by his side, "here is the second part of the question. How long will each of the pieces be? You have ten seconds to answer starting from . . . now!"

"Eight feet," said Paddington, almost before the master of ceremonies had time to start the clock.

"Eight feet?" repeated Ronnie Playfair. "You're sure you won't change your mind?"

"No, thank you, Mr. Playfair," said Paddington firmly.

"In that case," said Ronnie Playfair as he triumphantly banged the gong, "I must ask for the five pounds back. The answer is one foot. If I had a piece of wood eight feet long and I cut it in half, I would have two pieces four feet long. And if I cut those in half, I would have four pieces two feet long. And if I cut each of those in half, I would have eight pieces one foot long."

Having finished his speech, Ronnie Playfair turned and beamed a self-satisfied smile on the audience. "You can't argue with that, bear," he exclaimed.

"Oh, no, Mr. Playfair," said Paddington politely. "I'm sure that's right for *your* piece of wood, but I cut mine the other way."

Once again the smile froze on Ronnie Playfair's face. "You did *what?*" he exclaimed.

"I cut mine down the middle," said Paddington. "So I had eight pieces eight feet long."

"But if you're asked to cut a plank of wood in half," stuttered Ronnie Playfair, "you cut it across the middle, not *down* the middle. It stands to reason."

"Not if you're a bear," said Paddington, remembering his efforts at carpentry in the past. "If you're a bear, it's safer to cut it down the middle."

Ronnie Playfair took a deep breath and forced a sickly smile to his face as he handed Paddington a large bundle of notes.

"I think you'll find they're all there, bear," he said stiffly as Paddington sat down on the stage and began counting them. "We're not in the habit of cheating people."

Ronnie Playfair looked anxiously at his watch. The program seemed to be taking a lot longer than usual. Normally he would have got through at least five contestants by now.

"There are only five minutes left," he said. "Do you want to go on for the final prize of five hundred pounds?"

"Five hundred pounds!" exclaimed Judy in a tone of awe.

"If I were Paddington," said Mrs. Brown, "I'd stop now and make sure of what I've got."

The Browns grouped themselves even closer round their television screen as one of the cameras showed a closeup picture of Paddington considering the matter.

"I think I would like to carry on, Mr. Playfair," he announced at last amid a burst of applause.

Although Paddington was not the sort of bear who normally believed in taking too many chances as far as money was concerned, he was much too excited by all that had taken place that evening to think clearly about the matter.

"Well," said Ronnie Playfair in his most solemn voice, "here, for a prize of five hundred pounds, is the last question of the evening, and this time it's a much harder one."

"It would be," said Mrs. Brown, holding her breath.

"If," continued Ronnie Playfair, "it takes two men twenty minutes to fill a fifty-gallon bath full of water using one tap, how long will it take one man to fill the same bath using both taps? This time you've got twenty seconds, starting from... now!"

Ronnie Playfair pressed a button on the clock by his

side and then stood back to await Paddington's answer.

"No time at all, Mr. Playfair," said Paddington promptly.

"Wrong!" exclaimed Ronnie Playfair as a groan went up from the audience. "I'm afraid this time you really have got it wrong. It will take exactly half the time.

"I'm very sorry, bear," he continued, looking most relieved as he gave the gong a bang with his hammer. "Better luck next time."

"I think you must be wrong, Mr. Playfair," said Paddington politely.

"Nonsense," said the master of ceremonies, giving Paddington a nasty look. "The answer's on the card. In any case, it's bound to take *some* time. You can't fill a bath in no time at all."

"But you said it was the same bath," explained Paddington. "The first two men had already filled it once, and you didn't say anything about pulling the plug out."

Ronnie Playfair's face seemed to go a strange purple color as he stared at Paddington. "I didn't say anything about them pulling the plug out?" he repeated. "But of course they pulled it out."

"You didn't say so," cried a voice in the audience as

several boos broke out. "That bear's quite right."

"Give him the money!" cried someone else as several more voices added to the general uproar.

Ronnie Playfair seemed to shudder slightly as he withdrew a silk handkerchief from his jacket pocket and patted his brow. "Congratulations, bear," he said grudgingly, after a long pause. "You've won the jackpot!"

"What!" exclaimed Paddington hotly, giving Ronnie Playfair one of his hardest ever stares. "I've won a *jackpot?* I thought you said it was five hundred pounds."

"That *is* five hundred pounds," said Ronnie Playfair hastily. "It's the top prize of all. That's why it's called a jackpot."

As the applause rang through the theater Paddington sat down on his suitcase, hardly able to believe his ears. Although he knew there must be five hundred pounds in the world, he had never in his wildest dreams thought he might one day see it in one big pile, let alone be told it was his.

Ronnie Playfair held up his hand for silence. "One final question before we end the program," he exclaimed. "And there's no prize for this one. What are you going to do with all the money?"

Paddington considered the matter for a long time as the audience went very quiet. When you usually counted your money in terms of how many buns it would buy, it was very difficult even to begin to think about a sum like five hundred pounds, let alone decide what to do with it, and when he tried to think of five hundred pounds' worth of buns he grew quite dizzy.

"I think," he said at last, as the camera came closer and closer, "I would like to keep a little bit as a souvenir and to buy some Christmas presents. Then I would like to give the rest to the Home for Retired Bears in Lima."

"The Home for Retired Bears in Lima?" repeated Ronnie Playfair, looking most surprised.

"That's right," said Paddington. "That's where my Aunt Lucy lives. She's very happy there, but I don't think they've got very much money. They only have marmalade on Sundays, so I expect they would find it very useful."

Everyone applauded Paddington's announcement, and the applause grew louder still a few moments later when Ronnie Playfair announced on behalf of the television company that they would see to it the Home for Retired Bears in Lima was well supplied with marmalade for at least a year to come.

"After all," he said, "it isn't every week a bear wins the jackpot in one of our quiz programs."

"Well, I never," said Mr. Brown, mopping his brow

as the program came to an end and the captions began rolling past on the screen over a picture of Paddington as he stood in the middle of the stage receiving everyone's congratulations. "I never thought when we bought a television set it would come to this."

"Fancy Paddington giving it away," said Jonathan. "He's usually so careful with his money."

"Careful isn't the same as being mean," said Mrs. Bird wisely. "And I must say I'm very glad. I never did like the thought of all those bears only having marmalade on Sundays.

"After all," she added amid general agreement, "if it hadn't been for Aunt Lucy, we shouldn't have met Paddington. And if that doesn't deserve a bit of extra marmalade, I don't know what does."

CHAPTER FIVE

A Sticky Time

MRS. BIRD PAUSED for a moment and sniffed the air as she and Mrs. Brown turned the corner into Windsor Gardens. "Can you smell something?" she asked.

Mrs. Brown stopped by her side. Now that Mrs. Bird mentioned it, there was a very peculiar odor coming from somewhere near at hand. It wasn't exactly unpleasant, but it was rather sweet and sickly, and it seemed to be made up of a number of things she couldn't quite place.

"Perhaps there's been a bonfire somewhere," she

remarked as they picked up their shopping and continued along the road.

"Whatever it is," said Mrs. Bird darkly, "it seems to be getting worse. In fact," she added, as they neared Number Thirty-two, "it's much too close to home for my liking.

"I knew it!" she exclaimed as they made their way along the drive at the side of the house. "Just look at my kitchen windows!"

"Oh, dear," said Mrs. Brown, following the direction of Mrs. Bird's gaze. "What on earth has that bear been up to now?"

Looking at Mrs. Bird's kitchen windows, it seemed just as if in some strange way someone had changed them for frosted glass while she and Mrs. Brown had been out. Worse still, not only did the glass have a frosted appearance, but there were several tiny rivers of a rather nasty-looking brown liquid trickling down them as well, and from a small, partly open window at the top there came a steady cloud of escaping steam.

While Mrs. Bird examined the outside of her kitchen window, Mrs. Brown hurried round to the back of the house. "I do hope Paddington's all right," she exclaimed when she returned. "I can't get in through the back door. It seemed to be stuck."

"Hmm," said Mrs. Bird grimly. "If the windows

look like this from the outside, heaven alone knows what we shall find when we get indoors."

Normally the windows at Number Thirty-two Windsor Gardens were kept spotlessly clean, with never a trace of a smear, but even Mrs. Bird began to look worried as she peered in vain for a gap in the mist through which she could see what was going on.

Had she but known, the chances of seeing anything at all through the haze were more unlikely than she imagined, for on the other side of the glass even Paddington was having to admit to himself that things were getting a bit out of hand.

In fact, as he groped his way across the kitchen in the direction of the stove, where several large saucepans stood bubbling and giving forth clouds of steam, he decided he didn't much like the look of the few things he could see.

Climbing up on a kitchen chair, he lifted the lid off one of the saucepans and peered hopefully inside as he poked at the contents with one of Mrs. Bird's tablespoons. The mixture was much stiffer than he had expected, and it was as much as he could manage to push the spoon in, let alone stir with it.

Paddington's whiskers began to droop in the steam as he worked the spoon back and forth, but it wasn't until he tried to take it out in order to test the result of

his labors that a really worried expression came over his face, for to his surprise, however much he pulled and tugged, it wouldn't even budge.

The more he struggled, the hotter the spoon became, and after a moment or two he gave it up as a bad job and hurriedly let go of the handle as he climbed back down off the chair in order to consult a large magazine that was lying open on the floor.

Making toffee wasn't at all the easy thing the article in the magazine made it out to be, and it was all most disappointing, particularly as it was the first time he'd tried his paw at making sweets.

The magazine in question was an old one of Mrs. Brown's, and he had first come across it earlier in the day when he'd been at a bit of a loose end. Normally

Paddington didn't think much of Mrs. Brown's magazines. They were much too full of advertisements and items about how to keep clean and look smart for his liking, but this one had caught his eye because it was a special cooking issue.

On the cover there was a picture showing a golden brown roast chicken resting on a plate laden with bright green peas, gravy, and roast potatoes. Alongside the chicken was a huge sundae oozing with layer upon layer of fruit and ice cream, while beyond that was a large wooden board laden with so many different kinds of cheese that Paddington had soon lost count of the number as he lay on his bed licking his whiskers.

The inside of the magazine had been even more interesting, and it had taken him a while to get through the colored photographs alone.

But it was the last article of all that had really made him sit up and take notice. It was called "TEN EASY WAYS WITH TOFFEE," and it was written by a lady called Granny Green who lived in the country and seemed to spend all her time making sweets.

Granny Green appeared in quite a number of the pictures, and whenever she did, it was always alongside a pile of freshly made olde-fashioned humbugs, a dish of coconut ice, or a mound of some other sweetmeat.

Paddington had read the article several times with a great deal of interest, for although in the past he'd tried his paw at cooking various kinds of dinner, he'd never before heard of anyone making sweets at home, and it seemed a very good idea indeed.

All Granny Green's recipes looked nice, but it was the last one of all, for olde-fashioned butter toffee, that had really made Paddington's mouth water. Even Granny Green herself seemed to like it best, for in one picture she was actually caught helping herself to a piece behind her kitchen door when she thought no one was watching.

It not only looked very tempting, but Paddington decided it was very good value for money as well, for apart from using condensed milk and sugar, all that was needed was butter, corn syrup, and some stuff called vanilla essence, all of which Mrs. Bird kept in her cupboard.

After checking carefully through the recipe once more, Paddington took another look at the magazine in the hope of seeing where he'd gone wrong, but none of the photographs were any help at all. All Granny Green's saucepans were as bright as a new pin, with not a trace of anything sticky running down the sides, and even her spoons were laid out neat and shining on the kitchen table. There was certainly no mention of any of them getting stuck in the toffee.

In any case, her toffee was a light golden brown color, and it was cut into neat squares and laid out on a plate, whereas from what he'd been able to make out of his own through the steam, it had been more the color of dark brown boot polish, and even if he had been able to get it out of the saucepans, he couldn't for the life of him think what he would cut it with.

Paddington rather wished he'd tried one of the other nine recipes instead. Heaving a deep sigh, he groped his way across the kitchen and, stretching up a paw, rubbed a hole in the steam on one of the windowpanes. As he did so he jumped back into the

middle of the room with a gasp of alarm, for there, on the other side of the glass, was the familiar face of Mrs. Bird.

Mrs. Bird appeared to be saying something, and although he couldn't make out the actual words, he didn't like the look of some of them at all. Fortunately, before she was able to say very much the glass clouded over again, and Paddington sat down in the middle of the kitchen floor with a forlorn expression on his face as he awaited developments.

He hadn't long to wait, for a few moments later there came the sound of footsteps in the hall. "What on earth's been going on?" cried Mrs. Bird as she burst through the door.

"I've been trying my paw at toffee making, Mrs. Bird," explained Paddington sadly.

"Toffee making!" exclaimed Mrs. Brown, flinging open the window. "Why, you could cut the air with a knife."

"That's more than you can say for the toffee," said Mrs. Bird as she pulled at the end of the spoon Paddington had left in the saucepan. "It looks more like glue."

"I'm afraid it is a bit thick, Mrs. Bird," said Paddington. "I think I must have got my Granny Greens mixed up by mistake."

"I don't know about your Granny Greens," said Mrs. Bird grimly as she surveyed the scene. "It looks as if you've got the whole pantry mixed up. I only cleaned the kitchen this morning, and now look at it!"

Paddington half stood up and gazed around the room. Now that most of the steam had cleared, it looked in rather more of a mess than he had expected. There were several large pools of syrup on the floor and a long trail of sugar leading from the table to the stove, not to mention two or three half-open tins of condensed milk lying on their side where they had fallen off the drainboard.

"It's a job to know where to start," said Mrs. Brown as she stepped gingerly over one of the syrup pools. "I've never seen such a mess."

"Well, we shan't get it cleared up if we stand looking at it, that's a certainty," said Mrs. Bird briskly as she bustled around sweeping everything in sight into the sink. "I suggest a certain young bear had better get down on his paws and knees with a scrubbing brush and a bowl of water before he's very much older, otherwise we shall all get stuck to the floor."

Mrs. Bird paused. While she'd been talking a strange expression had come over Paddington's face, one that she didn't like the look of at all. "Is anything the matter?" she asked.

"I'm not sure, Mrs. Bird," said Paddington, making several attempts to stand up and then hurriedly sitting down again, holding his stomach with both paws. "I've got a bit of a pain."

"You haven't been *eating* this stuff, have you?" exclaimed Mrs. Brown, pointing to the saucepans.

"Well, I did test it once or twice, Mrs. Brown," said Paddington.

"Gracious me!" cried Mrs. Bird. "No wonder you've got a pain. It's probably set in a hard lump in your inside."

"Try standing up again," said Mrs. Brown anxiously.

"I don't think I can," gasped Paddington, as he lay back on the floor. "I think it's getting worse."

"That poor bear," cried Mrs. Bird, all thoughts of the mess in the kitchen banished from her mind as she hurried into the hall. "We must ring for Doctor MacAndrew at once."

Mrs. Bird was only gone a moment or so before the door burst open again. "The doctor's out on his rounds," she said. "They don't know when he'll be back and they can't even find his locum."

"They can't find his locum!" repeated Paddington, looking more worried than ever.

"That's his assistant," explained Mrs. Brown. "There's nothing to get upset about. We could try a strong dose of castor oil, I suppose," she continued, turning to Mrs. Bird.

"I've a feeling it'll need more than castor oil," said Mrs. Bird ominously as Paddington jumped up hurriedly with a "feeling better" expression on his face and then gave a loud groan as he promptly sat down again. "I've sent for the ambulance."

"The ambulance!" cried Mrs. Brown, going quite pale. "Oh, dear."

"We should never forgive ourselves," said Mrs. Bird wisely, "if anything happened to that bear."

So saying, she put her arms underneath Paddington and, lifting him gently, carried him into the living room and placed him on the sofa, where he lay with his legs sticking up in the air.

Leaving Paddington where he was, Mrs. Bird disappeared upstairs, and when she returned she was carrying a small leather suitcase. "I've packed all his washing things," she explained to Mrs. Brown. "And I've put in a jar of his special marmalade in case he needs it."

Mrs. Bird mentioned the last item in a loud voice in the hope it would cheer Paddington up, but at the mention of the word *marmalade* a loud groan came from the direction of the sofa.

Mrs. Brown and Mrs. Bird exchanged glances. If the

thought of marmalade made Paddington feel worse, then things must be very bad indeed.

"I'd better ring Henry at the office," said Mrs. Brown as she hurried out into the hall. "I'll get him to come home straight away."

Fortunately, as Mrs. Brown replaced the telephone receiver, and before they had time to worry about the matter any more, there came the sound of a loud bell ringing outside, followed by a squeal of brakes and a bang on the front door.

"Ho, dear," said the ambulance man as he entered the living room and saw Paddington lying on the sofa. "What's this? I was told it was an emergency. Nobody said anything about its being a bear."

"Bears have emergencies the same as anyone else," said Mrs. Bird sternly. "Now just you bring your stretcher, and hurry up about it."

The ambulance man scratched his head. "I don't know what they're going to say back at the hospital," he said doubtfully. "They've got an out-patients and an in-patients department, but I've never come across a bear-patients department before."

"Well, they're going to have one now," said Mrs. Bird. "And if that bear isn't in it by the time five minutes is up, I shall want to know the reason why."

The ambulance man looked nervously at Mrs. Bird

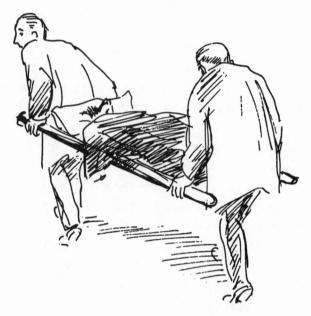

and then back at the sofa as Paddington gave another loud groan. "I must say he doesn't look too good," he remarked.

"He's all right when he's got his legs in the air," explained Mrs. Brown. "It's when he tries to put them down it hurts."

The ambulance man came to a decision. The combination of Mrs. Bird's glares and Paddington's groans was too much for him. "Bert," he called through the open door. "Fetch the number-one stretcher. And be quick. We've a young bear emergency in here and I don't much like the look of him."

Nobody spoke in the ambulance on the way to the hospital. Mrs. Bird, Mrs. Brown, and the man in charge traveled in the back with Paddington, and all the while his legs got higher and higher, until by the time the ambulance turned in through the hospital gates they were almost doubled back on themselves.

Even the ambulance man looked worried. "Never seen anything like it before," he said.

"I'll cover him over with a blanket, ma'am," he continued to Mrs. Bird as they came to a stop. "It'll save any explanations at the door. We don't want too many delays filling in forms."

Mrs. Brown and Mrs. Bird hurried in after the stretcher, but the ambulance man was as good as his word, and in no time at all Paddington was being whisked away from them down a long white corridor. In fact, he only had time to poke a paw out from under the blanket in order to wave goodbye before the doors at the end of the corridor closed behind him and all was quiet again.

"Oh, dear," said Mrs. Brown, sinking down on a wooden bench. "I suppose we've done all we can now."

"We can only sit and wait," said Mrs. Bird gravely as she sat down beside her. "Wait and hope."

*

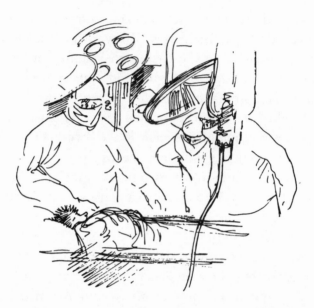

The Browns and Mr. Gruber sat in a miserable group in the corridor as they watched the comings and goings of the nurses. Mr. Brown had arrived soon after the ambulance, bringing with him Jonathan and Judy, and shortly after that Mr. Gruber had turned up carrying a bunch of flowers and a huge bag of grapes.

"They're from the traders in the market," he explained. "They all send their best wishes and hope he soon gets well."

"It won't be long now," said Mr. Brown as several

nurses entered the room at the end of the corridor. "I think things are beginning to happen."

As Mr. Brown spoke, a tall, distinguished-looking man dressed from head to foot in green came hurrying down the corridor and with a nod in their direction disappeared through the same door.

"That must be Sir Mortimer Carroway," said Judy knowledgeably. "That ambulance man said he's the best surgeon they have."

"Crikey!" said Jonathan in a tone of awe. "Fancy Paddington having him!"

"Quite right too," said Mrs. Bird decidedly. "There's nothing like going to the top. People at the top are always more understanding."

"I feel so helpless," said Mrs. Brown, voicing the thoughts of them all as they sat on the bench and prepared themselves for a long wait. They were each of them busy with their own thoughts, and although not one of them would have admitted it to the others, even the knowledge that such a famous person as Sir Mortimer Carroway was in charge didn't help matters.

"Good heavens!" exclaimed Mr. Brown a few minutes later as the door at the end of the corridor opened once again and the figure of Sir Mortimer appeared. "That was quick."

Mrs. Brown clutched her husband's arm. "You don't think anything's gone wrong, do you, Henry?" she asked.

"We shall soon know," said Mr. Brown as Sir Mortimer caught sight of them and came hurrying along the corridor, holding a piece of fur in his hand.

"Are you that young bear's... er... next of kin?" he asked.

"Well, he lives with us," said Mrs. Brown.

"He *is* going to be all right?" exclaimed Judy, looking anxiously at the piece of fur.

"I should think," said Sir Mortimer in a grave voice, but with the suspicion of a twinkle in his eyes, "there's every chance he'll pull through."

"Gracious me!" exclaimed Mrs. Bird as there was a sudden commotion at the end of the corridor. "There *is* Paddington. Don't tell me he's up already."

"A bad case of galloping toffee drips," said Sir Mortimer. "Most unusual. On the stomach too. Worst possible place."

"Galloping toffee drips?" repeated Mr. Brown.

"I think I must have spilled some on my fur when I was testing it, Mr. Brown," explained Paddington as he joined them.

"It probably set when he was sitting down," said Sir Mortimer. "No wonder he couldn't get up again."

Sir Mortimer chuckled at the look on everyone's face. "I'm afraid he'll have a bare patch for a week or so, but I don't doubt if you keep him on a diet of marmalade for a while, it'll start to grow again. It should be all right by Christmas.

"If you don't mind, bear," he said as he made to leave, "I'd like to keep this piece of fur as a souvenir. I've done a good few operations in my time, but I've never had a bear's emergency before."

"What a good thing Sir Mortimer had a sense of humor," said Mrs. Brown as they all drove home in

Mr. Brown's car. "I can't imagine what some surgeons would have said."

"Fancy keeping Paddington's fur as a souvenir," said Judy. "I wonder if he'll have it framed."

Looking out from behind Mr. Gruber's bunch of grapes, Paddington gave the rest of the carload one of his injured expressions. He felt very upset that everyone was taking his operation so lightly now that it had turned out all right, especially as he had a cold spot in the middle of his stomach where Sir Mortimer had removed the fur.

"Perhaps," said Mr. Gruber, as they turned into Windsor Gardens, "he just likes bears. After all, Mr. Brown," he added, turning to Paddington, "joking aside, it might have been serious, and it's nice to know there *are* people like that in the world you can turn to in times of trouble."

And to that remark even Paddington had to nod his wholehearted agreement.

CHAPTER SIX

Trouble in the Bargain Basement

SOON AFTER THE toffee-making episode, a change came over the weather. The air suddenly became crisper, and often in the mornings a thin film of ice covered the windows with a pattern of tiny ferns so that Paddington had to breathe quite heavily on his panes before he could see into the garden. Even when he did manage to make a hole large enough to see through, his effort was usually only rewarded by the sight of an even larger expanse of white outside.

Almost overnight great piles of fir trees arrived in the market, and on the carts brightly colored boxes of figs and dates put in an appearance alongside branches of holly and sprigs of mistletoe.

Inside the house there were changes too, as bowls of fruit and nuts began to appear on the sideboard and mysterious-looking lists were hastily tucked into jugs whenever he came into a room.

"Christmas comes but once a year," said Mrs. Bird when she met Paddington in the hall one morning on his return from the market, "and when it does it's time for certain young bears to have a bath. Otherwise they may find themselves left behind when we go on our shopping expedition this afternoon."

As Mrs. Bird disappeared into the kitchen, Paddington stared with wide-open eyes at the closed door for a moment or two and then hurried upstairs as fast as his legs would carry him.

The year before, Mrs. Brown and Mrs. Bird had taken him to a big London store in order to do the Christmas shopping, and although for some weeks past he had been keeping his paws firmly crossed in the hope that they would take him again, the news still came as a great surprise.

Paddington spent the rest of the morning hurrying round busily making his preparations for the big event. Apart from having a bath, there was so much to do in the way of making out lists and sorting through the various things he wanted to take with him, not to mention finding space for a hurried lunch, that it seemed no time at all before he found himself being helped off a bus as it stopped outside a large and familiar-looking building in one of the big London streets.

"I thought we would try and do most of our shopping at Barkridge's," explained Mrs. Brown when she saw Paddington's look of surprise. "It's so much easier if you can get everything in one shop."

Paddington peered up at the building with renewed interest, for he hadn't visited Barkridge's store since his very first shopping expedition, and it looked quite different now all the Christmas decorations were up. Apart from gay displays in all the windows, the outside of the building was a mass of twinkling lights that hung from some of the biggest Christmas trees he had ever seen in his life, and altogether it looked most inviting.

"I think I'd like to do some shopping by myself, Mrs. Brown," he exclaimed eagerly. "I've got one or two special things to buy."

Mrs. Brown and Mrs. Bird exchanged glances. "I suppose we could let him go down to the bargain basement," said Mrs. Bird as they entered the shop. "If we wait at the top of the stairs, he can't come to any great harm."

Paddington pricked up his ears at Mrs. Bird's words. He had never been down to a bargain basement before, and it sounded most interesting.

Mrs. Brown looked at him doubtfully. "Well," she said, "it *is* Christmas. But you must promise to be back here in half an hour. We've a lot to do."

"Thank you very much, Mrs. Brown," said Paddington gratefully as he picked up his belongings and hurried off in the direction of some nearby stairs.

"Hmm," said Mrs. Bird, voicing both their thoughts as Paddington disappeared through a door at the bottom. "That bear was in too much of a hurry for my liking. I've a nasty feeling in the back of my mind we're letting ourselves in for trouble."

"Even Paddington can't come to much harm in half an hour," said Mrs. Brown optimistically. "Not with shopping to do."

"If he gets as far as the shopping," said Mrs. Bird darkly.

Unaware of the way he was being discussed, Paddington stood for a moment blinking happily in the bright lights of the bargain basement. If anything, it was even more crowded than the upstairs had been, and there was so much to see it was difficult to take it all in at one glance.

In front of him was a big signpost with arrows pointing the way to the various departments, and after studying it for a moment or two he decided to investigate the one marked KITCHEN AND HOUSEHOLD. Apart from the fact that he felt sure the household department of a big store like Barkridge's would be bound to have something suitable for Mrs. Bird's present, he had just caught sight of another interesting notice pasted on the wall. It said THIS WAY TO THE FREE DEMONSTRATIONS, and it definitely needed looking into.

Following the arrows, Paddington made his way along a corridor until he found himself standing in a large area full of pots and pans. All around, people were shouting and jostling, and as he put his head down and pushed his way through, he suddenly discovered to his surprise that he had come up against a large table behind which stood a man in a white coat. The man appeared to be doing something with a piece of old carpet and a bottle, and he didn't look very pleased at the way things were going.

"Look at that!" he shouted, holding up the piece of

carpet as Paddington stood on tiptoe in order to get a better view. "Only one coating of Instant One-Dab Cleaning Fluid and already this old piece of carpet looks like new!

"Come on, ladies," he cried in a hoarse voice. "There must be *someone* who wants to buy a bottle. It not only cleans carpets—just one dab on your kitchen sink and you'll be able to see your face in it. Mirrors, furniture, floors—there's nothing in the world that can't be improved by Instant One-Dab Cleaning Fluid. I'm not asking the world for it. I'm not even asking much. All

I want for this giant-size economy bottle is the trifling sum of one pound."

Pausing for breath, the man looked at the sea of faces in front of him. "Some people can't see a bargain when it's held in front of their nose," he said crossly as no one moved.

"Take this piece of stuff here," he continued, reaching out across the table and picking up a shapeless object which he held up for everyone to see. "You couldn't have anything much dirtier than this. Most of you would probably have thrown it away years ago. Yet I guarantee that with one dab of my cleaning fluid it'll come up as good as new."

"What!" cried Paddington in alarm as he clambered up on his suitcase. "That's my hat you've got!"

"Your hat?" exclaimed the man, dropping it hurriedly. "I beg your pardon, sir. I didn't realize anyone was *wearing* it. I thought it was one of my old scraps. I keep a few of them by me for demonstrations, you know..."

The man's voice trailed away as he caught Paddington's eye. "I was only trying to get rid of your stains," he said lamely.

"Get rid of my stains?" repeated Paddington, hardly able to believe his ears. It had taken him a long time to collect all the different stains on his hat. Some of them

were so old he had almost forgotten how they had got
there in the first place, and some had even been made
by his uncle in Peru.

"Those aren't ordinary stains," he exclaimed hotly.
"Some of them have been handed down."

"Handed down?" echoed the man. "You can't hand
a stain down."

"Bears do," said Paddington firmly.

The demonstration man gave a nasty look. "Well, if
you want to hand them down anymore," he said,
waving the bottle of cleaning fluid dangerously close
to Paddington's hat, "I suggest you get lost. This is
very powerful stuff, and if the cork comes out acciden-
tally I shan't answer for the consequences."

Grabbing his hat, Paddington pulled it tightly down
over his head and pushed his way through the crowd,
out of range of the man's bottle. He didn't think much
of the first demonstration he'd seen, even if it had
been free, and he hurriedly made his way in the direction of the second one in the hope that it might prove
more interesting.

As he approached the next crowd, Paddington
paused for a moment and sniffed the air. To his surprise, there seemed to be a strong smell of pancakes,
and as he squeezed his way towards the demonstration

it got stronger and stronger, until by the time he reached the table he felt quite hungry.

This time the man in charge had a small camp stove in front of him and he was holding a frying pan in the air while he addressed his audience.

"How many times," he cried as Paddington reached the table, "how many times have you ladies broken your fried eggs in the morning? How many omelets

have you spoiled at lunchtime? And have you ever kept count of the number of times you've tried tossing a pancake only to find it stuck to the pan?"

Holding up the frying pan for everyone to see, the demonstration man paused dramatically. "Never again!" he cried as he waved it in the air. "Go home today and throw your old pans in the garbage. Buy one of my Magic Non-Stick frying pans and nothing— ladies, I repeat, *nothing*—will ever stick again. Why, it's so simple," he went on, "even a child of five can't go wrong.

"Come along, sir," he exclaimed, pointing to Paddington. "Show the ladies how to do it. Stand back, everyone," he called as he handed the frying pan to Paddington. "The young gentleman with the whiskers is going to show you all how easy it is to toss a pancake with one of my Magic Non-Stick frying pans."

"Thank you very much," said Paddington gratefully. "I might buy one for Mrs. Bird's Christmas present," he explained. "She's always grumbling about her pans."

"There you are," said the demonstration man triumphantly. "My first sale of the morning. Fancy all you ladies being put to shame by a young bear gentleman.

"I can see you know your frying pans as well as your onions, sir," he continued as Paddington gripped the frying pan firmly in both paws and closed his eyes as he prepared to test it. "Now, just a quick flick of the paw, and don't forget to catch the pancake on the way down. Otherwise..."

Whatever else the man had been about to say was lost as a gasp went up from the audience. "Here," he cried anxiously, "what have you done with it?"

"What have I done with it?" said Paddington with interest as he opened his eyes and peered at the empty pan.

"That was my demonstration pancake," cried the man, looking all around. "And now it's gone!"

The problem of where the pancake had disappeared to was suddenly solved as a disturbance broke out at the back of the crowd and a woman started to push her way through to the front.

"My best hat!" she exclaimed. "Covered in pancake mixture!"

"Never mind your hat," cried someone else. "What about my coat?"

As more and more voices joined in the uproar, Paddington decided to take advantage of the confusion. Picking up his suitcase and shopping bag, he hurried out of the Household Department, casting some extremely anxious glances over his shoulder as he went. He didn't like the look of things at all, and he decided he'd had quite enough of free demonstrations for one day.

It was as he was hurrying in the direction of the stairs and safety that Paddington suddenly stopped in his tracks again and peered up at the wall. In front of him was a large poster that he hadn't noticed before, showing a man in a white beard and a long red coat sitting astride a rocket. But it wasn't so much the picture that caught his eye as the wording underneath.

It said:

TRIPS TO THE MOON
VISIT FATHER CHRISTMAS IN THE MOON ROCKET
GET YOUR FREE PRESENT
TWO POUNDS ROUND-TRIP!

After the words a broad red arrow decorated with holly pointed the way towards a door, in front of which stood a group of people.

Paddington considered the matter for a moment. Two pounds seemed very cheap for a trip to the moon, especially as it had cost Mrs. Brown almost as much for the three of them on the bus and they hadn't even been given a present at the end.

Although he'd promised Mrs. Brown and Mrs. Bird to stay in the bargain basement Paddington felt sure they wouldn't mind in the circumstances if he took a short trip. At that moment the doors opened and the matter was decided for him as he was caught up in the rush of people all pushing and shoving to get through. In fact, it all happened so quickly he only just found time to hand his money to the man in uniform before the doors clanged shut behind him.

"Thank you very much," called the man, touching his cap as Paddington was swept past him. "A merry Christmas to you."

Paddington tried to raise his hat in reply, but by that time he was so tightly jammed against the wall at the back that he hardly had room to breathe, let alone move his paws. In fact, he was so squashed that it only took him a moment or two to decide very firmly indeed that he didn't think much of rockets. Apart from the fact that it kept stopping, it was so crowded he couldn't see a thing. And when it did finally reach the top of its travel, even more people pushed their way in before he had a chance to clamber out, and it started to fall back down again without his having so much as caught a glimpse of Father Christmas.

Altogether Paddington wasn't sorry when he heard the man in charge announce the fact that they were back in the bargain basement again and it was time to get out.

"I'd like my present now, please," he exclaimed as he pushed his way out behind the other passengers.

"Your *present?*" said the man in uniform. "What present?"

Paddington gave the man a hard stare. "The one the notice says you get," he explained.

The man looked puzzled for a moment, and then his face cleared as Paddington pointed to the poster. "You want Father Christmas on the fourth floor," he said. "We don't give presents here. This is the elevator, not a rocket."

"What!" cried Paddington, nearly falling over backwards with surprise. "This is an elevator? But I gave you two pounds."

"That's right, sir," said the man cheerfully. "Thank you very much. It isn't often we elevator operators get a Christmas tip."

"A Christmas tip?" echoed Paddington, his eyes getting larger and larger.

"Very kind of you it was," said the man. "And now, if you'll excuse me, I've another load to take up."

With that he clanged the doors shut, leaving Paddington fixed to the spot as if he had been turned into a pillar of stone. He was still rooted to the spot several minutes later when Mrs. Brown and Mrs. Bird came hurrying up, accompanied by an important-looking man in striped trousers.

"Where on earth have you been?" cried Mrs. Bird. "We've been looking everywhere for you."

"Are you all right?" asked Mrs. Brown anxiously. "You don't look very well."

"Oh, I'm all right, thank you, Mrs. Brown," said Paddington vaguely as he recovered himself. "And I haven't been on earth—at least, I have, but I didn't think I had and it cost me two pounds."

The rest of Paddington's explanations were lost as the man in the striped trousers bounded forward and shook him warmly by the paw. "My dear young bear," he exclaimed, "I'm the floor manager. Allow me to thank you for all you've done."

"That's all right," said Paddington, looking most surprised as he raised his hat.

"Non-stick frying pans have never been one of our most popular lines," said the floor manager as he turned to Mrs. Brown. "And as for the cleaning fluid ... now look at them both." He waved his hand in the direction of two large crowds in the distance. "They're both selling like hot cakes. Since this young bear demonstrated the frying pan, our man can't wrap them fast enough. And after our other assistant

removed the pancake stains from the customers' clothes, he's been rushed off his feet. Anything that gets a young bear's pancake stain out without leaving a mark must be good.

"You must let me know if there's anything we can do to repay you," he continued, turning back to Paddington.

Paddington thought for a moment. "I was doing some special Christmas shopping," he explained. "Only I'm not really sure what I want to buy. It's a bit difficult for bears to see over the edge of the counters."

"In that case," said the floor manager, snapping his fingers in the direction of one of the assistants, "you shall have the services of one of our expert shopping advisers. She can look after you for the rest of the day, and I'm sure she'll be only too pleased to help you with all your needs."

"Thank you very much," said Paddington gratefully. He wasn't at all sure what it was all about, but whatever the reason, he felt certain that with the help of anyone as important-sounding as a shopping adviser he ought to be able to get some very good Christmas presents indeed.

As she bent down to pick up her shopping, Mrs. Brown caught Mrs. Bird's eye. "I wish someone would tell me how Paddington gets away with it," she said.

"You'd have to be a bear yourself to answer that one," said Mrs. Bird wisely. "And if you were, the question wouldn't arise anyway. Bears have much more important things to think about."

CHAPTER SEVEN

Paddington and the Christmas Pantomime

"HAROLD PRICE?" said Mrs. Brown. "Wants to see me? But I don't know anyone called Harold Price, do I?"

"It's the young man from the big grocery store in the market," said Mrs. Bird. "He said it had something to do with their amateur dramatic society."

"You'd better show him in then," said Mrs. Brown. Now that Mrs. Bird mentioned it, she did vaguely remember Harold Price. He was a rather pimply-faced young man who served behind the jam counter. But for the life of her, she couldn't imagine what that had to do with amateur dramatics.

"I'm so sorry to trouble you," said Mr. Price as Mrs. Bird ushered him in to the living room. "But I expect you know there's a drama festival taking place in the hall round the corner this week."

"You'd like us to buy some tickets?" asked Mrs. Brown, reaching for her handbag.

Mr. Price shifted uneasily. "Well... er... no, not exactly," he said. "You see, we've entered a play for the last night—that's tomorrow—and we've been let down at the last moment by the man who was going to do the sound effects. I was told you have a young Mr. Brown who's very keen on that sort of thing, but I'm afraid I've forgotten his first name."

"Jonathan?" asked Mrs. Brown.

Mr. Price shook his head. "No, it wasn't Jonathan," he said. "It was a funny sort of name. He's been on television."

"Not *Paddington?*" said Mrs. Bird.

"That's it!" exclaimed Mr. Price. "Paddington! I knew it was something unusual.

"I wrote this play myself," he continued eagerly. "It's a sort of mystery pantomime, and we're hoping it may win a prize. The sound effects are most important, and we must have someone reliable by tomorrow night."

"Have you ever met Paddington?" asked Mrs. Bird.

"Well, no," said Mr. Price. "But I'm sure he could do them, and if he'll come I can let you all have free seats in the front row."

"That's most kind of you," said Mrs. Brown. "I don't know what to say. Paddington does make rather a noise sometimes when he's doing things, but I don't know that you'd exactly call them sound effects."

"Please!" appealed Mr. Price. "There just isn't anyone else we can ask."

"Well," said Mrs. Brown doubtfully as she paused at the door. "I'll ask him if you like—but he's upstairs doing his accounts at the moment, and I'm not sure that he'll want to be disturbed."

Mr. Price looked somewhat taken aback when Mrs. Brown returned, closely followed by Paddington. "Oh!" he stammered. "I didn't realize you were a... that is... I ... er ... I expected someone much older."

"Oh, that's all right, Mr. Price," said Paddington cheerfully as he held out his paw. "I'm nearly four. Bears' years are different."

"Er... quite," said Mr. Price. "I'm sure they are." He took hold of Paddington's outstretched paw rather gingerly. Mr. Price was a sensitive young man, and there were one or two old marmalade stains he didn't like the look of, not to mention a quantity of red ink from the debit side of Paddington's accounts, which somehow or other managed to transfer itself to his hand.

"You're sure you hadn't anything else planned?" he asked hopefully.

"Oh, no," said Paddington. "Besides, I like theaters and I'm good at learning lines."

"Well, they're not actually *lines*, Paddington," said Mrs. Brown nervously. "They're noises."

"Noises?" exclaimed Paddington, looking most surprised. "I've never heard of a noises play before."

Harold Price looked at him doubtfully. "Perhaps we could use you in some of the crowd scenes," he said. "We're a bit short of serfs."

"Serfs?" exclaimed Paddington.

"That's right," said Mr. Price. "All you have to do is come on and say 'Odds bodikins' every now and then."

"'Odds bodikins'?" repeated Paddington, looking more and more surprised.

"Yes," said Mr. Price, growing more enthusiastic at the idea. "And if you do it well, I might even let you say 'Gadzooks' and 'Scurvy knave' as well."

"Perhaps you'd both like to go into it all down at

the hall," said Mrs. Brown hastily as she caught sight
of the expression on Paddington's face.

"A very good idea," said Mr. Price. "We're just
about to start a rehearsal. I can explain it as we go
along."

"He did say it's a pantomime?" said Mrs. Bird when
she returned from letting Paddington and Mrs. Price
out.

"I think he did," replied Mrs. Brown.

"Hmm," said Mrs. Bird. "Well, if Paddington has a
paw in it, there'll be plenty of pantomime—you mark
my words!"

*

"Here we are," said Mr. Price as he showed Paddington through a door marked PRIVATE—ARTISTS
ONLY. "I'll take you along and introduce you to the
others."

Paddington blinked in the strong lights at the back
of the stage and then sniffed. There was a nice smell of
greasepaint and it reminded him of the previous time
he had been behind the scenes in a theater, but before
he had time to investigate the matter, he found himself
standing in front of a tall, dark girl who was stretched
out on a couch.

"Deirdre," said Mr. Price. "I'd like you to meet the

young Mr. Brown I was telling you about. He's promised to lend a paw with the sound effects."

The dark girl raised herself on one elbow and stared at Paddington. "You didn't tell me he was a *bear*, Harold," she said.

"I didn't know myself... actually," said Mr. Price unhappily. "This is Miss Flint, my leading lady," he explained, turning to Paddington. "She's in bacon and eggs."

"How nice," said Paddington, raising his hat politely. "I should like to be in bacon and eggs myself."

"You look rather as if you have been," said Miss Flint, shuddering slightly as she sank back onto the couch. "I suppose the show *must* go on, Harold, but *really!*"

Mr. Price looked at Paddington again. "Perhaps you'd better come with me," he said hastily, leading the way across the stage. "I'll show you what you have to do."

After giving Miss Flint a hard stare, Paddington followed Mr. Price until they came to a small table in the wings. "This is where you'll be," said Mr. Price, picking up a large bundle of papers. "I've marked all the places in the script where there are any sound effects. All you have to do is bang some coconuts together whenever it says 'horses' hooves,' and there's a record player for when we have any music or thunder noises."

Paddington listened carefully while Mr. Price explained about the script, and he examined the objects on the table with interest.

"It looks a bit difficult," he said when Mr. Price had finished his explanations, "especially with paws. But I expect it will be all right."

"I hope so," said Mr. Price. He ran his hands nervously through his hair and gave Paddington a last worried look as he went back onto the stage to join the rest of the cast. "I do hope so. We've never had a bear doing the sound effects before."

Mr. Price wasn't the only one to feel uneasy at the thought of Paddington taking part in his play, and by the time the following evening came round everyone in the Brown household was in a high state of excitement as they got ready for their outing. Mr. Price had been as good as his word, and he'd not only given Paddington a number of tickets for the family, but he'd slipped in an extra one for Mr. Gruber as well, and even Mr. Curry had promised to put in an appearance.

Paddington went on ahead of the others as he had one or two last-minute adjustments to make to his record player, but he was waiting at the door to greet them when they arrived just before the start of the performance. He was wearing a large rosette marked OFFICIAL in his hat, and he looked most important as he led the way down the crowded aisle to some seats in the front row before disappearing through a small door at the side of the stage.

As the Browns settled down in their seats, a roll of thunder shook the hall, and Mrs. Brown looked up anxiously. "That's very odd," she exclaimed. "Thunder at this time of the year. It was just starting to snow when we came in."

"I expect that was Paddington testing his sound effects," said Jonathan knowledgeably. "He said he had quite a few claps to do."

"Well, I wish he'd turn the volume down a bit," said Mrs. Bird, turning her attention to the stage as the curtain began to rise. "That ceiling doesn't look too safe to me."

"I think someone must have forgotten to pay the electricity bill," whispered Mr. Brown as he adjusted his glasses and peered at the scene.

Mr. Price's play was called

The Mystery of Father Christmas and the Disappearing Plans, and according to the program the action all took place one night in the hall of a deserted castle somewhere in Europe.

From where they were sitting, the Browns not only found it difficult to see what was going on, but when their eyes did get accustomed to the gloom, they found it even harder to understand what the play was about.

Several times Father Christmas came through a secret panel in the wall holding a lighted candle in his hand, and each time he disappeared he was followed after a short interval by Mr. Price playing the part of a mysterious butler. If Father Christmas was acting strangely, Mr. Price's actions were even more peculiar. Sometimes he came on waving the secret plans with a triumphant expression on his face, and at other times he looked quite sinister as he shook an empty fist at the audience to the accompaniment of a roll of thunder.

Behind the scenes Paddington was kept very busy. Apart from the thunder, there were the coconut shells to be banged together whenever anyone approached the castle, not to mention clanking drawbridge noises and creaking sounds each time a door was opened.

In fact, there was so much to do it took him all his

time to follow the script, let alone watch the action on the stage, and he was quite surprised when he looked up suddenly in the middle of one of his thunder records and found it was the intermission.

"Very good work, Mr. Brown," said Harold Price as he came off the stage mopping his brow and stopped by Paddington's table. "I couldn't have done it better myself. I don't think you missed a single cue."

"Thank you very much," said Paddington, looking very pleased with himself as he returned Mr. Price's thumbs-up sign with a wave of his paw.

Quite a lot of people had come and gone in the first half of Mr. Price's play, and altogether he wasn't sorry to sit down for a while and rest his paws. In any case, the serfs had to put in several appearances during the second act, and he was anxious to practice his lines while he had the chance.

It was some minutes after he had settled himself underneath the table with the script and a jar of marmalade that he noticed an unusual amount of noise going on at the back of the stage. It seemed to have something to do with Harold Price having mislaid his secret plans. Several times his voice rose above the others, saying he couldn't go on without them because a lot of his most important lines were written on the back. Paddington scrambled out hurriedly in order to investigate the matter, but by the time he stood up everything had gone quiet again, and order seemed to have been restored as the curtain went up for the second act.

Paddington was looking forward to the second half of Mr. Price's play, and even though a lot of people were still creeping around behind the scenes with anxious expressions on their faces, he soon forgot about it as Father Christmas made his entrance and approached Miss Flint's couch in the center of the stage.

From the little that could be seen of him behind his beard, Father Christmas looked most unhappy as he addressed Miss Flint. "I had hoped to bring thee glad tidings," he cried in ringing tones. "But alas, I am undone, for *I have lost the secret plans!*"

"You've *what?*" exclaimed Miss Flint, jumping up from her couch in alarm. Miss Flint had spent the intermission in her dressing room, and she was as surprised as anyone to learn that the plans really were missing. "What have you done with them?" she hissed.

"I don't know," said Father Christmas in a loud whisper. "I think I must have put them down somewhere. Er... nice weather we've been having lately," he continued in a loud voice as he played for time. "Hast thou read any good books lately?"

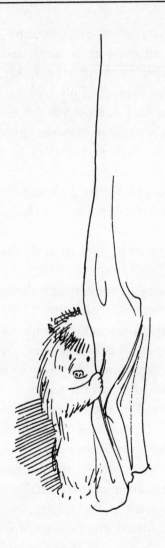

From his position at the side of the stage, Paddington looked even more surprised than Miss Flint at the sudden turn of events. Mr. Price had explained the play very carefully to him, and he felt sure no mention had been made of any character called Tidings. Then there was the question of the cloak. Father Christmas appeared to be wearing his cloak in exactly the same way that he'd worn it all through the play, and yet he'd definitely said something about it having come undone. Paddington consulted his script several times in case he'd made a mistake, but the more he looked at it, the more confused he became.

It was as he turned round to the desk in order to play one of his thunder records, just to be on the safe side, that he received yet another surprise, for there, lying in front of him, was a dog-eared pile of papers with the words *Secret Plans—Property of Harold Price* written in large letters across the front.

Paddington looked at the papers and then back at the stage. A nasty silence seemed to have come over the audience, and even Father Christmas and Miss Flint appeared to have run out of conversation as they stared at each other in embarrassment.

Coming to a decision, Paddington picked up the secret plans and hurried onto the stage with a determined expression on his face. After raising his hat several times to the audience, he waved in the direction of the Browns and Mr. Gruber and then turned towards the couch.

"Odds bodikins!" he cried, giving Father Christmas a hard stare. "I've come to do you up."

"You've come to do what?" repeated Father Christmas nervously, clutching the candle in one hand and the end of the couch in the other.

"I'm afraid I can't see anything about Glad Tidings in my script," continued Paddington. "But I've found your secret plans."

Paddington looked very pleased with himself as a burst of applause came from the audience. "Scurvy knave!" he exclaimed, making the most of his big moment. "Gadzooks! You left them under my coconuts!"

"I left them *where?*" said Father Christmas in a daze as Paddington held out the plans and exchanged them for the candle.

"Under my coconuts," explained Paddington patiently. "I think you must have put them there during the intermission."

"Fancy leaving your plans under a bear's coconuts," hissed Miss Flint. "A fine spy you are!"

While Miss Flint was talking, a glassy look came

over Father Christmas. So much had gone wrong already that evening it didn't seem possible anything else could happen, but there was definitely a very odd odor coming from somewhere.

"Can you smell something burning?" he asked anxiously.

Miss Flint paused. "Good heavens!" she cried, hurriedly taking the candle away from Paddington. "It's your beard—it's on fire!"

"It's all right, Mr. Christmas, I'm coming," called Paddington as he climbed up onto the couch. "I think I must have held the wick too close by mistake."

A gasp of surprise went up from the audience as Paddington took hold of the beard and gave it a tug.

"Well, knock me down with a feather," said a voice near the Browns as the whiskers came away in Paddington's paws and revealed the perspiring face of Harold Price. "Fancy that! It was the butler all the time—disguised as Father Christmas!"

"What a clever idea," said a lady in the row behind. "Having him unmasked by a bear."

"A most unusual twist," agreed her companion.

"My play!" groaned Harold Price, collapsing into a chair and fanning himself with the secret plans as the curtain came down. "My masterpiece—ruined by a bear!"

"Nonsense!" exclaimed Miss Flint, coming to Paddington's rescue. "It wasn't Mr. Brown's fault. If you hadn't lost the plans in the first place, all this would never have happened. Anyway," she concluded, "the audience seems to like it—just listen to them."

Mr. Price sat up. Now that Miss Flint mentioned it, there did seem to be a lot of applause coming from the other side of the curtain. Several people were shouting "Author!" and someone even appeared to be making a speech.

"I feel," said the judge as they joined him on the stage, "we must congratulate Harold Price on his pantomime. It was undoubtedly the funniest play of the week."

"The *funniest*," began Mr. Price. "But it wasn't meant to be funny..."

The judge silenced him with a wave of his hand. "Not only was it the funniest, but it had the most unusual ending I've seen for many a day. That serf bear," he said as he consulted a piece of paper in his hand, "his name doesn't seem to appear on the program, but he played his part magnificently. Remarkable timing—the way he set light to your beard. One false move with his paw and the whole lot might have gone up in flames! I have no hesitation," he concluded, amid a long burst of applause from the audience, "in awarding the prize for the best play of the festival to Mr. Harold Price."

Harold Price looked rather confused as the applause died away and someone called out, "Speech!"

"It's very kind of you all," he said, "and I'm most grateful. But I think I ought to mention that although I wrote the play, young Mr. Brown here had quite a large paw in the way it ended. I shouldn't be standing here now if it wasn't for him," he added as he turned to Paddington amid another outburst of clapping, "and I wouldn't like to think he'd gone unrecognized."

"How kind of Mr. Price to give Paddington some of the credit," said Mrs. Brown later that evening as they made their way home through the snow. "I wonder what he meant when he said Paddington had a paw in the ending?"

"Knowing Paddington's paws," said Mrs. Bird, "I shudder to think."

Mr. Gruber and the Browns looked back at Paddington in the hope of getting some kind of an expla-

nation, but his head was buried deep in his duffle coat and he was much too busy picking his way in and out of their footprints to hear what was being said.

Paddington liked snow, but while they'd been in the

theater rather too much had fallen for his liking, and he was looking forward to warming his paws in front of the fire at Number Thirty-two Windsor Gardens.

Apart from that, the sight of a Christmas tree in someone's window had just reminded him of the date, and he was anxious to get home as quickly as possible so that he could hang up his stocking.

There were still several more days to go before the holiday, but after watching Mr. Price's play that evening, Paddington didn't want to take any chances, particularly over such an important matter as Father Christmas.

About the Author

I WROTE MY FIRST children's book in 1957 and it came about largely by accident.... I was sitting at the typewriter one morning when my gaze happened to alight on a toy bear I had bought my wife for Christmas. We called him Paddington, so I typed the words: "Mr. and Mrs. Brown first met Paddington on a railway platform. In fact that was how he came to have such an unusual name for a bear, for Paddington was the name of the station."

Suddenly I wanted to write more about this small character. Where had he come from? What was he doing in London? What were his reactions to life in England and the curious complications we humans make for ourselves? Until that time I had always thought up stories and then tried to people them with characters. Suddenly, I learned a very simple fact of fictional life: If you create a believable character and you place it into a situation, events will develop naturally of their own accord.

The hardest part with Paddington is not getting him into trouble—he does this of his own accord—but getting him out of it in a way which is morally justifiable; someone must always benefit from his misdeeds, however tenuously.

I once received a letter from a child who said she liked my books because they made pictures in her head. It was the nicest compliment I've ever heard.

—Michael Bond, excerpted from *Children's Books and Their Creators,* Houghton Mifflin Company, 1995

Have You Read These Big Bestsellers from SIGNET?

THE DOMINO PRINCIPLE

BY ADAM KENNEDY

A SIGNET BOOK

NEW AMERICAN LIBRARY

TIMES MIRROR

For Regan and Jack

Who could these men be? What were they talking about? What authority could they represent? K. lived in a country with a legal constitution . . . all the laws were in force. . . .

FRANZ KAFKA, *The Trial*

PART ONE

Now that it's over, or almost over, I can see that it never was what I wanted it to be. The things I needed weren't available. Not to me.

It starts when you're very young. They tell you things that aren't true. They ask you to believe that a man by himself is a valuable thing, that his identity is sacred, that he can go as far, do as much, win as many prizes as he's able. All he needs is strength and courage and honesty.

It's a beautiful story. It's irresistible. Especially to people who don't have anything. They learn it early, just as their parents and grandparents learned it before them. They need to believe it, so they do.

Every man's a free man. His destiny is his own. That's the way they teach it. They also teach you that it's wrong to question it. They find ways to punish the people who do.

So it goes on that way, an imperfect circle you can only break by dying.

Then, of course, it all comes apart. That's the final punishment. The ones who believed the most and questioned the least, end up believing in nothing.

2

They brought me up to Ditcher's office on a Thursday afternoon. Bowkamp, his deputy, came down to the carpenter shop to take me up himself. That wasn't the usual procedure at Hobart. It wasn't usual for Ditcher to stand up when you came into his office either. But that's what he did when I walked in.

There were a hundred and thirty-six men in maximum security. Ninety-five blacks, twelve Puerto Ricans, three Chinese, two Mexicans, one Piegan Indian, and twenty-three white Caucasians. Only two of them had ever gone past eighth grade. Oscar was one. I was the other.

The Monday before I went up to see Ditcher, Oscar walked across the yard during the morning break and handed me a cigarette.

"I keep hearing things about you," he said.

"What kind of things?"

"Nothing definite. Just something floating around. Your name keeps coming up."

The guards didn't like Ditcher. They spread stories about him to anybody who would listen. They said he changed his socks three times a day and his shirt twice, washed his hands every ten minutes, and put on rubber gloves before he took a leak. He was a pale, dried-up, starched and antiseptic-looking bastard, no question about it, but that first day I talked with him in his office he only washed his hands once.

"The carpenter shop," he said. "Right?"

"Yes, sir."

"You like that work?"

4

"Yes, sir."

He opened a folder on his desk and flipped through some papers. "You've been here, let's see, how long?"

"Five years."

"Just over," he said.

"Yes, sir."

"You've got a clean chart, I have to say that for you. Not a mark here as far as I can see." He looked up at me. "With your background . . ." he seemed to forget what he was going to say. He sat for a long moment cleaning his fingernails with a paper clip. "I mean, there ought to be some work around here that would be more interesting than the carpenter shop."

That night, when we were in our bunks with the lights out, Oscar said, "What happened with Ditcher?"

"Nothing. He just stroked me a little and that was it."

"What do you mean?"

"He said I was a good inmate. Instead of being a carpenter, I should have a better job."

"Bullshit. If you're a model prisoner, I'm the Virgin Mary."

"I'm telling you. That's what he said."

"Maybe he's hot for your body."

"I don't think so."

"Next time you see him, tell him you got a fifty-five year old cellmate with hairy legs and no morals . . ."

"I'll do that."

". . . I mean, if there's gonna be any favors handed out, I want to get in line."

3

A couple days later, Bowkamp came after me again. This time he said, "Bring your gear." I put some tools in a box, hefted it on my shoulder, and followed along up to Ditcher's office. Before he went in, Bowkamp said, "Leave your toolbox here in the hall."

This time Ditcher didn't ask me to sit down. He said, "We need some shelves built in the conference room down the hall. It'll be several days' work."

"Yes, sir."

"I mean when I send down for you, don't come up without your tools."

"Yes, sir."

Ditcher turned to Bowkamp. "Go unlock the conference room and take Mr. Tagge in there. Tell him we'll be with him in a minute or two."

After the deputy left, Ditcher turned to me. "This Mr. Tagge is a man from the outside. He wants to talk to you. He may need to talk to you more than once."

"Yes, sir."

He stood up behind his desk. "I've got my instructions. So it's something you've got to do. And you're not to talk about it to *anybody*. That means Spiventa. You open your mouth, it'll be your ass. Understand?"

"Yes, sir."

"Anytime I have you brought up here, it's to put up shelves. Just in case anybody gets nosy."

"Yes, sir."

The man waiting in the conference room looked like the senior vice-president of a New York bank. Dark suit, white shirt, striped tie, neat gray hair, thin and brushed back, clean-shaven, and rimless glasses. Ditcher tried to act as if he were in charge but his voice gave him away. It was thin and tight.

"This is Roy Tucker, Mr. Tagge."

Mr. Tagge stood up, loose and strong and easy, crisp and calm and sure of himself. He held out his hand and shook mine. "How do you do, Mr. Tucker. I'm Marvin Tagge." He indicated a chair. I hesitated and he said, "Sit down. Please. No pressure. We're just going to have a little talk." He turned to Ditcher then and said, "Thank you, Warden." Ditcher left, closing the door behind him.

Tagge offered me a cigarette, lit one himself, and sat down across the table from me.

"All right," he said. "Let's not waste time. I represent a group of people who are interested in your situation. They want to help you if they can. How does that sound to you?"

"You mean parole?"

"No. I have nothing to do with that end of it. Besides, as I understand it, your sentence was very specific. No parole consideration till you've served twenty years."

He got up and walked to the window. "Let me put it this way. If things work out, I'm sure we can help you. But at the moment I can't give you any details. I have to ask you to accept it on faith. Accept *me* on faith. Later, I'll be able to tell you more."

"Let me get this straight. You want to help me and you want nothing from me in return. Is that it?"

Tagge smiled. "No, that's *not* it. We will definitely want something in return."

"Like what? I'm in here for at least fifteen more years. I can build shelves or make you a nice breadboard. But that's about it."

"You're going too fast, Mr. Tucker. We're not positive you're the man for us. That's why I'm here to talk with you. When *we* know, *you'll* know. Then, you can decide."

"Where does Ditcher fit in?"

"He doesn't. This is between you and me."

"You mean you tell Ditcher what you want and he'll do it?"

"That's right."

"Good," I said. "Then get me out of maximum security."

"All right."

"And my cellmate, Spiventa. Get him out too."

"All right," he said. Then I stood up and pushed my chair back. I looked at him for a minute. "I don't know who you are, Mister, but I think you're handing me a first-class line of horseshit."

Tagge smiled again. "No, I'm not. You'll see."

That afternoon, Spiventa and I were moved out of maximum security and into a cell with a shower, a toilet, and beds you could sleep on.

"How'd you arrange this?" Oscar said.

"I didn't arrange anything."

"You mean the warden decided we were a couple of worthwhile guys, so he's doing us a favor? Is that it?"

"All I know is what Bowkamp said. We've got a good record so—"

"So nothing. It doesn't play like that. There's no reward system in the pen. They take things away but they never *give* anything. That just ain't the way it works."

"It must be. Here we are."

"That's what I mean. It's a square egg. The only thing that figures is that there's some connection with those two trips you made to Ditcher's office."

"I told you about that. I was up there—"

"I know. Putting up shelves."

"That's it."

"That's *not* it," he said. Then he grinned. "But I'm not fighting it. Whatever you're doing, keep it up. Maybe we'll get a color television next, and two or three eighteen-year-old pussies. We'll watch football games and play hide-the-wienie every night."

Tagge settled back in his chair and lit a cigarette.

"All right. We've made some progress. You found out that I can deliver what I promise."

"I know you got me out of maximum security."

"That's right. Now, let's go on from there." He zipped open a flat leather briefcase, took out a file folder, and opened it on the table in front of him. "We need a man. We think it's you. What I have to do is convince myself, then convince my people."

"And who's gonna convince me?"

He grinned, took his glasses out of his pocket, and put them on. "That's the easy part. Everybody knows it's better to be *out* of prison than *in* it."

"Is that what we're talking about?"

"*That's* what we're talking about." He looked at me over his glasses. "I can see I have your attention now."

"That's right."

He looked down at the folder and rearranged a couple of the pages. "I'm going to read what we have about you. Not all the details. Just the important ones. If you don't correct me, I'll assume that what I see here is the truth."

I sat there looking at him, trying to guess what I was getting into. And once I got in, how I could get out. I decided it was simple. I could get out whenever I wanted to. Just up from the chair, out the door, and back to the carpenter shop. Back to maximum security and fifteen years, minimum, of wood shavings, sawdust, and the screech of machinery in my ears.

"One thing," Tagge said, "I don't want this to have

a threatening tone . . . I know Ditcher told you these conversations have to be kept secret."

"He didn't put it that way exactly. He told me to keep my mouth shut or it would be my ass."

Tagge nodded and went on. "If there's even a suspicion of any leak, everything will come to a stop. You'll be put in a situation where you can't communicate anything you've heard to anyone. And Ditcher and I will deny that I was ever here. Do you understand that?"

"I understood it from the beginning."

"Good. Let's go on." He adjusted his glasses and began to read: " 'Roy Tucker. Born in Underhill, West Virginia, January 27, 1942. Parents dead. A sister, Enid, living in Toronto.' How does she happen to be in Canada?"

"Her husband didn't want to go to Vietnam and get his balls shot off, so he went to Canada. She went with him."

"Are you in touch with them?"

"No. I'm not in touch with anybody."

"Not even your sister?"

"Especially not her."

"Why is that?" he said.

"Because her husband's a pain in the ass. The only smart thing he ever did in his life was beat the draft. From the day he started up with Enid, he's spent most of the time telling her what a prick her brother is. And she believes him. So I can get along without either one of them. He'll make his ten thousand a year kissing somebody's ass up there in Toronto. She'll get fat as a cow, they'll have half a dozen more kids, and they can all go to hell as far as I'm concerned."

"The fact that you're in prison . . . did your sister and her husband . . ."

"You mean now? This trip?"

"Yes."

11

"That was part of it, I guess. She wrote me a dreary fucking letter telling me she didn't want her kids to know their uncle was a jailbird. Words to that effect. But it started long before that. I've been in and out of jail since I was fifteen. You've got it all there in your folder. My mother died when I was twelve; Enid went to live with our aunt in Ohio; my dad ran off to Bluefield with some floozy; and I started proving to everybody how tough I was. I stole anything I could get my hands on, got drunk, got in fights, breaking and entering. You name it. For eight years, all the time I was *out* of jail, *all together*, only added up to a year and two months. So my sister and her husband decided they'd be better off without me."

"You said the only smart thing your brother-in-law did was stay out of the Army. If you feel that way, why did *you* go in?"

"I didn't have much say in the matter. I was picked up for armed robbery in Wheeling, and the judge gave me a choice. Three years in the Army or three years in the pen. I took the Army. If I had it to do over again, I'd go to jail."

Tagge looked at me for a while and didn't say anything. Then he looked down at the folder again. "I'd never know that from looking at your service record. Perfect discipline chart, high motivation, top-rated marksman in your outfit, promoted from private to sergeant in two years, three decorations . . ."

"I played the game. I'm good at that. I know when I'm outmaneuvered. I can play by anybody's rules if I have to."

"It says here you received a severe wound. . . ."

"I was shot in the ass if you call that severe. 'Multiple lacerations of the gluteus maximus.' That was the medical description. Looks impressive on a Purple Heart certificate but it's not that serious. A hell of a lot better than some other places I could think of."

12

"You were eligible for discharge after you left the hospital. But you refused it. . . ."

"The hell I did. That's what it says in my papers but that's not the way it was. They sent me to a hospital in Japan and a doctor there decided he was going to make a man out of me. Major Applegate was his name. He fucked me up good, but I can't say I didn't like him. He was just a young guy, in his thirties, I guess, but he was a hell of a doctor. And he had some missionary blood in him. Bound and determined to save me from a life of crime and horseshit. So when I got healed up to where I could sit down without putting an air cushion under me, Applegate fixed it so I could stay on at the hospital, as a medical aide, instead of being discharged. It looked like I was volunteering to finish out my enlistment. So everybody around the hospital treated me like a fucking hero. They even wrote me up in the newspaper they had there at the rehabilitation center. And I went for it. Applegate had me brainwashed to where I thought I really *could* turn myself around and end up doing something besides going to jail. I hustled my ass those last eight months in the Army. Half the time I did double shifts in the hospital. I was really switched on. And Applegate was clucking over me like a mother hen. By then he'd got the idea that not only was he gonna save my soul, he was gonna turn me into a doctor. And, like I say, I started to believe it. I came out of that Army separation center like a steer out of a loading chute. I was twenty-six years old and I had the world by the ass. At least that's what I thought. But it didn't work out that way."

"What happened?"

"You know what happened. It's all in that file."

That night in the chow line I was walking behind Oscar, and behind me were two guys from the cell next to ours—a rangy, keg-chested bastard named Harley and a towheaded kid they called Nebraska.

Harley had a mouth. He'd been zapping Oscar and me ever since we moved over from maximum security, keeping it up in a nonstop mumble, so you could get the sense of what he was saying but never quite catch all the words. Behind me in the line, I heard him start up again, in a husky, fruity whisper.

". . . some fancy stud he is . . . big carpenter . . . very mean . . . maximum security . . . but a good friend of the man upstairs . . . pushin' his tool in the warden's office, I hear . . . up there in the warden's office screwing himself an early parole . . ."

I wheeled around, grabbed him by his shirt front and one ear, spun him once, and rammed his head into the cement-block wall. When he turned back to me with his hands out, clutching, I kicked him hard between the legs, and when he slumped over I kicked him twice in the face.

They took us back to the cell without any food. After they slammed the door, Oscar said, "What got into you?"

"Nothing."

"Nothing? You call that nothing?"

"I had a bad afternoon. I wasn't in the mood for that bastard's mouth."

"How much you bet they move us back across the yard?"

"Why you? You didn't do anything?"

"I didn't? Who do you think was handling Nebraska while you were busy with his girl friend?"

"You always told me you were too smart to fight."

"I am. But I couldn't stand there and watch you get scratched to death."

I shared a cell with Oscar for two years before he told me anything about himself. Then, one day he started talking.

"You heard about the guy who was born with a silver spoon in his mouth—in my mouth there was a bread stick. My old man owned an Italian delicatessen in New York, on Columbus Avenue, in the West Eighties.

"In those days it was a great neighborhood. Some people with a lot of money, a lot of people with some money, and a lot more just getting by. But they all liked to eat. So my dad did all right. I can still smell that store. Twenty kinds of salami, forty kinds of cheese, homemade pasta, peppers on strings, and pickles in the barrel.

"Everybody worked in our house. Anytime I wasn't in school, I was in the store. And my sister, Ada, was in the back with my mother, making salads and pasta and hors d'oeuvres, anything the customers wanted.

"My dad's idea was that when you were depending on people for your living it was up to you to give them what they asked for. 'When a customer asks a question,' he used to say, 'there's only one answer . . . yes, sir. Or yes, ma'am. We're serving the public and if we don't do it right, somebody else will.' He had the same ideas about school. 'For your sister it's different. She'll get married and have a family. But you need to learn things so you can get ahead. When the teacher talks, you listen. It doesn't matter if you like him or not, he knows something you *don't* know and you're there to find out what it is.'

"So I listened. I worked my ass off to get good marks in school, and the rest of the time I worked my ass off helping out in the store.

"Economics. 'That's the thing to study,' my dad said. 'Find out about money. And business. That's the way to get ahead.' So I did. I lived at home and worked in the store and went to college. And that's *all* I did.

"When I graduated, in the summer of 1942, I enlisted in the Marines. My father said a man had to fight for his country. I fought all right, for three solid, fucking years. When I got mustered out I felt like an old man.

"I went back to New York and the next thing I knew I was in graduate school at Columbia and still working in my father's store. I got married to an Italian girl I'd known since I was six years old, we had two kids in two years. Then I started teaching economics in a high school on West End Avenue. And evenings and weekends I worked in that God-damned store.

"For almost fifteen years I stayed there. I stuck it out till 1960. Then, one nice summer evening, about a week after my fortieth birthday, I peeled off my apron, took three hundred dollars out of the cash register, walked out of the store, and took a cab to the bus terminal on Eighth Avenue. I got on the first Greyhound heading west, and I never went back."

"Where'd you go?"

"Everywhere. I covered this country like a rug. But mostly in the West. I liked it out there. And I stayed away from the cities. Any town over fifty thousand was too big for me. When I needed money, I'd get some kind of a job and work for six weeks or so. Then I'd go on a toot. Drinking and whoring around, balling anybody I could get my hands on. And when the

17

money ran out, I'd go back to work, work a while, then screw off again. After a couple years of that I fell in with a pair of ex-cons. And they took me over. I mean, they really educated me. Next thing I knew, I'd stopped working altogether. When we ran out of money, we'd roll a drunk or two. Or we'd stick up a gas station and away we'd go.

"One thing led to another. Until one night some asshole came around the corner with a shotgun when I was knocking over a filling station in Kansas, and I shot him. From then on, it was nothing but running and killing. A man in a drugstore in Salina, a state trooper in Iowa.

"Finally, I had to look for some city to hole up in. So I went to Chicago, found myself a juicy lady, and disappeared for a few weeks. Till one day my girl friend blew the whistle on me. For some reason I never understood. The police walked in one night when I was half-gassed and wrapped me up.

"Iowa claimed me so they sent me to Fort Dodge for trial. I no sooner hit jail out there than this cunt from Chicago, the same one who'd turned me in, showed up with three or four gorillas from Gary and broke me out again.

"We holed up in some God-forsaken place in South Dakota for a couple months, me and this woman and her friends. Finally the money ran low, and we headed back East looking for some banks to knock over.

"We found all kinds of banks. Mattoon, Illinois, Sterling, Illinois, Greencastle, Indiana. Then we rolled into Logansport, Indiana, and the shit hit the fan. Somebody pushed the alarm button, the bank guards started shooting, and all hell broke loose. But we blasted our way out and headed for the car.

"We almost made it. But some hay-seed cop outsmarted us. He took the elevator to the roof of an office building next door and perched up there with a

18

rifle, picking us off like ground hogs as we ran from the bank to the car. He was a good shot, too. Four for four. I was the only one he didn't kill.

"It took the jury about thirty seconds to reach a verdict. And it took the judge about ten seconds to pass sentence. But he took the time to give me a lecture first.

" 'You're a man with some background, an education, a respectable war record. How can such a man as yourself turn a gun on innocent people?' I just stood there with my eyes down, trying to look like Jesus Christ, and hoping for the best. But inside my head I had an answer for him: Ask any soldier, you bastard. It's like getting laid. After the first one, the others come easy."

The next morning, before breakfast, they marched me up to Ditcher's office. He was pacing back and forth behind his desk, his jaws clamped together, and his face as white as a piece of dough.

"Leave the prisoner here," he said to the guard. "You wait outside." As soon as the door closed he said, "Because of you we have a man in the infirmary."

"Good. I hope he dies."

That stopped him. He walked over to his chair and eased down in it.

"I swear to Christ," he said. "I give up."

I stood there with my hands behind my back, looking down at him, waiting for him to rewind. Eventually, he pulled everything together.

"Look, Tucker, this isn't any everyday-discipline gig. You're not a boob and we both know it." He waited again. I kept looking at him. Finally, he went on. "There's something serious in the works. You know that as well as I do. You probably know *more* about it than I do."

He got up and started to pace again. "I'll tell you the truth. I don't want to know any more than I do already. And what I know is *nothing*. You understand that? Just remember I told you that. I don't know *anything* about what's going on. But I know it's important. And if you do anything to blow it, it'll be my ass along with yours. You know what I mean?"

"No, sir."

"I mean I want you to cool it. Be inconspicuous.

For five years you've been no trouble around here. So for Christ's sake, don't start now."

"When you say there's something important going on, you're talking about Mr. Tagge? Is that right?"

"I didn't say that. Don't put words in my mouth. I didn't even mention his name. As far as I'm concerned, when you're in that conference room you're putting up shelves. If there's anybody there with you, I don't know anything about it. And I don't want to know."

"But you took me in there to him. That's how I met him in the first place."

"All right. I took you in there. But that's *all* I did. Anything else, I don't know anything about." He paced back and forth. Then he said, "But don't tell Tagge I said that." He stopped walking and looked at me. "You know what I mean?"

"I guess so."

"I got a job to do here. I don't want to get in over my head. I don't want to get fucked up, you understand? I don't want anybody to fuck me up."

After lunch that day, the guard came to get me again and I went up to the conference room with my tools. Tagge was waiting there.

"You've got Ditcher all excited," he said after I sat down.

"Something's got him excited."

"It's all right," Tagge said. I talked to him. He's in a better frame of mind now." He opened the file folder in front of him and put on his glasses. "I want to ask some questions about your trial."

"There's not much to tell. They indicted me for first-degree murder, the jury thought they proved the case, and they convicted me."

"And your wife was convicted too?"

"That's right. They said she was an accessory. Before the fact or after the fact. They couldn't decide which. So they gave her five years, just to be on the safe side."

"The trial was in Marion County, Indiana."

"That's right. Indianapolis."

"Were you living there?"

"No. I was living in Chicago. But the man died in a motel out by the Indianapolis airport. That's where they said I killed him."

"Let's get back to your wife for a minute. I take it she's out of prison by now."

"That's right."

"*Do* you know where she is?"

"No."

"Why not?" he said.

"We're not in touch with each other."

"Any reason?"

"What's the point? Why should I hang her up? She's out and I'm in. I'll either be here fifteen more years or I'll be here till I keel over."

"If you feel that way about it, why did you get married?"

"That's a good question."

"It says here you were married in the Marion County jail after you were both convicted."

"That's right."

"And now you don't know where she is?"

"No. But she knows where *I* am. There's no mystery about that."

"Does she write to you?"

"She used to. But after the first year or so I asked the mail guy here to send them back as soon as they came in. So I don't know if she still writes or not. Like I said, I don't want to hang her up."

"But what if you got out. . . ."

"I'm *not* out. I don't even *think* about getting out. One day at a time. That's the only way to survive in this shit-house."

He gave me a long look. Then he said, "This man you killed . . ."

"*I* didn't say I killed him. The prosecutor did."

"All right—this man you were convicted of killing, Bert Riggins, how did you come to know him?"

"I worked for him. I drove his car and washed it and greased it and did whatever else he told me to do."

"Did you like that job?"

"Not much."

"Did you like Riggins?"

"Nobody liked Riggins."

"Then why'd you work for him?"

"Because I had a record. How many ex-cons do you have working in your office?"

He didn't answer. He studied something in the folder for a minute, then he said, "What happened to Dr. Applegate? Last time we talked, you said he wanted to help you get an education after you got out of the service."

"That's right, he did. But he found out he'd bit off a bigger hunk that he could chew."

"How's that?"

"Well, I was twenty-six years old to start with. Number two, I'd only finished one year of high school. And number three, I had a record as long as my arm.

"Applegate didn't know all that till he got me to his house in Chicago, west of Chicago, Oak Park. I figured I'd better level with him so he wouldn't get some surprises later on. He took it pretty well, said it didn't make any difference. But I could see it made him think. Here he was with a wife and three kids and he was getting ready to subsidize a guy who needed three years of high school and four years of college before he'd be able to even think about medical school. It wasn't a question of money. He was loaded and so was his wife. I just got the idea that he was having second thoughts about taking me on as a weight around his neck. Vietnam and Japan—that was one thing. Being home in Oak Park, Illinois, things looked different. One night I heard him and his wife having a big discussion in their bedroom. I couldn't make out what they were arguing about but I decided it was me. So I waited for a couple hours till everything was quiet. Then I sneaked out the front door and left. I stayed in a crummy hotel on the near North Side for a couple weeks, then I saw Riggins' ad in the paper. And I went to work for him."

"Did you tell him you'd been in jail?"

"Yeah, I did."

"He didn't mind?"

"He liked it, I think. Gave him something to use against me in case he needed it."

"How long did you work for him?"

"About a year. From March 'sixty-eight till February 'sixty-nine, when he died."

"How did he die?"

"I drove him down from Lake Forest to Indianapolis the afternoon of February twenty-seventh. He was supposed to meet some guy who was flying in that night from Denver. We checked in the airport motel about five. He had a suite on the second floor and I had a single room, about thirty feet down the corridor. He told me he wouldn't be needing me till morning, that I could take the car and enjoy myself. So I drove into downtown Indianapolis about seven, found a place to eat, and went to a movie. When I got back to the motel, the police arrested me."

"It says here that Riggins died of a massive injection of morphine."

"That's right. And in his pocket they found a letter addressed to his lawyer saying he was afraid Thelma and I were planning to kill him, that I'd said something on the drive down from Chicago that made him suspicious. So they had the motive, they figured, and they went on from there. They got Applegate on the stand and he testified that I was trained to give injections when I was in Japan. So that was that. They hung me up to dry."

"Your lawyer was Arnold Schnaible? From Chicago?"

"That's right."

"What was his defense?"

"He said Riggins killed himself and tried to lay it on me."

"Why would he do that?"

"Because he was a son of a bitch, because he knew about Thelma and me, and because he was dying anyway. He had cancer all through his guts. He wouldn't have lived till summer. So, since *he* was going, he

25

figured he might as well screw us up for good measure. He gave himself the injection, got rid of the syringe somehow, went back to his room, and died. That was our case. But the jury didn't go for it. Not for a minute. Schnaible said if Riggins came to Indianapolis to meet some guy, why didn't that guy show up? And if I'd done it, why did I go into Indianapolis to have dinner and see a movie? The prosecutor said I did it to establish an alibi *after* I'd killed him. And the jury believed everything the prosecutor said."

"You have to admit it's a tough story to swallow, a man killing himself just to hurt somebody else."

"Not if you knew Riggins."

Tagge lit a cigarette and leaned back in his chair, squinting at me through the smoke. Finally, he said, "You can't be convicted twice for the same case so it won't hurt to tell the truth now. Did you kill Riggins or not?"

"No. But even if I did, I wouldn't be damned fool enought to sit here and tell you about it."

"Why not? I can't do you any damage."

"Maybe you can and maybe you can't. I don't know anything about you, who you are, where you came from, who you work for. You're just a guy in a three-hundred dollar suit who says he's gonna help me. Well, I'll believe that when I see it. The only kind of help I need is to get out of this hole. If that's not what we're talking about, you're wasting my time."

"That *is* what I'm talking about."

"No, you're not. You're digging up a lot of crap that's dead and buried. There's no new evidence in my case. I know that. I'm not gonna get pardoned. The only way I'll get out of here is by a miracle. Is that your specialty?"

"Not exactly. But I've got a good record for getting things done."

"Like I said, I'll believe it when I see it."

That night I lay in my bunk wide awake. Long after the lights were out. Things slowly began to come to life in me, whole sections of myself that I'd closed off, nailed shut, plastered over. For the first time in five years I let myself think about a different life, hope for something better. I admitted to myself that there was a world outside the walls, and I began to imagine myself as a part of it.

There was no logic to it. I couldn't make any sense of Tagge's presence of his words or his shadowy promises. But he did exist. He did have some purpose, whatever it might be, and that purpose seemed to involve me.

And whatever he wanted from me, or imagined he wanted, it had to happen outside the walls. Before he could use me in any way whatsoever, he had to get me out. Thin as the hope was, I did have some hope now. And it charged me up, opened my mind and my memory, and kept me awake, staring at the shadows the night lights made on the ceiling.

All the details of an everyday, outside life, some remembered, some imaginary, exploded in my head. Totally selfish, a series of images, all featuring me, nobody else, walking, riding, drinking the water, breathing the air, sleeping a quiet sleep on a wide clean bed.

I ate hot dogs at counters, sat in the bleachers at baseball games, strolled in parks, hailed taxis, rode buses and subways and trains, bought tickets and boarded planes, sat in movies, drank beer, shot pool, drove cars on back roads, ordered meals in restaurants with tablecloths, read newspapers on park benches, bought food in supermarkets, slept in clean pajamas, took long hot showers, and had a thousand shaves and haircuts in bright shops smelling of talcum powder.

I was anxious now for the next meeting with Tagge, eager to say whatever words he needed to hear. I'd allowed myself to handle the prizes and dream about the rewards. Now I had to move forward if there was any way to do it. I made up the speech in my head, lying there awake in the darkness: Whatever the bargain is, whatever you want from me, whatever I have to exchange for some kind of a life outside, I'm good for it. I won't question it or back down. Let's stop talking, for Christ's sake, and get on with it.

It was a week before they took me to the administration floor again. One of the guards, a hard-eyed old bulldog named Feaster, came for me.

"What about my tools?" I said.

"They're already there. Bowkamp had them sent up from the carpenter shop."

Bowkamp was waiting in the conference room for me, sour and cold, strictly business. "We want these shelves up as quick as possible. No more fuckin' the dog. All across that wall, floor to ceiling." He pointed at the narrow wall behind the conference table. "And the same thing on that wall down there." He pointed to the wall at the other end of the room.

Feaster sat in there with me all day, smoking cigars, sucking his teeth, and watching me work. I sawed and planed and sanded, working steady but not killing myself. And I waited for Tagge to show up. But he didn't come. Five days later, when I put up the last shelf, he hadn't come yet.

I was still lying awake at night. But I'd gone through all the pictures of myself on the outside. Now all I saw or thought about was Thelma. I'd pushed her away as long as I could. Now she settled in there with me in the dark and came to life, so real I could hear her and touch her.

She was six years younger than me, only twenty when I met her. She and Riggins had been married for almost three years, since she was seventeen. She was hill people, like me, and she'd wanderd up to Chicago from North Carolina with a couple of her relatives. She'd been working as a maid in somebody's house in Lake Forest when Riggins saw her. First he hired her to work for him, then he got her into bed, then he married her.

She was no match for him. Where she came from, people like her didn't say no to people like Riggins. And, once I'd started to work for him, I was no match for him either. He had a way of making you know it was his way or no way. You either went along with him or you went down the drain. He had her scared and he had me scared.

She wasn't looking to cheat on him and I wasn't trying to make time with somebody else's wife, certainly not his, but he pushed us together without knowing it. Or maybe he did know it.

Each one of us felt sorry for the other one, and everything else that happened grew out of that. We tried to keep it covered up but we weren't very good at hiding how we felt, especially Thelma, so we didn't fool him for very long.

Finally, she told him the truth, told him she wanted to leave him and go off with me. But he just went ahead with whatever he was doing and acted as if he hadn't heard her. Not long after that he was dead, I was in prison, and so was Thelma.

Her name before she got married was Thelma Chester. The men in her family had dug coal for a hundred and fifty years. When the mines in her town petered out, so did the family, little by little. They wandered off, or died, or went to jail, or went on welfare.

She was little and skinny with brown eyes and kind of reddish-brown hair, like a pup that starts out as the runt of the litter, then stays small because she's not strong enough to fight for her share of the food. But, all the same, there was something stubborn and tough inside her. And something warm and loving that no amount of neglect or abuse could make go away. Once we got hold of each other, there wasn't any question of us giving it up. No question at all in her mind, even after the trial, and none in my mind, either, till I'd sat in jail for a while and it started to sink in how long I was going to be there and what that meant. What it meant to me and more important, what it meant to her.

I wrote to her. It took me a long time to get it straight, exactly what I meant, so it sounded that way and not some other way altogether. Even then I guess it sounded hard-assed and cold-blooded, but I couldn't help that.

I told her I'd been thinking a lot, trying to figure out some answers for things, but no matter how I sliced it, I was going to be in prison till I was almost fifty years old and maybe a hell of a lot longer than that. And I couldn't make any sense out of her sitting around somewhere, making beds for a living or clerking in a dime store, while she waited for me to get out.

> So I'm not going to write to you any more. I want to, but I'm not going to. And I don't want you to write to me. I know it's going to hurt your feelings a lot, and it doesn't make me feel too good either but I can't think of any other way that won't hurt you more. Once you get used to the idea, it'll be better and you'll be able to work out some kind of a life for yourself.

Just that letter. Then I stopped writing. And I didn't read her letters. Except for the one when she answered mine. I carried it around in my shirt pocket for three years, till I'd sweated the ink away and the paper had worn through. But long before that happened I knew the whole thing by heart anyway. At least the important part, the part at the end.

> I wasn't surprised that you wrote the way you did. I'd been expecting it before this. I know how your head works. And I love you for writing those things. I know you're thinking about what's better for me. But please don't do it. Don't cut yourself off. You know I'll write to you whether I hear from you or not. Even if you don't read my letters, I still have to write them. It's the only connection I have with you and I can't give it up. I'm not trying to force you to do something you don't want to or don't think is right, but just remember that nothing's going to change as far as I'm concerned. And they can't keep you locked up in there forever.

It wasn't easy to send her letters back after that. But

I did. And after she got out on parole, when she came to Hobart on visiting day, I wouldn't see her. She came every time she could for six months but I never saw her. And finally she stopped coming. And I stopped thinking about her. I trained myself to. Just like I trained myself not to think about anything else on the outside.

But now, all of a sudden, I had a crazy, senseless notion that I might get out. I burned to now where she was. And how I could find her. She came to life again physically. For the first time in five years, I could feel her beside me on the bed, tiny and warm, slender and smooth as a child, whispering and laughing, lying under me and over me, touching and kissing, and sleeping with her head in the hollow of my shoulder.

I lay awake half the night and wrestled the hours all day waiting for Tagge. But he didn't come. I waited and suffered and sweated. Finally, I gave up on him. I knew the game was over. It had never made sense from the start. Who would have the power to bypass Ditcher and the whole fucking penal system and waltz me out past the walls and into the air? And, if somebody did have that power, why would they choose me? What need could they have, what motivation? What could I do for them that would make it worth their trouble? All the questions had negative answers. So I stopped asking them. I just hoped, gave up, then started hoping again.

Three weeks after I'd seen Tagge the last time and a week after the shelves in the conference room were built, installed, stained, and waxed, Bowkamp came for me again. But this time it wasn't Tagge.

I sat in the conference room alone for fifteen minutes. Then the door opened and a young guy walked in. About twenty-eight but with a soft boy's face that looked younger. Thin and wiry, medium height, hair brushed back, a suit that fit, and a button-down shirt. He looked like the men in the ads for those shirts. Easy and smooth and money in the bank.

He didn't say hello or introduce himself. He sat down across from me and said, "This won't take long. There are just a couple of things I need to know."

"Fuck you, Mister." I stood up and walked to the door. I turned the knob and pulled, but nothing happened. It was locked. I knocked on it with my fist.

"Wait a minute. What's the matter with you?" He was up, out of his chair.

"There's nothing the matter with me. What's the matter with you?"

"I guess I'd better get Ditcher in here."

"Go ahead. He can hear what I'm telling you. I'd like that."

He stood there staring at me.

"You can't threaten me," I said. "I'm already in jail, and I'm scheduled to be here for a long time."

"I wasn't threatening you—"

"Don't let this number on my shirt fool you. I'm a human being, you son of a bitch. You don't just

34

lean back with a fishy look on your face and start shooting questions at *me*. I don't even know who the hell you are. Or where you came from. You're nothing to me. Zero."

He didn't like what I was saying. He wasn't used to being manhandled. But I had him. I could see it in his face.

"Look . . . I'm sorry if I got in a rush. I'm Ross Pine. Marvin Tagge and I work together. He's in Mexico this week and we're getting in a bind for time, so he asked me to come see you."

He moved back to his chair and sat down. I sat down across from him. "That's better," I said.

"Like I said," he went on, "there are just a couple things we need to know." He didn't refer to a file the way Tagge had. He had it all in his head. "First . . . about Vietnam. We know you were wounded. How did it happen? What kind of an action was it?"

"Night partol. We came on a bunch of V.C.'s squatting around a fire, and we had a little shoot-out with them."

"You were with a combat unit?"

"That's right. Till I was wounded. After that—"

"I know about your duty in Japan." He took a pad out of his jacket pocket and made a note. "How many battle situations would you say you were in?"

"You mean fire fights?"

"That's right."

Right then, like a light switching on, it came clear. I knew what the conversations with Tagge had been about, I knew what they needed me for, and I knew the answers they wanted. "Sometimes twice a week. Sometimes three times a day." I sat there looking at him, waiting for the next question, wondering how he'd word it. He did a good job. Made it sound nonchalant, off-the-cuff.

"People who've never been in a war always wonder what it's like to kill another man."

"Are you asking me what it's like?"

"Yes. If you know."

"I know, all right. It's like swatting a fly."

He looked as if he wanted to make a note on his pad when I said that. But he checked himself. He shifted in his chair and said, "How can a man be certain? I mean in a battle situation . . ."

"You can't *always* be sure. But when it's face-to-face, dog-eat-dog, you know. I probably shot at two hundred men. I can't guarantee how many I hit, but I'll tell you this much: I've had a rifle in my hands since I was knee-high. I can hit a squirrel in the ear at a hundred yards."

I let that sink in for a minute. Then I said, "Five men I know for sure about. They were close enough to spit on."

He sat there, putting the next question together in his head and I sat waiting for it.

"The crime you were convicted for . . . Mr. Tagge says you're innocent, that the man actually killed himself."

"Too bad Tagge wasn't on the jury," I said.

"Isn't that what you told him?"

"I told him that was our defense. That was what my lawyer told the jury. But they didn't believe it. And I don't blame them." Then I told him what he'd come to hear. "I killed Riggins, Mr. Pine. And I'll tell you something else. If he came back to life, I'd kill him again."

I'd marked the deck and won the cut. But it was still somebody else's game. I knew that. And somebody else's rules. I knew that too. And the end of it was a long way off, down some road I didn't know. But I didn't care about that. The other choice was fifteen years in prison, smelling other people's feet and other people's urine, listening to screams in the night, and staring at walls. Anything was better than that. Any unknown commitment, any threat, any lonesome jump into the darkness was better. Even dying was better if it turned out that way.

"I'm not saying I like being locked up," Oscar said. "But I didn't like it on the outside, either. There's no time I can think of that I'd go back to if I had a choice. There's no place I've ever been that I'd like to be again. I just never got everything together at any one time. It was always shit, one way or the other. And I'll tell you something else: I don't think I'm much different than the next guy. Most people don't know what the hell they're doing. They get into some kind of a box—a job or getting married or whatever they decide is expected of them. And they clump around in there for a few years, pretending to like it and telling themselves how much *progress* they're making, but it's all bullshit. They're boxed in just as much as we are. The only difference is we *know* we're out of action and they don't. I've got more peace of mind now than I had when I was slicing salami or teaching school or knocking over banks. It may not be any kind of a life in here but at least it's something I can handle."

It was the night of the day I'd met Pine. Oscar was on a talking jag, unusual for him, and I sat there in the cell listening, half listening, my own thoughts full of tomorrow and the day after and all the other days I planned to buy.

"The food is brutal but it's no worse than most people eat on their own. If they stopped making potato chips and Seven-Up half the people in this country would starve to death. Do you know that? Did you ever stand at the checkout counter in a food market and see what people buy? All crap. They walk out with thirty dollars worth of packages and containers and three dollars worth of food. Salted and sugared, artificially colored, and pumped full of enough preservatives to give cancer to the whole fucking state of Texas."

We had an understanding between us, an agreement that we wouldn't talk about women. "It's bad enough thinking about them," Oscar said. "But it's a hell of a lot worse having some guy describe his old lady's pussy or moon about some blow job he got in Cleveland. It's the details that kill you, man. That's what you have to stay away from."

So we did. At least we tried to. But we both knew we couldn't keep it inside all the time. Once in a while a woman would come up, or women, from Oscar more often than from me, and he'd talk himself out. And I guess it made him feel better. Or maybe it made him feel worse. Anyway, this time I let him talk.

"You can get used to the food and the stink, freezing your ass in the winter and baking your balls in the summer. After a while you stop smelling the disinfectant and bug spray, your muscles stop aching from the beds. And you get used to living in a six-by-eight box with some ass-hole who scratches and farts and snores, some cretin bastard who never had an impulse that didn't originate in his belly or his pecker. You can find a way to live with all of that. You never get to like it but you build up scar tissue and numb spots, put blinders over your eyes, plugs in your ears, cotton in your nose. You wake yourself up, shoot some steel into your backbone, swallow some scalding coffee, smoke a cigarette, and push yourself, a couple of steps at a time, through another day. Then you link a couple of days together, and a few more, and you've got a week behind you. And, first thing you know, a month's gone past. And after what seems like six years, a year has passed, and you're still breathing, the heart's pumping, and things aren't so bad after all. Only ninety-eight more years to go.

"But the pussy part, being without a woman, you never get used to that. At least I don't. No matter what kind of a hammerlock I get on my own head, some little fox manages to squeeze in, twitching around, shaking her ass. No wonder half the guys in here end up going fruit. You get to the point where you'd stick your dick in a meat grinder if you could find one. I'll tell you the truth, much as I hated that whole comedy in New York, living by the numbers, feeling as if I was dying a little bit every day, still I don't think I ever would have left if I'd been getting any kind of action at home. Paula was a poor sad-assed excuse for a girl. She'd been so brainwashed by the nuns she couldn't take a piss without going to confession. If I put my tongue in her mouth she said forty Hail Marys before I could get it out. And she'd have killed herself before she'd go down on a man. I mean it. She'd bought the whole idea that fucking was just to get pregnant. If you had any fun doing it, you were heading for big trouble with the Pope. So she made sure she didn't enjoy it. And once we had the kids, she managed it so I didn't have any fun either. She complained to my mother, she complained to the priest, she had headaches and backaches and a cold every week. Instead of getting her period every twenty-eight days, she had periods that *lasted* twenty-eight days. Finally, I took a good look at her one day, fat and whining, her hair up in plastic curlers, her housecoat dragging on the floor, and I said to myself: Who needs her for Christ's sake? From then on, I let her alone. I screwed whatever teachers were available at the school where I taught, and every week or so I'd pick up a whore in the Village and have myself a real workout." He sat up on his bunk and lit a cigarette.

"You know I hate to admit it but it was my fault as much as Paula's that things didn't work out. I never should have married her. I never should have left Hawaii.

"When I hit the islands I was really an innocent kid. I mean I'd had a few fast bangs in alleys while I was growing up in New York, but nothing to prepare me for those little Oriental twats. There were two of them working in the PX on the base. I'd had pneumonia and I was in the hospital for a month. But as soon as I got on my feet, moving around, these two took me over. They had an apartment not far from the base and they moved me in. I had three weeks R and R but it seemed like a year. Those two little banana-eaters gave me a going-over that I didn't get over for months. Matter of fact, I'm not over it yet. That's what I meant above my wife. Even if she hadn't had a hang-up with the Catholic Church, that still wouldn't have solved my problem. I really never gave a shit about her. I couldn't forget about those short-legged little half-breed Chinks or Japs or whatever they were. I'd trade any five white women for just one of those little pissers."

"Listen, you bastard, if it's all the same to you . . ."

"I know. No more cock stories. Right?"

"Right."

I was geared for another long wait. I had to be. If Tagge was playing cat-and-mouse I couldn't let myself be suckered in. So I loosened up, ironed out the wrinkles in my head, and didn't try to second-guess myself on the things I'd said to Pine. And I waited.

This time it was only three days. And this time it was Tagge in the conference room. He started talking as soon as I sat down. He looked older. His face was gray. No small talk now. No smiles. He squared himself up in his chair like a man getting ready to pull in a marlin.

"All right," he said. "We're ready to go forward now. A week from today you'll be out of prison. Three days later you'll be out of the country. You'll have a passport in another name, a home with that name on the deed, and two hundred thousand dollars in the bank. Your wife will be waiting when you get there, and for all practical purposes Roy Tucker will be dead. Within a month you will have completed your work for us; you will be under no further obligation; and you'll be free to lead your life in any way you like. But we expect total secrecy from you. And you have to stay out of the United States for at least five years. After that, you can do whatever you want."

Fifty questions jumped into my head and stumbled over each other.

"What do you mean I'll be out of here? It's not that simple."

"That's *our* problem. We'll give you the details next time we see you."

"A week from today, you said."

"That's right. Tuesday."

"That part about my wife . . . I don't know where she is."

"That's all right. We know." He took an envelope out of his pocket, shook a sheet of paper out of it, and passed it across the table to me. It was a typewritten note without a signature.

> Dear Thelma:
> These two men, Marvin Tagge and Ross Pine, are friends of mine. They can help us. Please do whatever they ask you to. I'll see you soon.

"If you sign that, it will simplify matters when we contact your wife."

"Why do you have to contact her?"

"She won't be involved. We're just trying to protect her. We think she's better off with you."

"Well, I don't." I handed the note back to him. "I don't want her mixed up in it."

"It's up to you," he said. "If you don't sign it, we'll have your signature forged. By an expert."

"What's the point? I don't see why—"

"We want her to trust us. So she'll come voluntarily. We don't want her to be questioned by the police or the newspaper people. You can understand that."

"No, I can't. You're making a deal with me. Not my wife. If you're dragging her into it, I'm not interested."

He sat there looking at me for a long beat. Then he said, "Well, that's your choice." He put the envelope back into his pocket. "We can't very well force you to leave here." He pushed his chair back from the table. "We didn't put all our eggs in one basket. You must have guessed that." He stood up and walked to the door. He wasn't bluffing. He was halfway out the door before I stopped him.

"Wait a minute . . . look . . . I just want to be sure that Thelma doesn't get hurt or scared or anything."

He closed the door and turned back to me. "That's what *we* want. That's why we think she'll be better off with you." He came back to the table, took the note out, and handed it to me again. This time he handed me a pen, too. I signed it.

"Hang onto the pen," he said. "There's something else to sign." He slid a small file card across the table. "Write the name Harry Waldron three times on that card."

I did it and handed it back to him.

"That's the name you'll have on your passport." He took out a pocket camera and clicked half a dozen fast pictures of me. ". . . and we'll need a picture for it."

"In a prison outfit?"

"Don't worry. We'll fix that."

"You said 'out of the country.' "

"That's right."

"Where?"

"You'll know where when you get there."

"All this business about the house and the money in the bank—it's a good story—but why should I believe it?"

He stood up again. "It's a question of faith. We have faith that you're going to deliver for us. You need to have some faith, too. A week from today you'll be out of here. Just concentrate on that." When he got to the door he turned around. "Next Monday I'll tell you everything else you need to know. And just to make you feel better I'll bring the bankbook along. And the deed to your house."

He left me sitting there, staring at the bookshelves

44

I'd put up at the other end of the room and trying to pull everything together in some form I could deal with. But it didn't work. It was like trying to fold a pillow into a cigar box. As I sat there, staring, I started getting scared. My teeth didn't fit together right when I clenched my jaws.

Bowkamp came to take me back to the guard station. My legs were loose and unsure as I walked ahead of him down the corridor.

For the rest of that week I stumbled around like a drugged animal, spilling food, dropping tools, nicking my thumb with a saw, breaking drills, and scraping my knuckles on emery wheels. I struggled to keep my food down, couldn't concentrate, couldn't sleep. I felt feeble and slow and tentative. But it was all inside. Nobody noticed. Even Oscar looked at me as if I was the same person I'd always been.

Still the sickness continued, the symptoms were real. I was scared to death. Afraid to act, afraid not to, brutalized by the thought of all the years in prison, numbed by the power of smooth-spoken men like Tagge and Pine.

And through it all, like some struggling effort of the heart to heal itself, my mind kept sliding back to West Virginia, to the years before my mother died and my father fell apart, to the time when the size of the world was forty hilly acres and the sun marked the time.

There was no sense to it, no pattern or continuity. Just a series of pictures, jumbled and overlapping, with the sounds of the cattle and the mules, the hounds and the cats and the chickens, the roosters in the morning and the windmill squeaking, all mixed up together in the background. My dad in rubber boots, slogging his way through the mud from the house to the barn, a bucket in each hand. Or harnessing the mules, cuffing them on the side of the head to line them up, eating an apple, peeling it carefully, throwing the peelings and the core to the chickens, eating the rest, a bite at a time, from the point of the knife. Or chewing tobacco, a big lump inside his cheek, the long, slow walk from the kitchen table to the edge of the back porch, to spit in the loose dirt at the border of the flower bed.

Those things about my father, tall, thin, angular, and slow-moving, always came back first. It was *his* farm, his stamp was on it. The stock was his, the crops such as they were and the dogs. They feared only him, came only for his whistle.

My mother belonged to him, too. She didn't question it. And Enid and I of course were his, looking like his people, talking and moving like them, no resemblance at all to my mother's light-haired, small-boned relatives.

His thumbnail was split, a heavy healed-over seam straight down the center of it, a permanent mark—a badge of manhood, I felt when I was six years old. For years I watched my own thumb, waiting to see that ugly beautiful ridge appear.

Everything was physical for him. The world was made up of things he could handle, work with, shape to his needs. His hands were his life, strong and brown, thick skinned and rough. All of us focused on those hands. They did the building, the planting, the harvesting, milked the cows, held the rifle, the shovel, the spade, the hayfork. They made cradles, built toys, dug graves. They steered and supported and punished, hammered and sawed, polished, sanded, fitted, and painted designs on the furniture in the winter when we were snowed in.

His face was flat-planed, sculptured, and mostly immobile. His voice was thin and husky, little-used or needed. The hands did it all for him, said it all. When my mother died he cut kindling for two days, still chopping and sawing after dark with a lantern

47

sitting on a high stump. And three weeks later he lost his right hand in a mowing machine.

Everything fell apart quickly then. That winter, he brought a woman home with him from Buckhannon. Her hair was bleached almost white, Enid and I called her Cotton Top, and she had a voice that could cut and tear and peel the skin loose from your body. She and my father sat in the kitchen those cold months, drinking and fighting with each other. And in the spring they let the farm go for debts and went off to Bluefield together.

Mother's name was Esther. She was tiny and fair and as silent in her way as my father. She hummed and sang softly to herself over the churn, the stove, the washboard, kneading bread, snapping beans, putting up preserves, knitting, sewing, patching, sweeping, gardening, weeding. She was warm and easy-handed and tender when anyone was sick or hurt or heartbroken, but she too, like my father, did it with her hands, her presence, her body. Her instructions were simple, "We need firewood, Roy," her admonitions even simpler, *"Mind,* now." Or "Shame. *Shame,* Enid."

At the dinner table we sat silent. Once the prayer was finished, we passed food and ate and no one spoke. It was a silent house, and Enid and I were silent children. Whatever else our parents gave us, they gave us no survival tools. No words. No weapons. Looking for security, Enid married the first man who asked her, and I went to jail as quickly as possible.

On Sunday, the day before Tagge was due back, I said to Oscar, "Do you ever think of getting out of here?"

"Every day."

"The way you were blowing off the other day I thought maybe you were getting to like it."

"Bullshit. I'm getting used to the *idea* of it. That's all. I'm in here for life or ninety-nine years, the same thing. And with my luck I'll probably live to be a hundred. That means I've got forty-five years to go."

"You'll get a parole. Long before that."

"Big deal. So I'm seventy-five instead of a hundred. I'd be slobbering around the streets with holes in my shoes, drinking muscatel out of a paper bag."

"What about breaking out?"

"What about it? That only happens in movies. Look at this place. We're like sardines in a can. Concrete, solid steel, and guards in every corner."

"Guys get out all the time."

"Sure they do. But only if somebody on the outside *wants* them out. Somebody with money and time and connections. Bust-outs don't just happen. They're engineered. Guards get rich. And wardens. And all of a sudden a prisoner turns up missing. But it's never a surprise to anybody. Except the people who read about it in the paper."

"But if somebody on the outside was working for you, if they set it up, you'd go, wouldn't you?"

"You bet your sweet ass I would."

I opened the passport and saw a picture of myself and the name *Harry Waldron*. According to the date, the passport had been issued three years before. It was worn and soiled and the pages were half filled with entry and exit stamps, mostly from Central American countries.

"You have your own little business, Waldron Imports," Pine said. "You handle hospital equipment, and your territory is Central America and Mexico."

"Nobody's going to quiz you about it, so don't worry," Tagge said. "It's just a piece of information to keep in your head." He shoved a folded document across the table to me. "Here's the deed I promised to show you. It's in Spanish, but you'll see your name, Harry Waldron, as the owner. I guarantee you it's in perfect order."

"Why are all the addresses blocked out? How am I supposed to know where it is?"

"You're not," Pine said. "Not yet."

"And here's your bankbook," Tagge said. On the cover it said Crédito Nacional but the words under it were taped over. Inside, under deposits, it said 1,700,000 something or other. The name of the currency had been taped over too. "The rate of exchange is eight and a half to one. That means two hundred thousand dollars, the amount I mentioned to you."

"How do I know you're telling the truth?"

"You've got a life sentence and we're getting you out. Tomorrow. That should tell you something."

"When I'm *out* it will tell me something."

Pine sat forward in his chair, his forearms resting on the table. "In the northwest corner of the exercise yard, there's a steel door in the wall. With a guard stationed in front of it. At eight-thirty tomorrow morning, just before you're due to line up and march off to the shops, get yourself over by that door. Walk past the guard and say, "Tucker." Keep walking for fifteen paces, then turn and walk back to the gate. When you get there, it will be unlocked. Push it open, go through, and close it behind you. Directly ahead of you will be a green and yellow bakery truck that makes deliveries to the prison kitchen. Go straight to the truck, get into the back, and lie down. The driver will go through the side gate of the prison, and on out to the highway. He'll head west to the dunes. Some of our people will be waiting there in another car to drive you to Chicago. That's it."

"Sounds simple."

"It is," Pine said.

"What if somebody from the kitchen sees me getting into the truck?"

"They won't."

"What if they do?"

"Nobody can stop you except the guards. And they won't."

"Don't they check the truck at the gate?"

"Tomorrow, they won't. This is just as important to us as it is to you."

"Maybe. But if somebody starts shooting, I'm the one they'll be shooting at."

"No shooting. No trouble," Pine said. "We guarantee it."

"That's not good enough. I need Ditcher's guarantee."

"This has nothing to do with Ditcher—"

"He knows about it, doesn't he?"

"Yes, but—"

"Good. I want to hear him say it."

When Ditcher came into the room a few minutes later his face was the color of a plum. When he saw me all the color went away. "God damn it, I was told—"

Tagge cut him off. "We know what you were told. But we've hit a snag."

"I'm the snag," I said. "I want to make sure you know what's going on."

"I don't know anything." He turned to Pine. "You told me this would be done without me. . . ."

"Now we're telling you something else."

"I understand I'm walking out of here tomorrow," I said to Ditcher. "I want you to tell me how."

Ditcher turned from Pine to Tagge, found no support there, then turned back to Pine.

"Tell him," Pine said.

Ditcher took a deep breath and spit it out as if he'd memorized it and was glad to get rid of it. "Northwest gate of the yard, eight-thirty in the morning, the guard will let you out."

"What's his name?"

"Greber . . . You'll get in the bakery truck—"

"Who's driving it?" I said.

"Our man," Pine said.

"Go on," I said to Ditcher.

"—and the truck will go out through the side gate. That's all I know."

"No inspection at the gate?"

"No."

"What about an alarm?"

"It'll be at least an hour later," Tagge said, "when they miss you at the carpenter shop. By then you'll be with our people, heading for Chicago."

"Does that satisfy you?" Pine said to me.

"I guess so," I said. "There's just one more thing. I'm taking Spiventa with me."

There was a soft white silence. Then Ditcher said, "Jesus Christ."

"Out of the question," Pine said.

Tagge tried to smooth things over. "Maybe if we'd planned for it sooner. But you see . . ." He dried up.

"Sure, I see." I stood up.

"You're making a big mistake," Pine said.

"Yeah, I guess so," I said.

Bowkamp took me down in the elevator and along the corridor to the first security gate. Feaster was stationed there. "The warden called," he said when we walked up to him. "You're to bring the prisoner back upstairs again."

As we walked back I knew I'd turned them around. And I liked the feeling.

"Not me," Oscar said. "I don't buy it."

"What do you mean, you don't buy it? I broke my balls to ace you in on this."

"It stinks, Roy. It smells like a dead cat. You're gonna get racked up."

"Why? What's the point? Why would somebody weasel me out of here just to rack me up?"

"I don't know. That's the part that stinks. These guys are spooks. You don't know who they are or who they're working for. And all of a sudden they're gonna do you the biggest favor of your life. Does that make sense to you?"

"If I get out of here it makes sense."

"It's not for free, buddy. They're not gonna buy you a new suit and give you a one-way ticket back to West Virginia. You know that, don't you?"

"Hell, yes. I'm not stupid."

"Doesn't that bother you a little bit?"

"You're damned right it does. But sitting in this hole for the rest of my life bothers me a hell of a lot more."

"It's better than a coffin, isn't it?"

"You're too late on that one. I already asked myself that. A couple hundred times. And the answer's 'no.'"

"Great. You proved you're all guts and no brains. But it's not for me. I'll stay in here. And die a little bit at a time."

"Suit yourself. I'm not gonna kiss your ass."

He sat there on the edge of his bunk looking down

at the floor. Then he said, "Here's what I mean. You and I are a couple of bargain-basement items. This joint is full of guys like us. And nobody on the outside gives much of a shit. Am I right?"

"I guess so."

"Now, all of a sudden, these guys turn up, all ready to hand you the moon in a paper sack. Does that make sense to you? Who *are* they? Do you think a couple of ordinary sharpshooters can stroll into a prison, give the warden a little slow talk, and drive off with one of his prisoners? Not that I ever heard of. They have to be somebody big to do that. Don't they?"

"Big or little, who gives a damn?"

"I give a damn. They're somebody big. And they're up to something big. Big and dirty. Did you ever ask yourself what you could do for them that would be so valuable? You're damned right you have. And you don't have an answer—any more than I do. The first thing that pops in your head is they want you to kill somebody. You've thought of that, I'll bet."

"Yeah, I've thought of that."

"All right. There are a thousand guys on the outside that specialize in that work. And there's a price for every pocketbook. So why go to the trouble of flushing some poor ass-hole out of some crummy jail and handing the job to him. Does that make sense?"

"It doesn't have to make sense. All I want—"

"I know. All you want is *out*. Once you feel some grass under your feet, and those sparrows start shitting on your hat, everything's gonna be a piece of cake."

"Forget it, Oscar. You made your point. Let's drop it."

"I don't want to drop it. Because maybe I know the answer. Listen to this. Even a hired shooter is liable to have a wife and a family and friends. People who start asking questions if he disappears all of a sudden.

But in here it's another story. Right? If you're looking for a lost dog with no face and no name, no friends and no future, where do you go? To a prison. If a man's already missing from the outside the only place left for him to be missing from is a cell. Only the guards and the warden will notice he's gone. And if *they* don't notice . . . you see what I mean?"

"I see what you mean but it doesn't change anything."

"Remember when that poor bastard was knocked over in Louisville a few years ago? I can't stop thinking about that. They said the guy that shot him had busted out of jail not long before. He was living it up in Nevada, money and a car, having a hell of a time, for several weeks before the killing. No money coming in but a lot going out. Then later when he took off, he drove halfway across the country in a yellow Plymouth. The police *reported* that he left Louisville after the killing in a *yellow Plymouth*. And later he *admitted* that's what he was driving. But nobody saw him or picked him up. He moseyed on down to Florida and all the way to Argentina, living high on the hog. And finally, after things quieted down here, they nailed him, brought him back, sealed him up tight in some jail in the south, then whisked him back to prison. He didn't need a trial, they said, because he pleaded guilty. Pretty neat, huh? And I'll give you ten to one he dies in jail."

"So what?"

"So what? So somebody used the poor son of a bitch. They gave him some money, got him out of jail, and sold him a bill of goods. Whether he did the shooting or not is beside the point. The point is they had a patsy. They've still got him and they always will have. Even after he's dead, whenever somebody brings up the question about why he did what he did, they've got a readymade answer: 'Just a crazy jailbird who hated niggers.' "

"Who is this 'they' you keep talking about?"

"That's a good question. You tell me. Who are these two guys you've been talking to? Where do they come from? Who do they work for? You don't know, do you?"

"No."

"Damned right you don't. And you never will. Nobody ever knows who 'they' are. You don't usually even see them. But when you do, they wear good clothes and talk life professors and look as if they go to the barber twice a week. They're never black or Puerto Rican or Italian. They're never anything you can identify. They're just 'they.' They stay out of sight, mostly, and eat lunch together, I guess, and talk on the phone a lot. What they do is *manage* things. Money and wars and people. They know how to get the job done, no matter what it is, and they know how to cover it up, once it's done, mostly berause they've got dumb bastards like you and me to do the dirty work."

"You're nuts, Oscar. Nobody's after you to do anything. They don't even *want* you. They said if you came along, they're dropping you between here and Gary. Then you're on your own."

"Fuck 'em. They're not dropping me anyplace. Because I'm not coming."

"Suit yourself," I said.

When the bell went off at six in the morning, Oscar was already dressed. I slid down to the floor and he said, "You son of a bitch. I was awake all night because of you."

"Did you change your mind?"

"Not a chance. Did you change yours?"

"Not me. I'm going. And the best thing for you to do is forget I ever told you about it."

"Don't worry. I forgot it already."

He didn't talk on the way down to breakfast. And he didn't say a word while we were eating. Later, in the exercise yard, he played catch with a couple guys and didn't come near me.

Finally, just before eight-thirty, when I'd strolled close to the northwest gate, Oscar jogged over and fell in step beside me. "I'm going," he said.

"No, you're not. It's too late now."

"Fuck you. I'm going."

We passed the gate guard and I said, "Tucker." We went on fifteen steps, turned, and came back to the gate. The guard was standing in front of it, white as the belly of a fish. He stared at us, stock-still and dumb-faced.

Before I could say anything, Oscar leaned up to him and growled in his face, "Move it, you bastard. *Move* it! If we're not out of here in ten seconds, you'll be dead before lunch."

The guard's mouth dropped open but no words came out. He turned then, suddenly, pulled out the keys, and unlocked the gate. We slipped through and the gate clicked shut behind us.

22

Ten feet ahead, on the crushed-rock apron of the loading area, the bakery truck was waiting, its back door half open, its motor idling. We walked straight to it, climbed up in the back, and closed the door behind us. As the truck started to roll forward, the driver half-turned his head and said, "Lie flat on the floor."

I felt the truck move ahead slowly, thirty or forty yards, off the crushed rock and onto a paved surface. Then we stopped. I heard the lift gears of the wall gate begin to grind and the metal-capped heels of the guard walking over to the side of the cab. "They've had you runnin' out here for better than two weeks now. What's happened to Bernie?" The guard's voice.

"He was due back from his vacation today. But his wife's sister died down in Louisville. He drove down there last night," the driver said.

"Oh. Well . . . I'm sorry to hear that. If you see him . . ."

"You'll see him before I do, chances are. He ought to be back to work on Thursday."

There was a clanging jolt as the gate hit the top. The truck moved on through and the gate slid down behind us.

"Stay flat and keep quiet," the driver said. He speeded up, then slowed for a right turn, and entered a heavy stream of morning traffic. Oscar was lying on his stomach, his head resting on one arm. He winked at me and whispered, "I don't know how you'd get along without me."

I couldn't be sure of the time but it seemed like fifteen minutes fast driving. Then a turnoff, five minutes on gravel, and another five on what felt like packed sand. Finally we stopped, and the driver said, "All right. Roll outa there. On the double. You're changing cars." He got out of the cab, came around to the back, and opened the doors for us.

The sun was angling in across the lake and reflecting off the dunes. The glare blinded me. When I first stepped down out of the back of the truck I couldn't see. Then it came clear. Directly in front of us, fifty feet away, was a black Chrysler limousine, two strapping young guys standing in front of it looking at us, one of them in a gray chauffeur's uniform, the other one in a dark blue suit.

"All right. Move it," the truck driver said. "Let's get going."

"Take it easy with the orders, buddy," Oscar said. "We've had enough of that shit to last us a while."

I started toward the Chrysler. I could hear Oscar shuffling through the sand behind me, mumbling to himself. "Jesus, it's like fucking boot camp."

The man in the blue suit had a revolver in his hand. When I came close to him he said, "Tucker? Right?" I nodded my head and he said, "Back seat."

As I passed him he raised his arm and the revolver cracked and echoed through the dunes. I wheeled around and saw Oscar, ten feet behind me, blood spurting out of his chest. "You son of a bitch." I jumped sideways, grabbing for the gun arm but before I could reach it, the revolver cracked again. Then something heavy hit me just behind the ear. As I went down I saw Oscar sprawled on his back in the sand and I heard a voice say, "Get him into the car." Another voice, very faint, said, "Yes, sir."

PART TWO

I woke up slowly, floating, everything out of focus. I felt as if my blood had been drained off and replaced with warm milk. The ceiling wasn't quite solid. It shifted smoothly from side to side and an occasional ripple moved across its white surface.

I fixed my eyes on a spot just above my head, opened and closed them, staring, then relaxing, and after what seemed like a long time, the ceiling calmed over and stopped moving. I hitched myself up on my elbows and looked around.

At the foot of the bed three people were sitting— the man in a blue suit who'd shot Oscar; a gray-haired woman wearing glasses; and Ross Pine. When I spoke my voice sounded thin and faraway to me. "What time is it?"

"Four-thirty in the afternoon," Pine said. "You're in the Dorset Hotel in Chicago, on the seventeenth floor. Would you like some coffee?"

I nodded my head and the gray-haired woman went to a table by the door, poured a cup of coffee, put a spoonful of sugar in it, and brought it to me. Then she sat down again.

"You'll be here in Chicago for three or four days. This woman is Helen Gaddis. She'll be in touch with you while you're here. This man is Marty Brookshire. He's leaving Chicago this evening, but he'll be in contact with you later as our work goes forward."

I looked at Brookshire. Trim haircut, clear blue eyes, white shirt, gray tie. An unlined untroubled face, three years removed from the backfield, it seemed, of some Connecticut college. My impulse was very specific. In my mind I hurtled off the foot of the bed and wrapped my fingers around his well-bred, clean-shaven neck. But my body wouldn't support the instinct. The bones and muscles had been removed. Or so it seemed. I felt no pain, no tension. I had no physical self. I could look and listen and retain what I heard. But from the neck down I felt like cooked cereal. I fixed a look on Brookshire and tried to kill him with my eyes, but he sat with his legs crossed, cool and unhurt, listening to Pine and adjusting his cuffs.

"I want to see Tagge," I said.

"That's impossible. You won't see him again till you're out of the country."

My eyes came back to Brookshire. "You son of a bitch."

He looked at Pine and Pine stood up and walked to the side of the bed. "Let's get something straightened out. You'll be in contact with several of our people before this project is finished. *None* of them are required to take any abuse from you. In any way whatsoever."

"That son of a bitch killed Oscar."

"No, he didn't," Pine said. "*You* did. He was dead before he left the prison. You didn't outmaneuver us yesterday. You just thought you did. When we called you back and said it was all right for Spiventa to go along with you, we'd already made a decision about him. We had no choice. We're getting close to the bone now. A lot of people are involved and you're one of them. But you're only as valuable as your contribution. You understand that? We made a bargain with you and I assure you we'll keep it. But you are also expected to keep your end of it. I won't mince words with you. For the next few weeks of your life, we *own* you. You're bought and paid for. If you acccept that and do as you're told, everything will go smoothly. You'll be surprised at how easily things will work out. But if you *don't* accept it, if you have any idea of changing the rules on us, there is *no measure* too severe for us to take."

He turned and walked to the window, stood there with his back to the room. Then he came back to his chair and sat down.

"Do you have any questions?" he said. "It's important you understand *exactly* what I'm saying. If you don't, this is the time to talk about it. There won't *be* any time later. If you get into trouble, only Tagge or I can get you out. And we won't be around all the time. The people you'll be in contact with are programed to react. If you behave, *they'll* behave. It's as simple as that." He turned to the woman and said, "Place the call." She got up and went to the phone. With her back to me she spoke very softly into the receiver. "All right," Pine said, "that's enough business for the moment. Now we've got a surprise for you."

The woman put her hand over the mouthpiece of the phone and said, "There's a delay."

"How long?" Pine said.

"The operator says just a few minutes."

"All right. Tell her to put it through as soon as she can." As the woman went back to the phone, he said, "If you need to contact us for any reason whatsoever call the bell captain, identify yourself, and tell him your air conditioner isn't working properly. One of our people will be in touch with you in a matter of minutes."

I sat there listening to him, full-awake now, blood beginning to pump again in my body, my brain busy with alternatives.

There was no question in my mind about what I

was going to do. The image of Oscar sprawled in the sand with two bullets in him wouldn't leave my head. All the words and plans and veiled threats couldn't blot that picture out.

"Are you hungry?" Pine said. He was loose and relaxed, now, secure in the belief that he'd nailed me into position, that I'd be there when he needed me, starched and pressed, eager to please, docile as a bell-trained brute. I shook my head.

"You're not hungry yet?" he said.

"No."

"Well, you will be. And there are some excellent restaurants in this hotel. You like fish?"

"No."

"To bad. There's a fine seafood restaurant downstairs."

The phone rang then, and the woman picked it up. "It's the call," she said.

"Good," Pine said. He got up and took the receiver from her. He spoke softly with his head turned away. I couldn't understand anything he said. Suddenly, he held the receiver out to me. "Here's someone who wants to talk to you."

I'd spent five years trying not to think about her, forcing myself to forget what she looked like, what she sounded like, how she moved and spoke and how her skin felt. I'd blunted my nerve endings, blocked my senses, painted over as much as possible every picture of her. But when I heard her speak it all flooded back.

"Roy?" she said. Her voice was small and breathy and unsure.

"Hi, honey."

"Oh, God, Roy . . ."

"Don't cry."

"I can't help it. I was afraid . . . I thought . . ."

"It's all right, honey. Everything's going to be fine."

"I missed you so much . . ."

There was a break at the other end of the line. Then a man's voice said, "This is Marvin Tagge. I just want you to know that your wife is fine, and she's anxious to see you. I told her if everything stays on schedule, you'll be down here in three or four days." The line went dead. I put the receiver back in the cradle.

"Where is she?" I said to Pine.

"She's out of the country."

"God damn it. Will you stop playing games with me? Where is she?"

Pine sat there looking at me. Then he turned to Brookshire and the woman, and said, "I'll meet you downstairs in ten minutes." They got up and left the room. As soon as the door closed, Pine started talking. "I tried to explain things to you in a civilized way but I guess I didn't make my point. So I'm going to say it one more time."

He took out a cigarette and lit it. "I know your life story," he went on, "probably better than you know it. I know you've been through some rough times, you've had more kicks in the ass than you deserved. No question about it. But I guarantee you this . . . if you try to screw us up, if you try to get cute with me or Tagge or any of our people, you're going to see trouble like you never knew existed."

After he left I went over and stood by the window and looked down at the lake. I felt as if he was still in the room, jut behind me, with both my arms in a hammer lock. The call from Thelma had changed everything. It was their game. No rules but theirs. And still I stood there, struggling to find the escape hatch, knowing if I found it I couldn't use it. But looking for it anyway.

"All right," Pine had said before he left, "that's all

I can gell you. Just use your head and everything will be fine. You're registered downstairs as Harry Waldron. The bill is paid. All you have to do is drop off your key when you check out. Your passport is in the closet in the jacket of your brown suit. Your billfold, with papers and credit cards and money, is in your pants pocket. You've got five hundred dollars in cash. If you need more, contact our people. Gaddis will let you know your departure time. She'll give you the final detals and see that you get your ticket. Other than that, you're on your own. You're not a prisoner here. Nobody's standing guard outside your door. You can come and go as you like."

"What about the police?"

"What about them?"

"As far as they know, I broke out of Hobart this morning. They'll be looking for me, won't they?"

"No, I don't think so."

"What does that mean?"

"Let me put it this way. I guarantee you they won't be looking for you in Chicago."

"How can you guarantee that?"

He smiled and said, "You walked out of Hobart, didn't you?"

He got up and moved toward the door. "Just relax and enjoy yourself for a few days. Have a few good meals, walk in the streets, go to the movies, write a letter to your wife."

"Kinda tough to do when I don't know where to send it."

"That's right," he said. Then, "Well, write it anyway. You can hand it to her in a few days."

At the door he said, "You've got a lot at stake. We're counting on you being smart enough to remember that. We know you have friends in Chicago, like Schnaible, your lawyer, and Dr. Applegate, but we wouldn't advise you to get in touch with them. Even if you did, it wouldn't help you. And it could hurt them. A lot."

He stood there looking at me for a long beat, cool and polished, unflappable, able to cope, total faith in the future. Then he opened the door and left.

I walked over to the window and looked out. It was a beautiful fall day. The sun was cooling off now but it was still full light outside. I stared down at the beach for a long time, at the cars and buses on Lake Shore Drive. My mind was darting around like a desert animal looking for a hole. But I couldn't find one. All I could see was the shadow of a hawk. Finally, I turned away from the window, walked to the mirror on the wall above the bureau, and inspected myself.

You don't find many mirrors in a prison. Most men there aren't anxious to look at themselves, even if the mirrors were available. Whatever self-love or self-esteem you once had goes away quickly. And the looking-glass habit, if you ever had it, goes too.

So the man I studied there in the room that afternoon didn't please me or displease me or surprise me. I looked at him with curiosity. More that than recognition. More recognition than approval.

I was shorter than I wanted to be, the face was flatter and grayer than I remembered, the nose too large and not exactly centered, the eyes small and cloudy, jutting checkbones, and the teeth of a welfare child. The hair at the top of my forehead was thin, the furrows in my cheeks, a mark of my father's people, were deep, and my face had an expression, cold and detached, that didn't change when I cracked my mouth wide in a kind of smile.

The clothes I had on weren't right either. They were new and expensive, a dark red robe, blue cotton pajamas, and black slippers. They made my face look used, secondhand. I stripped off, still standing in front of the mirror, and looked at my body for the first time in a long time. White and thin, with knobby hard muscles, prominent tendons, sharp bones, and heavy veins in the arms. "You look like my father," Thelma had said the first time she saw me undressed. "Your body looks like a miner."

I went into the bathroom, filled the tub with hot water, and sat in it for a long time, not thinking of anything. I called downstairs then, had two bottles of beer and three cigars sent up, and I sat in the tub, drinking and smoking for more than an hour.

There was a toilet kit by the bathroom sink—razor, hairbrush, toothbrush, shaving soap, everything. I shaved and brushed my teeth and put some stuff on my hair to make it stay down. Then I got dressed.

The passport was there in my jacket pocket. And money in the billfold. There was a Social Security card, a driver's license, credit cards, and a draft card, all with the name Harry Waldron and an address in Norman, Oklahoma. There was a brown-plaid suit in the closet, a gray suit, and a tweed jacket on a hanger with a pair of gray pants.

They were expensive clothes, they fit me exactly, they were freshly cleaned and pressed, but they looked as if they'd been worn. Two pairs of shoes, one black, one brown, perfect fit, also expensive, also worn a little. Four ties on the rack, six shirts in the drawer, a dozen hankerchiefs, ten pairs of shorts, six pairs of socks, a trench coat and a soft brown hat in the closet, along with a leather briefcase, folders inside describing hospital equipment in Spanish and English, dimensions listed, and prices in ten or twelve different currencies.

After I got dressed, some color in my face now, feeling strange in the strange clothes, I sat down to look at the paper that had come up on the tray with the beer and cigars.

It was a very small story, on the next-to-last page of the first section, the only news item on a page of advertisements. The headline said, "Two Escape from Hobart" and the first paragraph told me what I already knew. But the second paragraph was interesting.

> The escape truck was found in the dunes along with the body of Spiventa. State Police believe he was shot to death by Tucker, who then escaped across the dunes taking the truck driver along as a hostage. A thorough search is under way all across the northern part of Indiana.

I put down the paper, got up, and went to the phone. "This is Harry Waldron, operator. Room seventeen-oh-five. I made a long-distance call this afternoon and I've misplaced the number I was calling. Would you please check your records and tell me what it was?"

"Yes, sir.

There was a pause. Then she said, "Waldron, Seventeen-oh-five?"

"That's right."

"Sorry, sir. I have no record of that call."

"I know the call was made. Will you look again?"

"Let me double check the exchange, sir. 'I'll call you right back."

Three minutes later, the phone rang. "I'm sorry, sir. They don't show it either. There's no toll charge at all against your phone today."

74

"There was a delay getting through," I said. "Someone there on the switchboard had to call me back. . . ."

"I'm sorry, sir. We don't show the call at all."

By eight o'clock that night I was so hungry I started to get dizzy. I decided to eat in my room. But when the waiter came to the door with the menu, I said, "I've changed my mind. How many dining rooms do you have downstairs?"

"Three, sir."

"Which one's the best?"

"Well, that depends on the kind of food . . ."

"Which one costs the most?"

"The Dickens Room."

Ten minutes later I was sitting at a table against the wall in a corner, three musicians playing at the far end of the room, silverware and glasses making a soft tinkling sound all around me, waiters in dinner jackets and women in beautiful clothes coming and going.

As I looked at the menu my memory ticked over the prison meal of the night before. Baked beans, rice, bread and margarine, coffee, and tapioca pudding. It was hard to conceive of that pasty mess in the same world with the things that were passing my table now on trays and carts.

When the headwaiter came for my order, I said, "Bring me a steak and whatever else you've got that goes with it. I'll leave it up to you."

"Very well, sir. Would you like the wine list?"

"No, thanks. I'm a beer drinker. Bring me a bottle of German beer."

"Will you have that now or with the food?"

"I'll have it now. No . . . wait a minute. Bring me

a bourbon and ginger ale now. And I'll have the beer with the steak."

The Dickens Room wasn't my speed. I knew it and the waiter knew it. I wanted to get up and walk, find a place where I could drink a few beers and have a cheeseburger. But I kept myself nailed to the chair. For once, I wanted to have the best. I needed to see what the best was like, no matter how uncomfortable it made me. Even if I didn't like it, it was something I owed myself, something I had to do. If the bubble broke, if six policemen came to get me in the night and hauled me back to Hobart, I had to have something to remember. A wide clean bed, a good meal, a couple of drinks, and a linen napkin on my lap.

After five years of macaroni and beans and rice and hominy and spaghetti, the steak was too rich for me. And too rare. I only ate a few bites of it. And I didn't like the salad dressing, so I passed on that. But I ate all the baked potato and the vegetables and five or six rolls with butter. And then I had a double order of strawberry shortcake with whipped cream on top. I drank a bottle of beer and finished off with another bourbon and ginger ale.

When the check came, I signed "Harry Waldron" across it without even looking to see how much it was. That was the best part of the whole dinner. When I got up to leave I took ten dollars out of my billfold and handed it to the waiter. That was the second-best part.

I strolled across the lobby, down the stairs, and out to the sidewalk. The doorman was hustling cabs, but I told him I wanted to walk. I turned right and headed toward Michigan Avenue, smoking one of the cigars I'd bought that afternoon. It was a soft, cool evening. I kept seeing my reflection in plate-glass windows as I strolled along, and I thought, It's not bad. It seems all right so far. It's not bad at all.

27

Three hours later I was still walking. I'd been in seven bars. On Rush Street, State Street, Division Street, North Clark, just strolling along, turning into a dark doorway whenever the impulse hit me, up on a stool like any other independent, free-spirited citizen, ten dollars on the bar, a look around to see how the place stacked up, and finally the order to the bartender.

Cool and easy. Plenty of time. No place to go. No hurry getting there. Just stir and sip, listen to the music, watch the people, snap a couple of swizzle sticks, study your reflection in the mirror behind the bar, then drink up, off the stool, out the door, and move on.

A solid activity, terrific security in it, observing all the unities, a beginning, middle, and end, a kind of classic structure, a series of blocks piled one on top of the other with nothing in mind other than the steady satisfying rhythm of the action.

At one o'clock I'd come full circle. A pink-lighted grotto in some basement three blocks west of the Dorset. Heading home, I told myself, warmed and enlightened and stimulated by the experience of the evening, but perfectly capable of recognizing how much of a marvelous thing was too much.

In the grotto, a naked girl was dancing to recorded music on a platform behind the bar, some simple back-and-forward steps with her feet, her hands making little circles at her sides, and her head tilting first one way, then the other, no expression on her face, just eyes and a nose and a mouth as the upper extremities of a moving naked body. No communication from her, no sensuality, it was a dance she was doing for herself in some private place, no eyes needed, none wanted. So no one really looked at her except in the most casual way, the way you look at a parrot when it moves suddenly on its perch.

When I found a stool and eased up on it, the bartender, a pale, light-haired and overweight young man, was saying to a man three stools away, "I have no patience with the son of a bitch. As far as I'm concerned he's a war hero. Period. All medals and citations and horseshit. What he knows about running a country you could stuff in your ear. He's dumb and stubborn and shot-in-the-ass with himself. But he's honest. You have to give him that. He's an honest man."

A girl slid up on the stool next to mine and said, "I'll bet you five dollars if I offer to buy you a drink you'll say no."

"You win," I said, and handed her five dollars. She waved it at the bartender and said, "New blood, Lefty. We need a couple drinks. I'll have gin and juice and my friend here wants—"

"I'll have a beer," I said. "I had enough bourbon to last me a while."

"Gin and juice and a bottle of Bud."

The bartender kept talking while he got the drinks, full concentration on the man sitting in front of him. "That's the twist. They needed him because he's honest. Now it turns out he's *too* honest. He won't let them steal any more. Threatens to send a few Senators to jail. So all of a sudden he's a liability. He's a threat. Either *he* goes or *they* go. Already they're talking about his health. Next thing you know he'll be in the hospital. And then he'll be dead. Mark my words . . . he's finished."

He set the drinks down in front of us and went off to the far end of the bar.

"Did you ever hear anybody like him," the girl beside me said. "That's Lefty for you. Too smart for his own good. Went to two colleges. University of Chicago out on the south side and a year or two up at Ann Arbor. Built a telescope when he was ten years old, ground the lenses and everything. Had a story in the paper about him a few months ago. Some rummy that comes in here wrote it, a really tacky little man. Happy hands. Anyway the story was called 'Brain Tends Bar.' And it went on to tell all about Lefty and how smart he is. He hated it when he read it, told the guy who wrote it not to come in here any more; but, from what I can tell, it was pretty much true. He's a guy who knows everything, but there's no place where he fits in. 'Overeducated,' the paper said. Does that make sense to you? Anyway, here he is pushing drinks. Been here four years that I know of, working the late shift and giving himself migraines from arguing politics with guys that are stupid or drunk or half asleep. Makes you wonder."

My eyes had adjusted to the light and I could see her better now. Her hair was cut short and it was gray. But her face looked young. Freckles and round cheeks and a dimple in her chin. She had on a tweed suit with a short skirt and a turtle-neck sweater. She looked like a girl who worked in an office.

"In case you're wondering," she said, "I'm not in the habit of picking up stray gentlemen. And I can afford to buy my own drinks. But I just stopped in for a nightcap. I went to the movie over an Oak Street, and I saw you wander in here right behind me, so I thought it might be pleasant to have a drink with somebody in a nice suit who doesn't look like a freak."

She lifted her glass and took a long drink from it. Then she said, "Now, that I see you close up, you look as if you've had a few. You're not drunk, are you?"

I shook my head and she said, "Do you live around here?"

"I'm staying at the Dorset."

"That figures. Where do you live when you're not on the road?"

"I guess you'd say I've lived all over. Right now I live in Oklahoma. I live in Norman, Oklahoma."

"Never been to Oklahoma. But I shared an apartment up on Diversey with a girl who came from there. Never understood half of what she said all that time. Terrible accent. Mush in her mouth. Couldn't pronounce half the letters in the alphabet. Is that typical Oklahoma?"

"I don't think so."

"No, I guess not." She emptied her glass. "Ready for another one?" I finished mine and she signaled the bartender. "I'm buying this time. You're so talkative and interesting I feel indebted to you." I heard a kind of muffled sound and I looked at her. There were tears on her cheeks. She sat there looking down the length of the bar and didn't try to wipe them away or hide her face.

The bartender came for our glasses then, looked at her, and said, "For Christ's sake, Ruby, knock it off. That's not gonna make you feel any better." She didn't answer, just sat there, and the tears kept coming. When he brought fresh drinks, she took a long swallow from hers, said, "Excuse me," and walked off along the bar toward the rest-room signs.

I sat there listening to the music from the loudspeaker and working away at my Budweiser, and after quite a while, ten minutes or so, she came back.

"Are you all right?" I said.

"I'm not gonna cry again if that's what you mean." She picked up her drink, then set it down again. "I don't want that damned thing. I'm going home." She slid off the barstool.

"Yeah. Me, too."

"Don't let me break up the party."

"You're not. I was leaving anyway."

As we were going out the door the bartender said, "Goodnight, Ruby," but she didn't look back and didn't answer.

When we were out in the street she said, "I live on Delaware not far from the Dorset. It's a little out of your way, but if you walk me home, I'd appreciate it."

At the corner, we turned east on Walton, and headed toward Michigan Avenue.

"You don't think I'm a hooker, do you?"

"No. Why would I think that?"

"Well, I'm not. I've got a good job. Executive secretary to the sales manager of a paper company. Napkins and facial tissue and, you know . . . john paper. Biggest paper company in Iowa. This is just our sales office here."

When we got to Michigan Avenue, she turned right. In the middle of the block she said, "I guess you wonder what I was crying about back there."

"No, that's all right."

"I was lying to you about Lefty. I didn't find out about him in the newspaper. I used to be married to him. Does that surprise you?" I didn't say anything and she went on. "I met him at Ann Arbor six years ago, when he was in school up there. We got married and lived together till he left Michigan. Then I divorced him. I mean he didn't divorce me. I divorced *him*. We didn't have a fight or anything. It just wasn't working. He was all wrapped up in his books and his ideas and he was so God-damned angry all the time. Not at me. I don't mean that. He was just mad at the world it seemed like. And he knew, even then,

82

while he was still in school, that he was going to have a rough time hacking it. He couldn't get along with anybody. People envied him. Or hated him. Or something. Or if they didn't, he thought they did. So things were always pretty tense around the house. He didn't act surprised when I said I wanted out, so I figured he wanted it too. And maybe he did. I'm still not sure about that. Anyway, we got a divorce and six months later I married a businessman there in Ann Arbor, owned a big roofing company. He was a sweet guy, treated me like a million dollars, but he bored me stiff. Or at least that's what I told myself. The fact was I couldn't get over Lefty. Isn't that sick? I think it is. I left number two and went to New York for a while. Then I got a job with the State Department and lived in Amsterdam for a year. And after that, I worked in California, in San Francisco, for a brokerage house. But all that time I knew I was kidding myself. I knew I'd be back in Chicago sooner or later. And I was right. Two years ago I came back here. I tracked Lefty down, and I finally found him in that bar we just left."

At Delaware she said, "I live just ahead there, in the middle of the next block." We crossed Michigan Avenue, heading east. "I don't know what I thought. That we'd get married again, or live together, or what. But I know I didn't expect it to be the way it is. What you saw there tonight, that's what it's like now. I sit at the bar with the rest of the customers, and if he talks to me at all, it's just the way he'd talk to anybody else. And still, I know he likes it that I come in. If I miss a night or two, he acts different. I know he still likes me even though he never says anything about it.

"Maybe he's trying to get back at you."

"That's what I thought at first. And I could understand that. But for *two* years?" After a moment she said, "It's weird. I know that. But the weirdest part of all is that I like it this way. I mean I don't *like* it, but I need it. I need to see him even under these circumstances. I know he's wrecking himself, throwing his life and his education away, but I'd rather have him where he is now, tending bar, if it means I can see him every day. I mean, as selfish as it sounds, I don't want him to go away someplace and make something of himself if it means he'll be away from me."

"But what good is it this way?"

"*No* good. But it's *something* at least. It's better than nothing."

We walked up in front of a wide solid building, a doorman standing just inside the glass doors.

"This is it," she said and before I could answer she said, "You can come up if you want to. Have a coffee or something."

"Thanks. But I think I'd better get back to the hotel."

She smiled up at me in a funny, vulnerable way. "I mean you can . . . you know . . . I *like* you . . . you can stay with me if you want to." She looked at my face trying to see the answer. "Maybe that sounds funny to you," she said then, "after what I just said about Lefty. But we're not . . . I mean Lefty knows. . . ." She folded her arms across her chest and shivered a little. "What would you say if I told you I made up that whole story about him, if I said we've never known each other at all except as a bartender and a customer? Does it sound better if I say I'm a thirty-two-year-old-girl who works in an office and lives alone and I . . . well, I get strange sometimes? I need to know . . . I want to feel . . . oh the hell with it. Look, I'm sorry, I'm getting cold. I'm going in now." She moved toward the entrance and I walked a step behind her. At the door, she said, "Let's just say you're a happily married man who doesn't cheat on his wife. That makes it better for me."

She turned and went in then. The doorman held the door open for her. I walked back to the avenue and on up to the Dorset.

In my room, in the center of the bed was an early edition of the *Chicago Tribune*. Marked in red crayon on the first page it said "Page 31." I turned to page thirty-one and found a three-inch story circled in red.

ESCAPEE IN CANADA?
Duluth. Sept. 26.

Avery Tunstall, 37, the bakery-truck driver from Hobart, Indiana, who was taken hostage in a prison break there earlier today was found, half-conscious this evening wandering in a field near Deer River. He told police that *Roy Tucker*, the convict who abducted him, was heading for the Canadian border when he pushed Tunstall out of the car. The car, a blue Pontiac, was later found abandoned near International Falls. Authorities believe that Tucker may have crossed into Ontario on a public bus.

I didn't sleep well that night. I lay on the bed in my clothes for a long time, staring up at the ceiling and listened to the hotel sounds gradually dying down. Once in a while I'd hear the hum of the elevator or the thinned-out sound of a car horn on Lake Shore Drive. But by three o'clock everything was quiet.

I got up and took a shower and put on my pajamas and robe. Then I flipped on the television set and watched the last twenty minutes of a Randolph Scott movie. After that I closed the drapes, carefully turned back the bed and got in it, arranged myself on the pillow, feeling the cool smoothness of the sheets, the clean firm mattress underneath me.

Every night in my cell, I'd had fantasies about such a bed. Now I was in it. It was better than any bed I could have imagined. But I couldn't sleep. I moved from my back to my side to my stomach, then back to my side. The air conditioner hummed softly and the room was dry and cool, but the bed felt too warm.

I took off my pajama top, peeled back the blanket, and lay under the sheet. After a while, I got up and tried to open a window but it was permanently closed. I put on my robe, sat in the chair, and read the paper from page one to the end. The first streaks of light were showing across the lake when I got back into bed. I pulled the blanket up over me and quickly fell asleep.

The phone woke me up. When I answered it a woman's voice said, "Who is this?"

"Who are you calling?"

"I can't hear you. Who *is* this?"

"It's somebody you just woke up. Who do you want?"

"Sorry," the voice said, and the line went dead. I clicked for the operator, and when she came on I said, "Don't put any more calls through here. I'm trying to sleep and you just gave me a wrong number. What time is it, anyway?"

"Six-fifteen, sir. Is this Mr. Waldron?"

"No. It's . . . I mean yes, it is."

"Mr. Harry Waldron. Right?"

"That's right."

"It wasn't a wrong number, sir. The lady asked for you and gave me your room number. Seventeen-oh-five."

"Then why did she hang up when I answered?"

"I don't know, sir. You don't want to be disturbed. Is that correct?"

"That's correct," I said and hung up the receiver.

I couldn't go back to sleep. By seven o'clock I'd shaved and got dressed, and I was out in the street walking south on Michigan Avenue. The sun was up, the sky was wide and blue, and there was hardly any breeze off the lake. The streets were almost empty. A few cars and early buses but nobody walking. Except me.

I kept going till I got to Chicago Avenue. I found a cafeteria, sat down at a window table where I could look out at the water tower, and ate breakfast. Eggs and sausage and toast and three cups of coffee.

When I left the restaurant, I turned right and followed Chicago Avenue all the way over to the lake. I crossed the drive and walked north on the sidewalk at the edge of the water. When I got to Walton, I sat down on a bench and looked out across the lake with the sun in my face and the traffic roaring on the drive behind me.

I wasn't scared now, the way I had been that day in the prison. But I had a hollow feeling at the bottom of my stomach. Somewhere along the line I'd missed something, somebody had said some words I was supposed to hear but hadn't. I kept seeing the house deed and the bankbook with sections taped over.

I wanted to disappear but I couldn't. I knew that was no answer. But I couldn't just sit and wait either, watching the jigsaw pieces slowly lock into place. All the things I couldn't do were very clear to me. The problem was to find something I *could* do.

There was a list of choices in my head. But it was a short list. Two names on it.

It was almost ten o'clock when I got up from the bench, crossed the drive through the underpass, and found a phone booth. I looked up both the numbers and wrote them down on a slip of paper.

I called Applegate first. At the office. A woman's voice answered. "Dr. Applegate's out of the city until later this afternoon. Are you a patient?"

"No, I'm a friend from out of town. I want to surprise him. I'll call back later on."

Then I called Schnaible. The girl on the phone gave me a set speech. "I'm sorry, Mr. Schnaible's dictating. Then he has to go into a meeting. If you'd care to leave you number . . ."

"I don't have a number. This isn't business. It's personal. So cut out the horseshit and put me through."

There was a silence at the other end. Then a tight little angry voice said, "I'll give you Mr. Schnaible's secretary."

Before the secretary could start her spiel, I said, "Just tell Schnaible that Roy is on the phone. He'll want to talk to me."

"May I give him your last name, please?"

"No. Tell him I just broke out of prison yesterday and I'm anxious to talk to him." I'd barely finished talking when his voice came on. "For Christ's sake, Roy, you shouldn't call here. I mean where are you? The paper said . . ."

"I'm at the Dorset Hotel."

"You mean you're in Chicago?"

"That's right."

"Look, Roy. You have to understand. I can't get involved. I can't even *talk* to you."

He hung up then and I stood there like a dummy with the dead receiver in my hand. I eased it back on the cradle and walked along the street to my hotel, trying to stay calm inside, trying to keep the anger down. And I did pretty well. At least I told myself I was doing pretty well. But as soon as I got inside the hotel I went to a booth and dialed Schnaible's number.

This time I got his secretary right away. As soon as I heard her voice, I said, "You tell Schnaible that if he doesn't get on the phone I'm coming to his office to see him. And if he's not there, I'll go to his house in Wilmette and wait for him."

When he came on he said, "Jesus, Roy. What do you want from me?" His voice sounded tired.

"I want to talk to you. It's twenty minutes to eleven now. I'll meet you at twelve o'clock. You tell me where."

There was a long pause. Then he said, "Lincoln Park Zoo. By the giraffe pen. You know where that is?"

"I'll find it."

When I got there, at two minutes before twelve, Schnaible was waiting for me. He was fifteen pounds heavier than I remembered. His hair was thin on top and gray all over. The first thing he said was, "Where did you call me from?" I told him I'd called from a booth.

"Both times?"

"I guess so. What's the difference?"

"Jesus Christ. Are you crazy?"

"What are you so nervous about? What difference does it make where I call from?"

He got a funny look on his face then, as if he'd said something he shouldn't have. "I'm just jumpy, I guess. Been working too hard." He looked around him. There weren't many people in the zoo. Some old ladies and a few nurses with babies in carriages. He pointed to a path winding off through the trees. "Let's walk over there. Give us a chance to talk."

He found a bench thirty feet off the sidewalk, partially hidden by some bushes. We sat down. "I'm sorry if I sounded unfriendly on the phone. But I was surprised. I didn't know what to say. I mean, I knew you broke out of Hobart yesterday morning. . . ."

"I'm surprised you saw the story. I was *looking* for it and I almost didn't find it."

"Oh, I saw it, all right. And then this morning it said you were up in Canada."

"Yeah, that's what it said."

"Jesus, I wish you were. You came strolling up that

walk a while ago like you owned the place. They must have your picture in every squad car in Chicago."

"No, they don't. Nobody's gonna pick me up. It was a setup, Arnold. I didn't break out. They *let* me out. I walked out."

"Why do you mean?"

"Just what I said. Somebody wanted me out, so they arranged it."

"*Arranged* it? What does that mean? Nobody can do that."

"They did it."

"I don't know how. And why would they want to?"

I let that one hang in the air for a while. Then I said, "I can't answer that. I thought maybe *you* could."

He wasn't good at covering up. As soon as I asked the question, his face told me the answer.

"I don't know what you . . . Look, Roy, we've been out of touch. I haven't seen you since that courtroom in Indianapolis."

"I know. But I thought maybe somebody had talked to you about me. These people had a lot of information. They had to get it from somewhere. And another thing. I never could figure out how they found me in the first place. There are thousands of guys in the pen. How do you zero in on one of them? What makes you say, 'This is the one we want.' "

"This is all flying past me, Roy. It's Greek."

"You mean nobody ever called on you and asked about me?"

"Not that I can think of," he said. "No. I'm sure of it. I'd remember if they had."

"I've never seen you so nervous."

"I'm not nervous. I just don't like being out in the open like this." He stood up. "Let's go sit in my car. We can cut through here and get to the parking lot."

As soon as we were inside the car I said, "Why did you ask me where I called you from?"

"I don't know. Just a casual question, I guess."

"No, it wasn't. You know it and so do I."

"Roy, I swear to Christ I'm telling you the truth. . . ."

I let him sit there and steam. He lighted a cigarette and rolled the car window down. Then I said, "Well, it's easy to find out. I'll tell them I talked to you and see what they say."

"For God's sake, Roy, take it easy. What do you want from me? All right, they *did* contact me. But if they knew I was talking to you . . ."

"Who are they?"

"I don't know. I don't want to know."

"What does that mean?"

"Look . . this is all I'm going to say. I don't know why they picked you, and I don't know what they want you for. But I can tell you this. If they killed you and me in this car right now, there'd be no arrest and no trial. And nothing in the papers. It would all be arranged from the top down, just the way your getting out of prison was arranged. Don't be stupid, Roy. I'm a lawyer. I see this shit all the time. It's the way things work. Just keep your mouth shut, do what they say, no matter what is is, and maybe you'll come out of it with your skin. Your only other choice is to put a bullet through your head. You made your deal and it's carved in cement. You can't outfox them. Just accept that. I'm telling you like a friend. The less you know about them the better."

I got out of the car then and stood in the parking lot and watched him drive away. And two hours later I was still there in the zoo, sitting in front of the tiger cage, sorting through what I knew, what I thought, what I suspected, and trying to figure out if I had a move. I stayed cool and relaxed, determined to think in straight lines. But all the lines kept curving back to the starting point.

It was after five when I got back to the hotel. I'd walked all the way, stopping on Division Street for a cup of coffee and a hamburger. When I came into my room, there was an envelope on the carpet just inside the door. I tore it open and found a white card inside, a typewritten message on it: WATCH THE SIX O'CLOCK NEWS. CHANNEL FOUR.

I sat in front of the television set watching the tail end of a film about the elk herds in Alaska and trying to stay awake. At a few minutes before six I went into the bathroom and splashed cold water on my face, took off my shoes and socks, and ran cold water on my feet.

When I got back to the television set, the program had just started. It was local news. Chicago and vicinity. For five or ten minutes I watched and listened but none of it made much sense to me. I was half expecting to see my own face. With some item, a day late, about my breaking out of Hobart. When Schnaible's picture came on, I stared at it for a second before it registered. Then I heard the newscaster's voice.

. . . dead in his car in the garage of his office building on North La Salle Street. Death came from a blow on the head. Nothing was taken from the car or from the victim's pockets. Police say they have ruled out robbery as a motive. Mr. Schnaible was born in Chicago and had been a prominent criminal lawyer here for the past ten years. Also active in state politics, he . . .

I switched off the set. My hand was shaking. I went to the phone and picked it up.

"Bell captain, please."

"Yes, sir. I'm ringing the bell desk."

"Bell captain . . ." a voice said.

"This is Mr. Waldron in seventeen-oh-five. My air conditioner's not working."

"We'll send a man up right away, sir."

I hung up, took off my tie and hung it in the closet, sat on the edge of my bed and put my shoes and socks on.

The door buzzer sounded then. I went to the door and said, "Who is it?"

"I believe you called about your air conditioner?"

"Yes. Just a minute." I took my handkerchief out of my pocket, folded it into a long strip, and wrapped it around the knuckles of my right hand. Then I opened the door.

He had blond hair, crew-cut. He was wearing an expensive suit and a polka-dot tie. He looked as if he'd gone to the same school, graduated in the same class with Pine and Brookshire. "Mr. Waldron? My name's Henemyer."

He was also a half-head taller than me and thirty pounds heavier. So when he closed the door behind him I didn't wait for him to turn around. I hit him as hard as I could, behind his left ear. When he turned I hit him three times in the stomach to bring his head down. Then I brought both my fists down on the back of his neck and my knee up under his chin. I opened the door again, then, and dragged him down the hall to the exit stairs. I pushed the fire door open, eased his weight forward across the edge of the top step, and let him go. He slid down the half-flight of stairs on his side and ended in a sprawl on the landing.

I went back to my room, put on my tie and jacket, and took the elevator down to the lower lobby. All the phone booths were full. I ran up to the main lobby and found one free. I dialed Applegate's office number. It rang five times. Then a woman answered.

"I'm calling Dr. Applegate . . ." I said.

"I'm sorry, the office is closed. This is the answering service."

"Where can I reach him?"

"He'll be checking in with us. Would you like to leave your name?"

"No, thanks. I'll try him later."

I stepped out of the booth, and walked across the lobby to the house phone. "Bell captain, please." I stood there and watched him pick up the receiver, forty feet away from me.

"This is Mr. Waldron in seventeen-oh-five. There's something wrong with my air conditioner."

"Yes, sir."

"Please send Gaddis this time."

On the way to my room, I opened the fire door and looked down at the landing. Henemyer was gone.

31

I'd barely got inside the room when my buzzer sounded. I opened the door and Gaddis was standing there. She had a frozen look on her face. She walked past me and sat down in the chair by the window. I sat down on the bed facing her. I was afraid to start talking. I didn't trust the ugliness inside of me.

"Yesterday, Pine stood here and told me that you people *own* me. He's wrong. *Nobody* owns me. He also said if I didn't behave, you'd show me trouble like I've never seen before. He's right about that. Yesterday I saw Spiventa get shot, and this afternoon you had somebody kill Schnaible. I'm not kidding myself. I know if it wasn't for me, neither one of them would be dead. And if you wonder how that makes me feel, I'll tell you. It makes my stomach turn over. But if you were trying to *teach* me something, I want you to know I haven't learned it. I'm in over my head with you people. I *know* that. You've got me by the short hair. But don't fool yourself that you've got me programed. You haven't and you never will have. You can't put me into a box like a file card. Tell your boss that. Or your committee, or whoever is running this fucking game of yours. I'm still holding back. I'm making up my *own* mind. One step at a time. I made a deal with Tagge and I'm not running away from it. But don't think that puts me in your pocket. I'll give back exactly what I get. If you try to muscle me I'll muscle back. You can kill me but you can't *break* me. You understand that?"

She didn't like to swallow it but she did. She nodded her head.

"One other thing. Wherever you're sending me, I want to leave tomorrow. I've had enough of Chicago."

32

When I came back to my room that night after dinner, the light on my phone was blinking. I asked for the message, and the operator said, "You can pick up your airline ticket at the Braniff desk, O'Hare Airport, tomorrow morning at seven o'clock. Your flight will leave at seven-forty-five."

"Where am I going?" I said.

"The message doesn't say."

I packed my bag, took a shower, and went to bed. Early. It was ten-fifteen when I turned off the light. I lay there on my back wondering if it was going to be a sleepless duplicate of the night before. The next thing I knew the phone was ringing.

"This is your wake-up call, Mr. Waldron. Five o'clock."

I had breakfast in my room, then took a cab to the airport. The girl at the Braniff desk had puffs under her eyes and a big mug of coffee in her hands.

"My name's Harry Waldron. Picking up a prepaid ticket."

"Where to?"

"I don't know."

"Have a heart, Mister. It's too early."

"My company made the reservation. I don't know the destination."

"Don't you have any idea?"

"Look, honey, I know it's early. But it's just as early for me as it is for you. Now do you want to feed my name into that computer or shall I call the supervisor's office and have them do it?"

She didn't answer. She sat down and tapped the keys of the computer and it started talking back to her. She looked up then and said, "That's our flight three-one-seven to Mexico City. With a stop in Fort Worth."

"Good. Now dig out the ticket and I'll leave you alone with your coffee."

"You must be a pleasure to be married to," she said.

"I'm not married. I'm a priest."

It was a first-class ticket. As soon as I sank in one of those big seats I went to sleep again. But when they came around with breakfast, twenty minutes after we took off, I ate again. Then I went to sleep again.

I didn't wake up till we passed over Oklahoma City. I read a magazine till we landed in Forth Worth. While the plane was on the ground, I went to sleep again. And I didn't wake up till we were air-borne. By then I was beginning to be healed. The steel wool in my head had dissolved, the bones had stopped aching, the muscles were able to respond.

Sleep is medicine for me. It always has been. And sometimes it's a drug. During the bad time with my father, after our mother died, both Enid and I slept like opium smokers, hour after hour, day and night, shutting out everything, seeing nothing, remembering nothing.

But it wasn't like that on the plane. It was simple and good. I felt clean and healthy and safe, away from the bad stuff and unaware of what was ahead, hoping that when I got off the plane in Mexico City I'd see Thelma.

I made a strong, specific effort to keep Oscar and Schnaible out of my mind. I couldn't handle that yet. I wasn't sure I'd ever be able to handle it. There was no plus-and-minus pattern I could develop that would exonerate me, take away the gut-pain and the guilt. So I had to do the next best thing. Paint it over.

Applegate was another matter. At least he was alive, slumped in a big chair in his house in Oak Park, sweater and corduroys, reading till two in the morning. When I thought of him, it was always there. Not in uniform in Japan, not in his doctor's smock, not with his family or his friends of his patients. I always thought of him alone in his den at home, deep in that chair, under a lamp, full concentration on a book.

It's hard to dredge up people from your life who bring nothing with them but good memories. It's always a mix. Even when you can't remember the bad things, even when you assure yourself they were never there, deep down, if you stir enough, you'll find sand in the lemonade.

I'm sure Applegate is no exception to this. But he certainly seemed to be.

He wished me well. It was as simple as that. He wanted things to be good for me. He tried very hard to share what he had. Maybe he felt guilty. Maybe he said to himself, Everybody didn't have my chances. The least I can do is try to give a leg up to some stumbling bastard. Like Tucker, for instance.

A lot of people say things like that to themselves. There's no shortage of good intentions in the world. It's the follow-through that's difficult, when you're faced with a choice between what's convenient and comfortable and what isn't. That's the sluff-off point. A lot of people don't show up for roll call after that.

33

Robert Kenneth Applegate. The thing that was hard to swallow when I first knew him and when he made it clear that he was going to make me over, whether he had cooperation or not, was not that he was a tall, good-looking, likable, talented, and successful son of a bitch, in the Army or out of it, but that he was so fucking young. Older than me, sure. But not very much. Not very much at all when you started to compare what he'd done with himself and what I *hadn't* done with myself. It made me want to avoid him those first weeks in Japan.

But he had an answer for that, too. "You're not competing with anybody but yourself. Remember that. That's enough of a struggle. Don't compare yourself with people who for some reason managed to get a head start on you."

If he'd been older I could have looked up to him, as they say, or admired him. But you can't admire some bastard who's that close to your own age. If they really outstrip you that much, you're bound to end up with some mixture of envy and self-hate. So you're stuck, if you're not careful, without a category. It's hard going if you think about it too much.

That was Applegate's trick. He never gave you time to think. He kept you on the move, at least he did me, the mind, the body, the feelings, the whole piece of equipment.

He never tried to pretend I was his best friend. We came from different strains, a beaver and a hawk, different nests, different feeding habits. He was some kind of golden animated trophy who'd never failed at anything, and I was his project. He was very frank about it. "I don't like to get drunk every night and look for whores. And I get tired of playing poker and shooting pool. So I'm going to spend six months of my spare time educating you. I'm going to make you hungry for everything you've missed. From now on, you'll never be satisfied with anything except the best you can get."

He was wrong about that. He didn't understand what it is to be programed for failure. He didn't know that it takes a long time to cultivate a taste for the good stuff. Most people will trade the best, any day, for something that's familiar. I came from generations of people who followed oxen and mules, shoveled dirt, chopped wood, grew plain food and ate it, and died in the beds they were born in.

My people don't buy stocks or bonds or run for office or go to college. They do what they've always done. At least they try to. And that's what I would have done if the situation hadn't forced me to do other things.

But Applegate didn't understand that. He was motivated upward. He didn't understand being motivated sideways. If he'd been in my shoes, faced by the fact that he couldn't go on to school, Applegate would have worked in a drugstore or as a hospital orderly and gone to school at night. That would have been his instinct. He couldn't understand that my instinct was to get a job driving somebody's car.

I said he was a reader. And that's what he was, more than anything else.

"It makes sense," he said. "It's all there. Everything that's beautiful or wise or significant has been written down at some time or other. How can anybody have the gall or the self-satisfaction to ignore all that? Who would want to? You read to feel alive, to bring things to life in yourself that you didn't know were there. All those folds and creases in your brain have some function, some potential, all the nerve endings are waiting to be stimulated. And it's all in the books. Everything. The whole fucking world is there if you know how to find it. Reading isn't an escape from life. It *is* life. It *creates* life."

I liked to hear him talk like that. And I believed everything he said. But I couldn't do it. I couldn't read like that. I tried but it just wouldn't work for me. You have to be able to be alone. You have to *want* it, to be calm and peaceful being by yourself. That's no good for me. I get crazy and jumpy when there's nobody around. I like people in the house, in the room, dogs and cats, talking and singing. When I'm by myself it's never because I want to be. Alone to me means punishment. It always has.

No one met me at the airport in Mexico City. I went to the baggage area, claimed my bag, then stood around for a while expecting to see some face I recognized. Or someone who recognized me. But nobody showed up. I took the escalator back upstairs and found the Braniff desk. "My name is Waldron. Do you have any messages for me?" The man behind the desk, coarse black hair, a wide, flat face the color of coffee, looked on the message rack and shook his head. "No, sir. Nothing for Waldron."

"Where's the bar?" I said.

"Just up those stairs."

I sat in the bar for an hour. I had three bourbons and a chicken sandwich. I was on my way to the Braniff desk again when I heard my name on the loud-speaker.

"Mr. Waldron. Mr. Harry Waldron. Please report to gate twenty-four in the blue boarding area. . . ."

The passengers were already boarding when I got to the gate. The destination card above the check-in desk said, "Guatemala City."

After we took off, I examined my ticket. Destination: Guatemala City-Tegucigalpa. I rang the call button and a stewardess came over.

"Where's Tegucigalpa?" I said.

"It's the capital of Honduras."

"Does this plane go there?"

"Yes, sir. First Guatemala City. Then Tegucigalpa."

I had a couple drinks. Then, they brought food. And after that I went to sleep. When I woke up it was raining outside. It rained all the way to Guatemala City. While we were on the ground, there was a full-scale electrical storm. It stopped raining just as we took off again.

Tegucigalpa is not a good place to land an airplane. Whoever started living there, however many hundreds of years ago it was, wasn't thinking about flying machines, didn't consider at all what the problems might be of setting a plane down in the middle of those mountains. I looked out the window as we made our approach, perfectly target-fixed, it seemed to me, on a three-thousand-foot slab of granite. When the stewardess opened the door of the cockpit for a second, I could hear the pilot laughing up there. That didn't make me feel better about the mountains. I decided to pull the shade and not watch. But when I felt the plane slide into a steep left bank I pushed the shade up again. The wing tip seemed to be five feet from the stone side of the mountain. But we pulled forty-five degrees around, dropped sharply, and eased down to the landing strip. Business as usual.

This time there was someone to meet me. An airline steward. He took my bag and hurried across the terminal with me trailing behind, down a long corridor, out across the concrete apron, and up the steps to a smaller plane. I was short of breath and out of patience when I sat down in my seat and he shoved the ticket in my hand. "Where the hell am I going?" "San José" he said. He was up the aisle, then, out the door, and it closed behind him. While the stewardess secured the lock bolts, the plane began to roll forward.

I didn't have to ask about San José. There was a flight map in the pocket in front of me. There was also a printed booklet about Costa Rica. On the first page it said: *Information of Interest to Retirees:*

The many charms of Costa Rica have induced people of many nationalities to retire here, where they can live in peace and harmony with 2,000,000 other inhabitants, where it is possible to enjoy full personal liberty in a peaceful, stable, and democratic society. . . .

"Full personal liberty"—that phrase kept bouncing back and forth in my mind. Did someone, writing that, think that anyone reading it would believe it? I turned the page to *General Description:*

Costa Rica is at the southern end of Central America, lying between Panama to the south and southeast, and Nicaragua which it borders on the north. The Pacific Ocean and Caribbean sea from the western and eastern boundaries, respectively.

It went on to say that San José is 3,480 feet above sea level; that the unit of currency is the colon, worth about twelve cents U.S.; that the official language is Spanish; and the national sport is soccer. Under *History* it said:

Costa Rica was discovered in September 1502 by Christopher Columbus on his fourth and last trip to the "Indias."

I skipped down to:

In contrast to most of the other countries in Latin America, Costa Rica has no tradition of military juntas or dictatorships. The last uprising was a civil war twenty-five years ago, and right after that the Army was abolished.

It sounded impressive. Then I saw a short paragraph under *Source of Population:*

The population of Costa Rica is mainly of Spanish descent. Of the aborigines that were inhabitants of the territory during the pre-Columbian era, there only remain a few thousand distributed in small tribes all over the country.

I put the booklet away and looked out the window for a while. I kept wondering who saw to it that the aborigines were "distributed in small tribes" instead of congregated in one big tribe. And whether the person who wrote that line about "full personal liberty" was an aborigine.

Tagge was waiting at the airport in San José, freshly barbered, solid, and smiling.

"I've got a little crop-duster out here to take us to Puntarenas. It's only a fifteen-minute flight. Then we drive twenty minutes down the coast to Juapála, and you'll be home."

"What about Thelma?"

"She's there. She said she was going to cook you a fine meal."

The sun was setting when we took off in the Cessna. We flew straight west, low through the mountains, and the sun kept burning ahead of us as the terrain dropped quickly to sea level. We could see the ocean when we came in to land at Puntarenas.

It was quiet in the car after the ear-splitting noise of the Cessna engine and the wind beating against the fuselage. The copilot of the plane drove the car, a forty-year-old La Salle limousine with a glass panel between the front and back, and Tagge and I sat in the back seat.

"I think you'll like the house," Tagge said. "It's all by itself up in the hills above the beach. But it's only a ten-minute walk down the road to Juapála. And just a short drive to Puntarenas."

"Does Thelma like it?"

"That's an understatement, I think. But you'll get a first-hand report in a few minutes."

"What have you told her?"

"Not much. I thought you could handle that

better than we can. She knows we helped you get out of prison, and that we brought her down here to wait for you. She didn't ask questions. From the time we gave her the note from you, she was anxious to co-operate."

"I'll have to tell her something," I said.

"She hasn't seen the papers. She doesn't know how you got out of jail. I think she believes we're an organization that tries to help innocent men, that we find new evidence and try to arrange a new trial."

"Did you tell her that?"

"Pine gave her some hints, I think."

"What if I don't want to lie to her?"

"Then don't." He lit a cigarette. "It's up to you. One way you get a lot of questions you can't answer. The other way you don't."

It was dark now, deep black suddenly, heavy vegetation growing up to the roadside, the sound of the surf in the distance off to the right.

"What about *my* questions?" I said.

"Do you have some?"

"What do you think?"

"I think if I were you, I'd only have one question in my mind right now. Would I rather be smelling the flowers and breathing the air in a beautiful spot on the ocean, having a drink, and talking to my wife, or would I rather be stuck in a cell in Hobart?"

We turned off the road and up a curving driveway to a house built on pilings, lights burning from the wide windows on the ocean side.

"You'll hear from us," Tagge said. "Meanwhile, enjoy yourself."

I opened the car door. "What if I'm not here when you come back? What makes you so sure I won't take off?"

"I'm not *sure*. But I'm reasonably confident. I

110

think you're smart enough to recognize an opportunity when it's handed to you."

I watched the car circle the driveway and disappear down the hill. When I looked up, Thelma was standing at the railing on the deck looking down at me.

"I can't believe it," she said. "I can't believe you're sitting there, eating a meal, and talking. I always hoped it would end up like this. I tried not to stop hoping. But it was hard, when the months went by, and the years, and I didn't have any word from you. And my letters kept coming back. . . . Now we're just sitting here in a different country with nobody to bother us, and I'm so flustered I don't know whether to laugh or cry. . . ."

I'd forgotten how small she was, how timid and vulnerable, frightened of lightning, wary of crowds, slow to speak or smile, eager to please, warm and kind and trusting, no armor or protective coloration at all, an innocent hill child from another time, trying to walk barefoot through rusty nails and broken glass.

She had started to cry when I came up the stairs and put my arms around her. Her arms were under my jacket and I could feel her hands, cold and shaking, through my shirt. We stood like that for a long time, holding onto each other, till she stopped crying and got quieter. Then she looked up at me and said, "We've even got some bourbon."

We sat out on the deck and had a drink with the trees and foliage and the night sweet and heavy around us. Then I stood in the kitchen and watched her fix supper. And all the time she never stopped talking, while we ate and later on the deck again drinking coffee and smoking strong dark cigarettes.

"I hated to leave Indiana. I wanted to stay close to where you were, even though you wouldn't see me or talk to me or anything. I lived there in Hobart, did you know that? I was there for over a year after I got out on parole. I answered an ad that a woman named Clara Onnerdonk had put in the paper.

"She was a seamstress, did alterations mostly. Had several dry cleaners who were her main customers. Whenever they had repairs or any kind of tailoring or sewing, they sent it over to her. But it got too much for her. They were throwing work at her so fast she couldn't handle it all. That's when she put an ad in for somebody to help her.

"We hit it off right away. She was a widow, living alone. She'd been a farm woman when her husband was alive. She liked to talk crops and stock and weather and recipes, how to cook this, how to bake that. So we got alone fine.

"She rented me a room upstairs for practically nothing, took it out of my wages, and she got me my own sewing machine. So I was really set. She'd made a big workroom out of her downstairs parlor and you should have seen the two of us working away there. Clara never stopped talking and laughing, the radio going, and both our sewing machines buzzing away. . . ."

She came to me suddenly then and put her arms around my neck. "Oh, God, Roy, don't let me rattle on so much. I don't give a damn about all that. Not now."

37

I played the same game with Thelma that Tagge was playing with me. I knew it as I did it. I thought the less information she had the happier she would be. And safer, maybe. Until I had something good to tell her, I decided it was better to tell her nothing.

"Do they know when you'll get a new trial?" she asked.

"Hard to tell. Sometimes it takes a while to set it up."

"All the time I was in prison, and afterward, when I was out but you were still in, I was really down in the mouth. I figured people like us didn't have a chance, that if somebody wanted us in jail we had no choice but to go. Now, all of a sudden, these men show up and all they want to do is help us. I can't believe it. And they're high-type people. I mean, when they tell you something, it's not hard to believe what they say."

"That's right."

"I've got a good feeling about things," she said. "I wasn't so sure before. I thought maybe there was something funny about it, us meeting here in a foreign country and all. But now I've decided it's just the way an educated person does things. Smooth and painless. Everything worked out ahead of time. Do you think we'll stay here till it's time for the trial?"

"I'm not sure. They'll let us know, I guess."

"I bet that trial will go one-two-three. And afterward it will say in the papers that you were innocent all along. I can't wait for that."

The more she talked, the more I realized I couldn't tell her what I knew. She couldn't handle it. So I nodded my head, made up answers that were pleasant to hear, and volunteered nothing.

Two days after I got to Costa Rica I drove up to Puntarenas with my bankbook in my pocket.

The teller sent me to a desk in the corner where a bald-headed man was sitting, polishing his glasses. When I told him my name he stood up, shook my hand, and had a chair brought up for me.

"It is a pleasure to have you, Mr. Waldron. Costa Rica makes a welcome for new residents from the United States. There are six thousand from your country who live here all the year."

"I know. I read the booklet on the plane coming down."

"No crime. No bad air, the life is good here."

"I hope so."

"No question. And you have a fine home. In a good situation. Juapála is a pleasant village. Now . . . how can I be of service?"

I told him I wanted five hundred dollars worth of Costa Rican money. He made a note on a piece of paper, handed it to a secretary, and said to me, "You will see that your money buys a lot down here. Perhaps later you will desire to move some moneys into our savings plan. Or buy bank certificates. If I may say, so, with the amount you have in your account, we can invest it so you can live on earnings and not disturb the principal." The girl came back with the money then and counted it out for me.

"That's good to know," I said. "Give me some time to get settled in. Then we'll talk about it again."

"Of course." He stood up and we shook hands, and I

said, "There's a chance I may want to buy some more real estate down here. In that case I'd have to take a lot of money out of my account. How do I go about doing that?"

"A simple request. Just as you have done today."

When I left the bank I walked down the street to a travel agency I'd seen as I drove into town. The girl at the desk spoke clear but limited textbook English.

"To Rio de Janeiro there are two flights each day. At eight hours and nineteen hours. Change aircraft in Panama City. One hour delay there."

Next, I went to a real-estate office with a sign, "English Spoken" in the window. A gray-haired lady wearing a heavy silver necklace talked with me.

"Of course we know that home. It's a fine piece of property."

"Yes, it is," I said. "But my business plans may change. If they do, I would have to leave Costa Rica on short notice. Would there be a problem selling my house?"

She smiled and touched her necklace. "Our problem is not to sell. Our problem is finding houses to sell." She leafed through a stack of papers and handed me a page with a list of twenty or thirty names on it. "These are buyers who cannot find a house to buy, bona-fide residents with cash in the bank. For a home like yours, I guarantee you we could find a suitable buyer in twenty-four hours."

That afternoon, a silver Mercedes pulled into our driveway and a thin dark man in a brown suit got out and climbed the stairs to the front deck. I walked to the top of the steps to meet him.

"Señor Waldron?"

"Yes."

"I am Captain Ruiz. I would like to welcome you to Costa Rica."

"Thank you."

"I am with the department of immigration at Puntarenas."

I started to offer him a drink, then decided against it. "Immigration? Does that mean I did something I shouldn't have?"

"Not at all. Normally we would ask you to come into the office to register with us but I needed to be in Juapála this afternoon so I thought I could save you the trip."

"Well . . . thank you."

"If you will give me your passport to take along I will have one of my clerks make out the registration. Then you can sign it next time you come into Puntarenas."

"Why don't I bring the passport in tomorrow morning, and we'll do it all at once?"

"We could do that." He smiled and held his hands out, palms up. "But since I have already made the trip . . ."

When I went to the bedroom for the passport, Thelma was asleep in her beach robe. She woke up as I closed the bureau drawer.

"Hey."

"Go back to sleep," I said.

"What's happening?"

"Just some local official. He has to look at my passport. He's waiting out on the deck."

"It's no problem, is it?"

"No. Just red tape."

After Ruiz left, Thelma and I walked down to the beach and went swimming. It was after four when we came back. While she took a shower I called the real-estate woman in Puntarenas.

"This is Mr. Waldron. I spoke to you this morning about my house in Juapála."

"Yes, I remember."

"I've just had the news I was waiting for. It looks as if I will have to sell the house."

"I see."

"I'd like you to find a buyer as quickly as possible. Can you do that?"

There was a short pause. Then she said, "Yes, of course, Mr. Waldron. You will hear from me very quickly, I'm sure."

Two days later Thelma and I drove to Puntarenas. "I just want to stumble around in some of the stores and get a Spanish-English dictionary and a lot of dumb stuff like that," she said. "You don't have to go with me if you don't want to."

"I've got a couple of errands myself. I'll meet you in an hour by the fountain in the square."

After I let her out and parked the car I walked into the real-estate office and found the lady I'd talked to before.

"Has anything developed yet?" I said.

"No, Mr. Waldron. Not yet."

"From what you said the other day, I thought . . ."

"I'm sure I will discover a buyer very soon. I will telephone you as soon as I know something of good news."

Before I left I asked her where I could find the immigration office. She walked to the door with me and pointed to a five-story office building down near the docks.

The building, when I saw it close, was bright green tile on the outside. Inside, it looked as though it had never been finished. Patches of raw plaster, cracks across the ceiling, and tiles missing from the floor. I didn't like the looks of the elevator either, so I walked up three flights to Ruiz's office.

"Captain Ruiz is in San José," his secretary said.

"When do you expect him back?"

"My English . . ." she said, and made a gesture with her hands.

I repeated it slowly. "When does he come here?"

"I don't know. Tomorrow perhaps."

"He has my passport. Can I get it back?"

She nodded her head and smiled. "Yes. From Captain Ruiz. As soon as he is back in Puntarenas."

When I met Thelma she said, "Is everything all right?"

"Everything's dandy. Let's make a tour."

We spent the rest of the day there, up and down the streets, in and out of stores and cafés. We had lunch at an open-air restaurant by the docks and watched the ferries pull in and out. When I paid the check I asked the waiter where the ferry went.

"Península de Nicoya," he said. "Very beautiful. *Playas hermosas.* Good to swim. Beautiful beaches."

"Can I take my car there?"

"Your car? *Sí.* On the boat."

When we walked out on the dock I said to Thelma, "You want to take a boat ride?"

"Sure."

"We'll ferry the car over and drive around. It stands to reason if cars can make the trip, there must be some roads to drive on."

"It's too late, isn't it? By the time we get there it will be time to come back."

"We won't come back. We'll find a place to stay all night."

"But I don't have any clothes."

"I'll buy you some clothes."

"I don't even have a sweater with me."

"I'll buy you a sweater. Come on. We'll give ourselves a party. We'll have a honeymoon on the peninsula."

She put her arms around my neck. "I thought that's what we've been doing for three days, having a honeymoon."

"That's all right. We'll have it some more."

We stayed five days. We drove north to Nicoya, then on to Santa Cruz, and across to the beaches on the west coast. From there we bumped and skidded our way south on the dirt roads, half-naked, laughing, and drunk on the wine, from one beach to another, sleeping in motels, sleeping in the car, sleeping on the ground on a blanket, freckled and suntanned, sand and sea salt in our hair, nothing to carry, nothing to pack, no deadlines or timetables, no books or maps. Cash and carry, sleep and eat, walk and run and swim, fall naked into bed or on some floor, or in the car, then up again and swim some more and on to the next spot, wherever that might turn out to be.

I wanted it that way. I wanted that time with Thelma. With money in my pocket and nothing to make either one of us think of anything we'd known or seen or been a part of at any other time in some other place. I wanted it crazy and unreal, with a different language in our ears, strange food and places, and faces that could never remind a person of West Virginia or North Carolina or Chicago or Indianapolis or the inside of a cell.

I knew when I drove off the ferry again in Puntarenas, the tangle I'd left behind would still be there, the people and puzzles, the things I couldn't figure out and the things I couldn't forget. But until that happened, until tomorrow started to push in on me again, I wanted something special and secret and private for me and Thelma. She wanted it too. And we had it, better than it could have been planned or dreamed about.

It was ten in the morning when we got back to
Puntarenas. Thelma waited in the car while I stopped
at the real estate office. The gray-haired lady was wearing her silver necklace again. She saw me coming
through the door and met me at the front desk, all
smiles.

"Nothing yet, Mr. Waldron."

"I don't understand."

"What do you mean?"

"I mean I thought you'd have a buyer by now."

"So did I. But sometimes we guess wrong. Just be
patient. Something will come up soon."

Ruiz wasn't in his office. Having coffee, his secretary
said.

"Where does he go for coffee?" I said.

"Sometimes he drives home."

"Did he drive home today?"

"I don't know."

I stood in front of her desk looking down at her.
I stared at her and didn't say anything.

"What is it?" she said.

I didn't move or change my expression. Finally, she
couldn't stand the silence. "I really don't know . . ."
she began. But she couldn't make herself believe it,
and she knew I didn't believe it either. So she told
me where he was.

It was walking distance from his office, the second
floor of a heavy old building looking out over the
harbor, with fans going on the ceiling inside and men

124

in white suits sitting around playing cards and drinking coffee. And smoking black cigars.

"I am happy to see you," Ruiz said.

"I looked for you at your office. I'd like to have my passport back."

"Of course. Tomorrow or day after, I think."

"You said it was a formality. It would only take a few minutes."

"Normally, that is true."

"What does that mean?"

"Once a year, my superiors in San José review all alien papers. While I was holding your passport, they requested it. It was just a matter of timing. Out of my hands altogether."

"You didn't even give me a receipt. Do you know that?"

"Not necessary. When your passport comes back I will deliver it in person. There is no reason for you to be unquiet."

When I got back to the car, Thelma said, "What took you so long?"

"Red tape again."

"No problems?"

"No problems."

When we pulled into our driveway, there was a car parked there. Inside the house, Tagge and Pine were waiting, in their shirt sleeves, collars open, a man with them I hadn't seen before, trim, cool-eyed, with steel-gray hair, a thin cigar in his hand. The air was heavy and hot in the room, the ashtrays were full.

"We've been here since early this morning. We've been trying to contact you for two days," Pine said as soon as Thelma and I came through the door.

Tagge cut in quickly. "It's all right, Ross. No harm done." He turned to me then, indicated the third man with a gesture and said, "Shake hands with our associate, General Reser—"

"Retired," the man said with a quick, muscular smile. "Tom Reser." He held out his hand to me.

"—Roy Tucker . . ." Tagge went on ". . . and his wife, Thelma."

Thelma and I both shook hands with Reser, and Tagge went on talking, painting the air with butter and honey. "Sorry to invade your house like this, Mrs. Tucker, but we didn't want to go back into town and run the risk of missing you. I must say, you two look like different people since the last time I saw you. Sun-tanned and rested. Costa Rica must agree with you."

"We like it fine," Thelma said. Then she turned to me. "I guess you've got things to talk about. I'll go and clean up."

As soon as she left the room Reser said, "Let's mosey out on the deck."

Pine had been looking at me with his jaw muscles twitching and his mouth pressed shut in a straight line. As soon as we got outside he said, "I'm losing patience with you, Tucker. In case you haven't figured out who's giving orders here, *we* are. When we say we'll be in touch with you, that means you're supposed to *be* here, where we can reach you."

I turned and looked at him and he kept on talking. "You're not doing us a favor. That's not the way it works at all. You're just a pair of hands to us—"

"That's enough, Pine." Reser clipped out the words like three pieces of wire.

"What does he mean by that?" I said to Tagge.

"It's all right—" Tagge said.

"No, it's not. What did he mean?"

"Why do we have to handle this man like a piece of glass?" Pine said. "If you don't straighten him out now—"

"Listen, you son of a bitch—" I started.

Tagge eased himself between me and Pine.

"All right. That's enough."

"Wait inside, Pine," Reser said.

"What?"

"I said open that door and close it behind you."

"Wait a minute. Let's get something clear—"

"Take it easy, Ross. Let's not forget who we are and what we're doing." Tagge turned and looked at Reser. "We all have to remember that." He took out a cigarette and lit it. "Now . . . ." he said. "Tucker and I need to talk. I think it's best if we talk alone." He nodded toward the door leading inside. "We'll be with you in a few minutes."

No discussion this time. Reser turned, crossed the deck, and went into the house. Pine followed him.

Tagge sat down at the table by the edge of the deck and I sat across from him. The umbrella made a wide disk of shade over us.

"Good climate down here. Hot and wet. I like that. Always have. I spent eight years in West Africa. Nigeria, Cameroon, the Congo, back and forth across the equator. Best time of my life. Other people slow down in the heat. I speed up. The head works better, the muscles feel loose and easy." He looked up at the sky. "The sun beats down, then a soaking rain, and the steam comes up out of the ground. Damned good for you, I think. At least it's good for me. As long as a person has a nap. You need an afternoon nap in this climate." He put his feet on the lower railing, crossed his ankles, and looked out over the trees toward the ocean.

"Let me tell you something about Pine," he said then. "He's a brilliant young man. One of the best minds I've come in contact with. Conceptual. But he's young. You can see that. And impatient. It's a long time and a long distance between the cookbook and the meal. He has trouble dealing with that fact. He's a snob, too. The intellectual kind. He thinks anybody who isn't as smart as he is isn't worth listening to. And since hardly anybody's as smart as he is . . . you see what I mean?"

"I don't give a damn how smart he is. I don't want to listen to his mouth—"

"Another thing is he's afraid of you. Gerald Henemyer, the man you threw down stairs in Chicago, is a friend of Pine's. It shook him up when he heard about that. Pine is not physical. Everything's tactical with him. He can't understand a man getting sore and punching somebody. It scares him."

Tagge lit a fresh cigarette from the end of the one he was smoking and flipped the butt out into the foilage around the deck. "No forest fires here," he said. "You couldn't start a fire out there with a flame thrower. Heavy and wet. I like that."

He sat there, relaxed in his chair and smoking.

Finally, he said, "At four this afternoon we're flying up to California. We've got a jet waiting. We'll fly direct to Long Beach."

"You mean I'm going with you?"

"That's right."

"How long will I be there?"

"I can't say exactly. A week or ten days. Maybe less. We expect the situation to develop fast once it starts."

"What situation are you talking about? What's going to develop?"

He gave me an open look and said, "I don't know the answers to those questions any more than you do. I know what I'm supposed to do because somebody tells me. And when the time comes, you'll know what you're supposed to do because somebody will tell you. But none of us," he indicated the room where Pine and Reser were waiting, "know the whole thing. We just know pieces."

I eased my chair around so I could get a clear look at his eyes and said, "There may be a problem. I don't have my passport."

"Why not?" he said. His face told me nothing.

I explained to him that about Captain Ruiz. When I finished he said, "Sounds like routine to me. Nothing to worry about. We gave you that passport so you'd have a piece of solid identification. That's all."

"You mean I won't need it to go to California?"

He shook his head. "And you won't need it to come back here. Just an entry card. And we'll take care of that."

"You mean some countries you need a passport to go in and out and some you don't?"

"That's right." He snuffed out his cigarette, turned, and smiled at me. "If I wanted to go to Brazil, to Rio de Janeiro, for example, I'd need a passport."

I sat there looking at him and I understood. It was impossible not to understand.

Tagge and Pine and Reser stopped talking and looked up as Thelma and I came into the room. There was a thick silence. I put the bags down and Tagge, after a look at Pine and Reser, came over to me.

"I'm sorry," he said, "this is awkward. And I guess it's my fault. I thought I'd made it clear but apparently I didn't. We can't take you along on this trip, Mrs. Tucker. . . ."

"Yes, we can. If I go, she goes," I said.

"I'm sorry. I understand how you feel. And we'd accommodate you if we could. But it's out of the question."

"No, it's not."

"I'm not just being arbitrary, Tucker. These aren't my decisions to make. I told you earlier, I have orders to follow and so do you."

"Maybe I do. But this is one order I won't take," I said. My look shifted from Tagge to Pine. As I looked at him, something came to life in his eyes. He moved across the room toward Tagge.

"We're tried to be flexible with you before," Tagge went on, "but circumstances are different here—"

Pine stepped in. "Marvin, I just had a thought." He eased away toward the windows and Tagge followed him. Thelma and I stood like two children waiting to be punished and watched them talking on the other side of the room.

Tagge turned and came back then. "Ross has an

idea and I'm sure he's right. We're being too rigid about this." He looked at Thelma. "Forget what I said. Of course you want to be with your husband. And you should be."

PART THREE

I remember in my schoolbooks it said that Los Angeles is the largest city, chief seaport, and principal industrial center of the state of California. And the largest city in area in the United States.

I had never been there but Thelma had. When she left Hobart she'd gone to San Bernardino to live with her cousin.

"I always thought I'd love California before I went there," she said. We were sitting in the back of a private jet flying north from Costa Rica, Tagge and the other two men up ahead, smoking and talking quietly.

"I liked to look at pictures of it," she said, "the orange groves and the palm trees, and everybody cool and comfortable, walking around in gardens in their shirt sleeves or summer dresses or sitting under umbrellas on the beach.

"And the movies . . . everybody gets excited about that, I guess. I've been looking at movie magazines since I was a kid, memorizing things I read in them, seeing pictures of those mansions with swimming pools and the stars in white cars with the tops down.

"So when Fay said I could come out here and live with her I was so flustered I didn't know what to say. I didn't want to leave Hobart, didn't want to be far away from you, but if I wasn't going to hear from you or see you or have a chance to talk to you I figured I could wait for you just as well out there with Fay as I could in Clara Onnerdonk's furnished room in Hobart.

"I was lonesome too. Mostly for you. But I needed to be with somebody my own age. I needed a woman friend from home, somebody who knew what I was like and how I felt about things. So when Fay said come on out, at first I didn't do it. But, finally, I went. And boy, did I get a surprise. I mean Los Angeles must have been a nice place once. If it wasn't, all those people wouldn't have flocked out there, would they? But now . . well you'll see when we get there . . . it makes you think it's a place where *cars* live and the people are just there as some kind of servants to keep the cars alive.

"It's hard to breathe there, too. I mean it. Some days there's a yellow cloud all the way from the ocean clear out to San Bernardino. Your eyes burn and water, and when you first go there you can't figure out what's wrong. Then they laugh and tell you it's just the smog. But it's not funny. It makes you think they'd laugh if somebody put rat poison in their coffee. I mean how can anybody be so crazy about living in a place that they love it even when it's terrible.

"The vegetables and the fruit don't taste good either. They're all fat and big and bright-colored, but when you put them in your mouth you can't tell what you're eating. A California tomato doesn't even *taste* like a tomato. It tastes like something that somebody invented or made in a fake tomato factory. When you eat *anything* that tastes good in California, you can bet it's shipped in.

"It's all desert, you know. Before they put a town there, it was desert. And that's the way it still makes you feel. Like nothing could grow there or live there. For all the fancy buildings and homes and traffic and money and people dressed up and whipping around, you get the feeling it's a place to die in, that everything and everybody you see came there to die."

I sat listening to her, feeling her shoulder against

mine, her hand on my arm, looking at the soft mountains of clouds outside the plane window, and wondering if I should tell her the truth. Or part of the truth. I wanted to keep her safe, to protect her in any way I could. And if I couldn't do that, I wanted to help her somehow to protect herself. I wanted to say, "Look, honey, I've painted myself into a corner. I'm a captive and so are you." But there was no way I could say it to her. She couldn't handle that kind of information. It would be too much for her. She'd want to run. She'd want me to run with her. And there was no way I knew to tell her the truth, that there was no place for us to run to.

It was dark when we landed at the Long Beach airport. Tagge walked Thelma and me through the terminal and put us into a car.

"You're going to the Sutter Hotel in Santa Monica. There's a room reserved for Mr. and Mrs. Waldron. You don't have to sit by the phone, but don't go too far. And don't stay away more than an hour or two at a time. I'll be in touch with you soon, probably tomorrow." He handed me an envelope. "Here's some walking-around money."

I liked the hotel. It looked the way a California hotel should look. On a high street, above the ocean, palm trees, a swimming pool just outside the lobby, and an endless parade of blond girls with long legs and men in white shoes with their shirts open to the waist. On the way to the elevator I saw Brookshire sitting in the lobby.

Our room was on the ninth floor, looking out on the park across the street, the beach two hundred feet down below, and the ocean beyond that.

As soon as we were alone in the room with the door closed, Thelma picked up the phone.

"What are you doing?" I said.

"I gotta call Fay. She'd kill me if she knew I was here and didn't call right away."

I walked over and took the receiver out of her hand just as the operator came on.

"Never mind," I said into the phone. "We'll place the call later." When I hung up the receiver, Thelma said, "What's the matter?"

"Nothing."

"Why can't I call?"

"I don't think it's a good idea."

"I just want to talk to her for a minute. Tell her I'm here. Fay's been awful nice to me. . . ."

"Use your head, honey. Just use your head."

"You mean because of . . . I don't know what you mean. . . ."

"I mean it isn't exactly front-page news that I'm out of jail . ."

"But it's all legal and everything. . . ."

"That's right. But I don't think it's a good idea to advertise it."

"Is that why we're using a different name?"

"That's part of it. Tagge doesn't want the newspapers deciding my case before he gets it into court."

I didn't like to lie to her. I'm not good at lying. But I didn't know what else to do.

"I still don't see what that has to do with me calling my cousin in San Bernardino. She's not gonna ring up the papers and tell them she just talked to me, is she?"

"I don't know what she's liable to do, and I don't want to find out. I just don't want you to talk to her. All right?"

"All *right*. You don't have to get mad."

"I'm not mad."

"Then why are you yelling at me?"

She went into the bathroom and closed the door and I could hear her crying. I wanted to go in and talk to her, but I didn't. I went out on the terrace and smoked a cigarette and looked at the ocean.

After a while I heard the bathroom door open and she came out on the terrace in her robe and put her arms around me.

"I'm sorry," she said.

"There's nothing to be sorry about."

"I don't care. I'm sorry anyway. I don't like to fight with you."

"It's all right," I said. "We're not fighting." I put my arms around her and kissed her. Then she leaned against me with her head on my chest.

"You want to hear something crazy. I was in there crying and feeling sorry for myself and trying to be mad at you, and all of a sudden in the middle of all that I wanted you to . . . you know . . . I started to feel all funny inside." She took my hand and put it between her legs.

"You don't feel funny to me," I said.

"I don't mean *funny*. You now what I mean."

I sat down on the chair and pulled her on my lap with her robe open there on the terrace in the cool air off the ocean.

"My God, Roy. Somebody's gonna see us."

"No, they're not. It's all right. This is California. People do everything outdoors in California."

"But we've got clothes on and everything."

"That's all right. It feels all right, doesn't it?"

"You tell me," she said.

Later I carried her inside and we undressed and lay on top of the bed with the moonlight coming in the window. We went to sleep like that.

We woke up at three in the morning, both of us. We were shivering from the night air. Thelma slid under the sheets and I found an extra blanket in the closet to put over her.

"That's better," she said. "Now I'm warm but I'm starving. Why am I so hungry?"

"We didn't eat supper. That might have something to do with it."

"My stomach feels like it's chewing on itself."

I picked up the phone. After a long wait a man's voice came on.

"Any chance of getting some food up here?" I said "We're starving to death."

"I'm sorry, sir. Room service stopped at two. But there's an all-night coffee shop on the lobby floor."

"Won't they send something upstairs?"

"I'm afraid not," he said. "They don't deliver."

I hung up and started putting on my clothes.

"It's all right," Thelma said. "Don't go out. I can stand it if I have to."

"Maybe you can. But I can't."

Twenty minutes later I was back. With four hamburgers, four chili dogs, a sack of french fries, and four containers of hot coffee. We sat in bed and ate every crumb of every sandwich, fought for the last french fry, and guzzled down every drop of the coffee. I put the empty sack and cartons in the wastebasket in the bathroom, got back into bed, and switched off the light.

"That's more like it," Thelma said.

141

"Did you have enough?"

"I ate so fast I can't tell yet." She rolled close to me with her head on my shoulder and her leg over mine. "I smell like a french fry," she said. "How would you like to be loved up a little by somebody with greasy hands and onion breath?"

"Let me think about it," I said.

"Too late. I already made up my mind."

She raised up then and lowered herself slowly on me. "That's more like it. Aren't you glad you woke up?"

There was a heavy fog outside the window. From far off we could hear foghorns.

"What time is it?" Thelma said.

I switched on the bed lamp and looked at my watch. "Five o'clock."

"That's what I get for drinking all that coffee," she said. "I can't sleep."

"I can't either. You want to fool around?"

"You're kidding. Do *you?*"

"Sure, why not?"

"Big talk. If it's all the same to you I'll wait a little while."

"Don't say I didn't ask you."

She put her head on my shoulder again. After a while she said, "I don't know if it matters to you but I didn't do anything with anybody while we were . . . while you were in jail."

"I didn't ask you."

"I know you didn't. But I'm telling you anyway."

"It's all right."

"You wouldn't like it if I did, would you?"

"Not very much, I guess."

"I mean you like it better that I didn't, don't you?"

"Sure I do. Anybody would."

"I though about you all the time. I kept you right in the front of my head so I could see you. I didn't even go out anyplace or hang around with people. So there was no chance of anybody getting any ideas or of me finding myself in some kind of a corner I couldn't get out of. In Hobart, there with Clara, it was like being in a convent. I mean I never even *saw* a man for days at a time. Just the mailman and people like that for a few seconds."

She rolled on her back then and bunched the pillow under her head. "When I got out to Fay's it was a little different because she and Pearse, that's her husband's name—did I tell you that—they liked to have a few drinks and play cards, so they most of the time had somebody over at the house. But their friends caught on quick that I was married. We told everybody you had an oil-drilling job down in Venezuela and I wasn't allowed to be there. So they knew I wasn't lookin' for any kind of playing around at all. With anybody. Fay and Pearse were funny about it. They looked after me like I was a ten-year-old girl who'd never had a date or been kissed or anything.

"Fay told me that Pearse really unloaded on Fred Bazley. He was a friend of theirs from the garage where Pearse worked, and he was the only one who didn't get the message about me. I mean he was some kind of a ladies' man. At least he *thought* he was. Sideburns and tight pants, and always had his sleeves rolled up tight to show his muscles. So he took one look at me and figured I was easy pickin's, I guess. But I straightened him out in a hurry. And just in case that wasn't enough, Fay followed right up on it. And finally, like I said, Pearse told him, in words he could understand, that I wasn't on the menu. That's the way Fay put it. She always had a funny way of saying things. But anyway, that turned Fred Bazley off once and for all. He got so he'd hardly speak to me when he came over to the house. He was so afraid I'd take it the wrong way. But after a while he got past that, and then he was just friendly and nice like anybody else."

144

She turned on her side with her face close to mine. "You see," she said, "I know what I'm doing. I'm not just some big-eyed kid from the sticks. I know how to take care of myself."

At eight in the morning the phone woke me up.
Thelma was still asleep, so I picked it up quickly. It
was a woman's voice. "Walk out the front entrance of
the hotel, cross the street to the park, turn right,
and walk two hundred yards. Someone will be waiting for you at exactly eight-thirty." She hung up.

I took a fast shower, shaved, and dressed. I found a
piece of hotel stationery and wrote, "Out for a walk.
I'll be back by ten." I left it on the bathroom sink
where Thelma would see it if she woke up.

Tagge was waiting for me, on a bench at the edge
of a bluff, high up above the coast highway.

It was damp and cold, heavy fog over the ocean and
a wave of ground mist rolling slowly across the grass of
the park between the rows of date palms.

"It's chilly," Tagge said. "Did you have breakfast?"

"Not yet. The call woke me up."

"Don't worry about it. I haven't been in bed at all."
He looked like it. His face was gray, dark under the
eyes, and his suit was rumpled.

"You want to get a cup of coffee somewhere?" I
said.

"No, I don't have time." He looked at his watch.
"Here's what I want you to do. At exactly eleven
o'clock, walk out the back entrance of the hotel, turn
right, and go down that street to Santa Monica Boulevard. There's a taxi stand there. Get a cab and tell
him to take you to the Akron on Sepulveda Boulevard.
He'll know where it is—"

"What's the Akron?"

"It's a store. When you get there, get out of the cab. A green Pontiac will be right behind you. Get in the back seat and the driver will take you where you're going. Reser will meet you." He pulled his coat around him. "Jesus, it's cold out here."

He fished a cigarette out of an inside pocket and lit it. "Off the record, I want to give you a tip," he said then. "You're in a tricky situation and I want to ease it for you if I can. I want you to come out of this neat and clean. And you can. But you have to keep your *head* out of it. You know what I mean? Don't try to figure it out. All the thinking's been done already. All the plans are made. This thing is like a train going downhill. You either ride it or it runs over you. But there's no stopping it. Don't misunderstand me. I'm not telling you this as some kind of a threat. But you're in a crack. You know it and I know it. So the best advice I can give you is to turn your *head* off. Get your sleep, stay loose, and do as you're told." He stood up and said, "Let's go."

We started down the walk leading to the hotel. After we'd gone a little way, he stopped. "Just remember what I said. Make it easy on yourself." He turned and walked across the grass. When he got to the curb, a car rolled up and he got into the back seat.

I went back to the hotel and had breakfast in the coffee shop. Then I went upstairs and let myself into the room. Thelma was still asleep.

The cab driver began talking as soon as I got in and closed the door. It sounded like a monologue that had started a long time before.

"The whole country's gone to shit. You know what I mean? Every question has four or five answers now. Nothing's right and nothing's wrong. God is dead, they tell me. Kids don't listen to their folks. The cops are getting paid off by the crooks. Every time somebody gets married in California, somebody else gets a divorce. The hippies are right about *that*, I think. They're wrong about everything else, but they're right about that. If you're gonna get a divorce six months after you get married, what's the point of gettin' married in the first place? You might as well get yourself a room over here in Venice and shack up with somebody till you get it out of your system. I'm not an old man. You can see that. But I'll tell you I don't recognize this country any more. Everybody's got his hand out. Something for nothing. That's the idea. I get these people in my cab. Big mouths, fancy clothes, expensive apartments. How do they do it? They don't work. They'll tell you right to your face. So where's the money come from? It's a mystery to me. I've been beatin' my brains out ever since I got out of the Navy in 'forty-five, tryin' to raise my kids, keep a roof on the house, food in the icebox. I never found any secrets. Nobody ever showed me how you get along without workin'. When I think of me and my buddies gettin' our asses shot off down there at Guadalcanal it makes me sick. What was it for? The

Japs ended up better off than we are. The Germans the same thing. We got fifty guys in the State Department whose main job is to kiss the Russians' ass. Does that make any sense to you? It sure don't to me. I'll tell you something else. The President and the Senators and all those bastards in Washington have got a helluva lot more in common with those pricks in the Kremlin, or in China, or Japan, or anywhere, than they have with the ordinary tax-payin' bastards like you and me who elect them and pay their salaries. We're patsies, my friend. The government ain't workin' for *us*, not by a damn sight. We're workin' for *them*. Jesus, those guys in Washington must be laughin' up their sleeves. You talk about thieves. Those bastards make the guys in jail look like boy scouts. You think they give up practicin' law so they can take a loss in income? Not much they don't. That law degree's a license to steal. Everybody knows that. But gettin' elected to Congress, that's a license to steal *big*. Someday, a long time after everything's gone down the drain, some smart guy will write it all up. And I guarantee you he'll say we got screwed like no other bunch of people ever got screwed before. What I mean is it's all rigged. We get to vote but the votes don't mean anything. If a good man gets in office, they either shut him up, buy him off, or kill him. They got Kennedy, they got his brother, and they almost got Wallace. Martin Luther King, they blew a hole in him. You think all that just happened? Bullshit. And look at that poor bastard they got in there now. All of a sudden he's got a bad liver or something. Do you believe that? I don't. No wonder he doesn't want to go into the hospital. If he does, he's a goner. They'll carry him out in a paper bag."

He pulled over then and said, "Here's the Akron, buddy."

I paid him and he said, "What do you think? Am I right?"

"Don't ask me," I said. I got out of the cab and walked back to the green Pontiac parked by the curb.

It was a forty-five-minute drive, south on the freeway. We turned west then, maneuvered through a tangle of streets jammed with trucks going to and from the harbor, and stopped finally in front of a gate with a guard station. A uniformed man was sitting inside.

My driver was a young girl, with long brown hair parted in the middle. She hadn't said a word from the time she picked me up till she stopped the car. She sat behind the wheel now, looking straight ahead till I got out and closed the door behind me. She started the engine and drove off.

The wire gate opened and a white jeep drove out. Reser, wearing blue coveralls and a golf cap, was driving it. He stopped beside me and said, "Hop in." Then he drove back through the gate and it closed behind us.

Matter-of-fact, no small talk, he went right to the subject, crisp and direct as a briefing session.

"We're got two patterns, A and B. *A* is the one we prefer because we have more control. *Total* control if we're able to go that route. But it may not happen that way. The objective may not sit still for it. So we had to come up with an alternate. It's crude in a way but it can work. We'll make it work if we have to. It has a kind of amateur smell to it that should work in our favor. So . . . we're giving it a dry run."

He pulled up and stopped, thirty feet from a medium-size helicopter. The pilot was already inside and the blades were turning. Reser climbed on board and I followed him.

It was a combat chopper, an H53, the kind we used to pick up wounded personnel in Vietnam. Light, maneuverable, and fast, easy to hover, with special side doors and good controls to slide them open and shut in a hurry.

Reser dropped into a bucket seat and motioned me to the one beside him. The pilot was a stocky guy, forty years old maybe. He kept his eyes straight ahead when we got in. As soon as we were in our seats, the doors slid shut and we lifted off.

Reser had to raise his voice now, but I could hear him all right over the motor noise.

"Three things going for it, this plan. Speed, surprise, and the fact that we get to run through the moves. The other trick we only get one chance at." He looked at his watch. "Twelve-ten . . . travel time included we'll be back on the ground by one-twenty."

The helicopter was out of the harbor area now. We headed southwest, a thousand feet over the water. The ocean was clear and blue, no clouds in the sky, sailboats sliding back and forth across the smooth water.

As we moved away from the mainland, Reser pointed ahead and to the right. "That's Catalina. We'll head south and a little east of there. There's a rough spot that most of the boats steer clear of. That's where we'll do our maneuver."

I was trying to remember exactly what Tagge had said about following orders. The helicopter helped. I half expected to see the gray, burned-over ground of Vietnam when I looked down. And Reser's voice sounded like all the officers I'd ever served under. Even the weapon, when he took it out of its case and handed it to me, was no surprise. I'd carried an exact twin of it for months.

"It's a weapon you're familiar with," Reser was saying. "The weight's the same. And the balance. But everything else is custom. It's almost totally silent, it has the sights of a hunting rifle, and the barrel's as close to a hundred per cent true as any tools can make it. The ammunition's hollow-nosed, explodes on contact. It's a beautiful piece."

I hefted it, settled the stock against my shoulder, and sighted through the window. I shortened the strap and tried again. Reser left his seat and made his way up to the pilot. I could see them talking but the words didn't carry. We started a straight-down, steady drop as Reser came back to his seat.

"We're gonna hover here. This is the spot."

As we came down a hundred feet over the water, Reser called to the pilot, "Hit the doors." Immediately, the door by my seat slid open and I felt the sea air against my face. "That seat of yours swivels," Reser said. "Get it where you want it and we'll lock it."

I reached down and released the catch, turned the seat so I faced straight out through the door, nothing to block my arms or my vision. I sighted at the water.

"Here comes your target," Reser said. He slid a big cardboard carton forward. It was full of gallon-size paint cans. He picked them up by their bales and threw them out the window. They hit the water and floated on the swell like a family of ducks. The pilot held the ship in a tight, steady hover, adjusting to a light breeze flowing toward us from the west.

"You're on," Reser shouted to me. "There are ten of them down there. If you get them all in twenty cracks I'll be happy."

I got them all in twelve, ten fast explosions of red paint from the half-filled cans.

"Ten for twelve in sixteen seconds," Reser said. "You win the Kewpie doll." He called to the pilot. "Let's go."

The chopper lifted in a wide left circle and angled toward the mainland. I handed the rifle back to Reser and he slid it into the case. I could still feel the stock against my cheek, the weight of the barrel in my hand, the hard ridges of the trigger against my finger.

It was an old instinct with me, an old sensation. An air rifle when I was five, a .22 when I was six, days in the woods with my dad shooting squirrel, nights with a lantern hunting possum.

At that time, in that place, a rifle was more than what it did. It was part of the life, a part of the house and the family. It brought food in and kept strangers out, it was the right and the strength and, if necessary, the law. The feel of it meant something. The weight of it, the jolt against the shoulder, the smell of burning powder, all triggered sensations and memories older than your own body. It was a kind of identity, very real, and I felt it strongly, in spite of myself, that afternoon over the ocean off California.

"Do you know this coast up ahead?" Reser said.

"No."

"Used to be great. But it's a dead loss now. In a few years they say it'll be one big city from San Diego all the way up to San Francisco. It's not far from that now." He went up forward to the pilot again. When he came back he said, "We're heading north, across the east edge of Los Angeles. We'll target in the national forest, southwest of Bear Canyon." He looked at his watch again. "Right on the money."

I looked out the window on the right as we edged

close to the coast. The water was pale green along the beaches. I could see square, walled white houses, red tile roofs, palm trees in long lines, and the bright blue rectangles of swimming pools with grass all around.

"Looks pretty good from up here," Reser said. "Down there, it's something else. A bunch of tired people with tired ideas eating avocados and breathing each other's exhaust fumes."

He looked out the window, full concentration, as we flew north across the tangled maze of the city. "Pasadena," he said finally. Then, "And here comes the national forest." Below us now were mountains, rough and tree-covered. After ten minutes or so Reser said to the pilot, "Okay, Lenny. Coming up."

"I'm on it," the pilot said. We slowed forward speed and settled into an easy forward angle. The door slid open again.

"Fix your seat," Reser said. I did. Facing out, right angles to the thrust of the helicopter.

"This is it," Reser said, "the way it's gonna be. We'll come down to two hundred feet, hover twenty seconds, then haul-ass out again. That's how much time you'll have."

It was a walled compound in a clearing on a mountain-top, trees all around, stone paths winding to a rambling tile-roofed house, red roses against the green of the lawns, a swimming pool, and a shaded tennis court.

"Right here, Lenny. Freeze it," Reser called to the pilot.

"Got it."

The engine softened and we hovered high above the house, half hidden by a wooded ridge.

"That will be our position, dead on that path going down to the pool. We'll know when he's coming, and we'll be here. Like I say, you'll have twenty seconds. The way you shoot, that's more time than you need."

I sat there like a customer in a movie seat. Steady, comfortable, a straight line of unobstructed vision.

"All right?" Reser said. I nodded my head and he shouted to the pilot, "Let's go home."

We whipped around in a steep climb and headed southwest, climbing to a thousand feet or more and roaring ahead, clouds forming now and slipping past quickly outside the windows. Reser lit a cigar and sat back in his chair.

"My wife always had it in her head that we'd retire to La Jolla. She spent a few years there when I was in Korea, and she thought it was the greatest place since . . . you know what I mean. Couldn't wait to drag me down there and start looking for a house. Well, she got me there all right but we didn't look for a house. We spent three nights in a motel that was half rest home and the other half whorehouse, with a discotheque blasting on the hill fifty yards behind us. So I said, 'Honey, if I had my choice between this place and a five-year stretch in the Philippines as a buck-ass private, I wouldn't hesitate. I'd be on that plane for Manila before they had the engine warmed up.'"

He kept talking and smoking, all the way back. I looked out the window and let all kinds of pictures run back and forth in my head. Like one of those little books where you flip the pages and your eye thinks it's seeing a motion picture. All kinds of pictures, all places and times, running together without any pattern or time sequence. West Virginia was there. And Vietnam. And the insides of a few jails. Japan, Oak Park, and Chicago. The Dorset Hotel and the Lincoln Park Zoo. Sailboats on the water, beaches and palm trees, and great heavy houses like squares of white cake. I kept seeing a close-up view of the house in the mountains where we'd hovered for an endless twenty seconds. It kept easing back, nudging me for some reason, teasing me in some soft nonspecific way, coming forward clearly, fading slowly, then rushing forward again, asking to be labeled or recognized or identified as something besides an anonymous rich house in an unfamiliar forest.

Suddenly then it locked in. As we settled down, like ammonia fumes cutting through my head, I knew that house. I knew who lived in it.

52

After we came down, Reser and I walked across the landing area and into the parking lot. Pine was waiting for us.

"How'd it go?"

"It went fine till a couple of minutes ago," Reser said. "Smooth as silk. But now I don't know."

"What does that mean?"

"He says he won't do it."

"He says what?"

"Ask him yourself," Reser said.

Pine turned to me, trying to stay even. But his neck started getting red. "What's he talking about?"

"I won't do it."

"The hell you won't. We're under the gun and we can't start over now. You're a part of this plan and the plan is going to work."

"Not with me it isn't."

"Now you listen to me—"

"No. You listen to me. What kind of a simple-minded son of a bitch do you think I am? Did you think I wouldn't guess what you're up to? I was in prison but I wasn't buried. They have newspapers, even in prison. I don't know what I thought I was bargaining for, but it sure as hell wasn't something as crazy as this. Do you think this is going to fade away after it's done? You think you're going to sweep it under a rug?"

"That's not your problem. . . ."

"The hell it's not."

159

"Every possibility has been dealt with. It's a tight plan. No loose ends."

"Bullshit. It's *all* loose ends. It's dynamite and it's gonna blow up in your face."

"You didn't think it was something easy, did you?" Reser said. "We didn't get you out of prison to mow somebody's lawn."

"I'm not talking about easy," I said. "I'm talking about crazy. This like going after Fort Knox with a can opener. It's not a question of whether you can do it. It's a question of what you do *afterward*. The world's not big enough. There aren't enough places to hide."

"I told you we have two plans," Reser said. "This one today is our second choice."

"What's the difference," I said. "Either way he ends up dead, doesn't he?"

Pine had been standing there quietly, looking at me. Now he said, "Do you think we'll let you walk away from this?"

"Let me put it this way. If I have the choice of putting a bullet in my head or jumping off a ten-story building, I'll make the jump. The odds are bad but they're better than no odds."

Pine stood there in the sun in the center of the parking lot looking at me. Finally, he smiled. "You're right. The odds are bad."

He looked off toward the entrance gate as the green Pontiac pulled in and stopped. "There's your driver," he said. "She'll take you back to Santa Monica." He turned and walked off toward the three-story building at the back of the parking lot. Reser followed a few steps behind him.

53

The driver let me off in downtown Santa Monica and I walked to the hotel from there. I was hungry. I called upstairs from the lobby to see if Thelma wanted to come down for a late lunch. There was no answer. When I went to the desk for the key I asked the clerk if he'd noticed what time my wife went out.

"No, sir, I didn't." He checked the box. "The other key's not here. Maybe she didn't come to the desk when she left."

I went up in the elevator and unlocked the door. The room was neat, the bed made up, fresh towels in the bathroom. I took a quick look around to see if she'd left a note, but I couldn't find anything.

I went back down to the coffee shop and had some lunch. Then I went upstairs again with the afternoon paper. I lay down on the bed to read it. But before I got past page three I went to sleep.

It was late afternoon when I woke up. I felt cold and cramped. I took a hot shower and put on a clean shirt. I finished reading the paper, looked at television for ten minutes, then went back downstairs to the desk.

The same clerk was still on duty. "I haven't heard anything from my wife and I'm a little worried," I said. "You haven't seen her in the lobby here, have you?"

"No, sir."

"And you're sure you didn't see her go out?"

"I'm afraid not. If she didn't drop off her key . . ."

"Yes, I know," I said. I walked over to the plate-glass window and watched the people diving and swimming in the pool outside. Then I strolled past the elevators to the bar, dark and cool, with goldfish swimming in a tank and Hawaiian music playing. I had a lousy rum drink with too much sugar in it. After ten minutes or so I went back upstairs again.

I looked in the closet and Thelma's dresses were hanging there. And a coat. Also two pairs of slacks on a pants hanger and three pairs of shoes on the floor. I looked in the chest of drawers at the foot of the bed. Neat piles of stockings, blouses, handkerchiefs, and underclothes. And a nail kit in a plastic bag.

I had supper in my room that evening. I didn't want to be away from the phone in case she called. I sat there looking at the food, pushing it around with my fork, and trying to eat it, with the television set going in front of me. Finally, I gave up on the food and started to wheel the table out to the hall. As I opened the door, two girls were standing there, young women, as if they were about to knock. One of them was tall and thick, the other was short.

"Oh, you scared me," the tall girl said.

"We were just getting ready to knock."

They stepped back so I could wheel the table through and leave it against the wall. "My name is Nan Garrity and this is my friend Sue Rimer. We're from Columbus, Ohio, out here for a vacation."

"We don't mean to be nosy," the short one said, "but we were down at the desk when you were asking about your wife. We think we saw her go out. We saw you two together when you checked in."

"Come in," I said, holding the door open. They looked at each other and the tall girl said, "Oh, no. That's all right. We're running out somewhere. We just thought . . ."

"Does your wife have a long red robe, like a house-coat?"

"Yes, she does," I said.

"Well, then it must have been her. About one-thirty this afternoon we saw her going down in the elevator. She had her robe on, and slippers, and she looked sleepy, as if she just woke up."

"Was she by herself?"

"No. There was a young man with her. Good-looking. And an older woman, with gray hair."

It all snapped into focus then. "Just a minute," I said. "Let me check and see if her robe is here." I turned and went inside, into the bathroom. She usually left her nightgown and robe on the hook behind the door. They weren't there. I hadn't expected them to be.

I went back to the two girls in the doorway. "I guess you saw someone else," I said. "Thelma's robe is right where she left it this morning."

They gave each other a look and I said, "Thanks, anyway. I have a hunch she just went to a double-feature or something." They started a kind of awkward sideways retreat toward the elevators. I smiled at them and closed the door.

I opened all the drawers in the chest at the foot of the bed. Then I checked the shelves in the closet and the floor of the closet and the cabinet underneath the sink in the bathroom. I opened our luggage and looked inside. There was only one place left to look, the deep drawers in the bedside cabinets. It wasn't on my side. I went around the foot of the bed and slid the drawer open on her side. There on its side was her purse. I knew the story now. I knew she was gone and I knew why. I had a flash of Pine's face as he said, "You're right. The odds are bad."

I went to the phone and picked up the receiver. When the operator came on it hit me suddenly that there was nobody for me to call. No capitulation number. No place to surrender.

I hung up, went into the bathroom, washed my face and hands, and came back to the phone again. I called down for the afternoon paper and a bottle of bourbon. I was surprised at how calm I was.

I understood it all now. They knew there was only one way to turn me around and they'd done it. They'd let me sweat for a few hours, then somebody would make the call, either Tagge or Pine, and I'd say, "You win. You pressed the right button. Just tell me what and where and when and I won't give you any more trouble. I promise."

The bourbon arrived, the paper, and a bucket of ice. I made myself a drink and sat down with the paper. All I had to do was sit in my room, order up food and liquor and newspapers, stay near the phone, and wait.

I waited for five days. I never left the room. After the second day I didn't take a drink. After the third day I couldn't eat. I hadn't shaved or taken a shower or changed my clothes.

I waited. Nothing else. I sat in the chair by the window, watching the light change, and listening for the phone. And at night I stayed in the chair with a blanket over me, struggling to stay awake, or partially awake, scared that I'd go to sleep and not hear the phone ring.

There was no doubt in my mind that the call would come. It had to. It was the logical next step. I told myself that a hundred times a day. And I believed it.

But the logic got weaker and thinner, the words began to lose meaning, like a singsong repeated over and over. By the fifth day I'd stopped listening for the phone.

Finally, I went to a phone booth in the lobby and called Chicago. I dialed direct to Applegate's house in Oak Park. A woman answered.

"Is this Mrs. Applegate? Rosemary?" my voice didn't sound familiar to me. It was dry and thin and cracked.

"No. Mrs. Applegate isn't here. Who is this?"

"I'm a friend of Dr. Applegate's. I'm calling long distance from California. I have to talk to him."

"I'm sorry. The doctor's out of town and so is his wife. I'm staying here with the children."

"Where is he?"

"You say you're a personal friend?"

"Yes. It's important."

"Well . . . I'm sorry but they're in Scotland."

"That's all right. I'll call him there. Where are they staying?"

"That's the problem. I don't know. If you'd called yesterday I could have told you. They were in Edinburgh. . . ."

"Where? What hotel?"

"That's what I'm saying. They left there this morning. They'll be driving through Scotland and England. I don't expect to hear from them for five or six days. . . ."

I hung up and stood there looking at the phone for a long time. Then I went up to my room for my jacket, back downstairs in the elevator, and out into the street, holding a piece of paper in my hand. With the address of the police station written on it.

It was after midnight, light traffic and nearly no one on the sidewalks. I stumbled along like a sleepwalker. The words I planned to say stopped and started and tangled together in my head:

My name is Roy Tucker. I escaped from a prison in Indiana last month. You've got to help me find my wife.

When I got to the police station, I walked past it and turned into the first bar I came to. I had a drink. Then I went into the men's room to wash my face and hands and slick my hair down with water. Now I was ready.

But when I walked out of the bar I crossed the street to a diner and had a cup of black coffee. Then I ate a doughnut and drank another cup of coffee. I sat there at the counter looking at the waitress, listening to the music, soaking it all up, trying not to think about Hobart.

I stalled and drank coffee and tried to find some other way. But there wasn't any other way and I knew it. So I got up finally, paid the check, stepped outside, and started across the street toward the police station.

Down the block a car pulled out from the curb and came toward me. I stopped in the middle of the street to let it go past, but just before it reached me it slowed down. As it rolled past I saw Thelma looking out at me from the back seat.

I ran alongside and tried to get hold of the door handle but the car speeded up, swerved, and knocked me down in the middle of the street. When I got up, the car was pulling slowly away, a hundred feet down the block.

I ran after it as it crept along the dark street. When I'd almost caught up, the car started going a little faster, staying just away from me, just out of reach. I could see other people in the car through the back window but I couldn't recognize anyone.

They played seesaw with me, keeping me running, slowing enough to let me almost catch up, then speeding away, stalling till I'd almost come even, then away again. My chest was burning, my mouth was dry, and I could feel the sweat pouring down my back. But I could see Thelma's head through the back window and I kept going, shaking and stumbling and struggling to catch up, straining to get my hands on that car door, my teeth grinding together and my breath rasping in my throat.

Finally, I couldn't run any longer. I staggered and fell and got up on shaky legs and stood there, looking at the car ahead. They sat there waiting as I walked toward them. Then the car raced suddenly down the block and turned into a dark parking lot.

Half-jogging, half-walking, I followed along behind. When I came to the parking lot, Tagge was waiting for me at the curb. I was too winded to talk. We stood there in the light from the street lamp looking at each other. Then he turned and started across the lot toward the car and I walked beside him. Another car pulled in behind us. I felt the headlights on me, and I heard the door open and close but I didn't look around.

Tagge walked to the far side of his car, the opposite door from where Thelma was sitting. He turned to me and said, "You're going to see a very happy face. I promise you that." He opened the door and said, "Go ahead."

As I leaned over to get in, the other back door opened. Thelma screamed, and a man reached in and dragged her out of the car. I felt a shove from the back and I sprawled across the seat as both doors slammed.

It was like the car that had taken me from Hobart to Chicago. The doors had no handles on the inside, the windows wouldn't open, and there was a thick slab of shatter-proof glass between the front and back seats.

As the car screeched ahead, out of the parking lot, I looked back and saw Thelma struggling between Tagge and another man who were dragging her to the other car.

I pounded on the glass and yelled at the driver till my throat was raw. But he kept his eyes straight ahead.

I sat in the back seat of the car, trying to find some way to get rid of the knot in my stomach. They'd jammed me into the tight end of the funnel and there was only one way to go. On down the cramped passage to the opening. There was no space to maneuver in, no choices.

They were right about Thelma. That was the part I couldn't handle. I could buck long odds, or hopeless odds, when I had nothing to lose but myself. I'd done that all my life, tossed my future into the pot and cut the cards. I'd won a few and lost a lot more that I'd won. And I was ready to do it again. Eager to do it. But not with Thelma. With her in the game, the bluff broke down. I couldn't play any more. They'd guessed right about that.

The car rolled along a wide boulevard, bright street lights on either side, rows of palm trees, and green lawns sloping away into the dark, with driveways curving around in front of great white houses, wide squares of flowers and shrubs in front of them.

I'd seen houses like that in Lake Forest when I worked for Riggins, great statements of prosperity and superiority, not just a place to sleep and eat but a painful, aching announcement that the people inside knew some secret that I would never know. Who *lives* there? Where do they come from? Who could put together such permanence in one lifetime? I never came close to the answers but I couldn't stop asking the questions.

This night, those houses and lawns, that quiet

snotty richness were part of what I was fighting, that easy unshakable power, that drive to preserve itself no matter how, that mixture of impotence and complacency that produces year after year, men like Tagge and Pine and Reser.

As I sat in the sealed cage of that back seat like a trapped animal, all the hot violence pulled back inside me and turned cold. Knowing I had no chance to win, I began to plan the details of my defeat.

Losing the war didn't scare me so much as I thought about winning some battles. Or at least *fighting* battles, gouging lawns, scraping paint off those smug rich houses.

As we pulled through a stone gateway and up the drive, floodlights switched on in front of the house. Pine, Henemyer, and Brookshire came out on the porch and down the steps, combed and scrubbed and well pressed, hungry eyes looking for a meal.

As they walked to the car I slumped in the seat and closed my eyes.

The engine stopped. I heard a click, releasing the door locks, and the driver got out of the front. Then the back door eased open and I heard somebody say, "What happened to him?"

"He was going crazy back there," the driver said. "Looks like he wore himself out."

"All right. Let's get him inside the house." Pine's voice.

I felt a pair of hands on me, straightening me up in the seat. "He's dead weight," a voice said. "Feels like he's out cold. Give me a hand."

Another pair of hands took hold of my legs. Between the two of them, they lifted and pulled me out of the car, one of them supporting me on either side.

Dirty fighting is like shooting ducks. You have to aim at one particular duck. If you aim at the whole flock, you'll miss them all. And if you're fighting with more than one man, you have to concentrate. One at a time. No matter what the other two or three are doing to you. They may overpower you in the end but not till you've done a lot of damage.

I started with Henemyer. He bent over in front of me to lift up my legs so they could carry me into the house. He was in perfect position. I slipped two fingers inside his nose and ripped up as hard as I could. The blood came out of his face like a fountain.

Brookshire came to life behind me then and tried to pin my arms but I slammed my head into his face and drove him back against the car. He fell half-in, half-out of the back seat and I slammed the door on his legs.

When I turned back the driver was moving in on me with a wrench and Pine was trying to avoid getting himself dirty. I caught up with him on the porch of the house, grabbed him by the wrist, spun him around, and hammered his hand against one of the pillars. I slammed it against the stone three times before the driver got himself in position behind me and put me out with the wrench.

I felt as if I was falling in sections, in slow motion, gradually down to my knees, then forward from the waist, a slow roll to the right, then down on one shoulder and over on my back, with everybody shouting from a long distance away and Pine moaning and crying about his wrecked hand. Then it all fuzzed over and went soft and black and silent.

When I woke up it was still dark outside. I was lying across a wide bed in an upstairs bedroom and a floor lamp was burning over a chair in the corner. Helen Gaddis was sitting in the chair.

As soon as I opened my eyes and sat up, she went to the door and opened it. "He's awake," she said.

I felt clearheaded and rested. There was a sore place on the back of my neck but my head didn't ache. When I stood up, though, the muscles and tendons reacted wrong, one beat too slow, a time lag between the impulse and the action. A new sense of rhythm, a feeling that I was standing to one side watching myself move, learning old actions fresh after some long time of forgetting.

I sat down slowly on the bed as Tagge and Pine and Reser came in, closing the door behind them. They stood at the foot of the bed and looked down at me. Each of them made a little speech. As if they'd rehearsed it. Tagge spoke first.

"You may feel woozy for a minute or so. Disoriented. But that will go away. You're not drugged. You're able to function in a normal way. Physically at least. We've just slowed your motor down. Some of your hardnosed instincts have been temporarily shut off. Do you understand what I'm saying?"

"Yes."

"You're going to be peaceful and agreeable for the next few hours. Otherwise perfectly normal. You feel all right, don't you?"

"Yes."

173

Tagge looked at Reser then, and Reser said, "We'll be leaving here at four in the morning, thirty minutes from now. Tagge and I will ride in the car with you, and one of us will be with you all the time till we're back here in the house. That should be not later than seven-thirty."

Reser looked at Pine. His left hand was bandaged and resting in a black sling. His face was pale and his eyes were pink and angry. But he was in tight control of himself.

"You know by now," he said, "that this is critical business. You have no choice but to do what is expected of you. Do you understand that?"

"Yes."

"If you try, in any way, to sidetrack or sabotage the work we have to do this morning, your wife will be dead in a matter of seconds. The people who are with her have clear instructions. It's very important that you understand that. Do you?"

"Yes," I said. And I did. I understood everything. I accepted everything. I felt like a child's toy, waiting to be placed on the floor, fully wound, pointed in some arbitrary direction. "I understand," I said.

When they operated on me at the field hospital near Qui Nhon, they gave me sodium pentathol as an anesthetic. They told me to count to ten backward. I got to seven before I went out. No sensation at all. No fading. No sinking. Just out. But coming conscious again was another matter. Soft lights, shifting panels of color, screens of pink smoke, yellow tides coming in and receding, dead silence, no music or wind-sounds. A glowing, warm sensation of floating. No tension or hazard. Just mindless, directionless being, an awareness of it, a feeling that the senses were keen and capable, that all was well, that no adjustments were necessary or possible.

The difference now was muscular. I felt strong and balanced, fine-tuned as an athlete. Not floating at all. Very much on the ground, sprinting between the chalk lines, hurdling ahead through white-marked lanes, accepting the route without question.

It was exactly four in the morning when we left the house and got into the car, Brookshire driving, Tagge sitting beside him, and Reser in the back seat with me, smoking a cigarette, whistling softly between his teeth. As soon as we pulled out into the street, Tagge put on a set of earphones and started adjusting the dials of a two-way radio sitting beside him on the front seat.

The streets were dark and silent. Brookshire drove carefully till we turned on to the freeway. Then he got into the fast lane, very few cars on the road, and headed east, then north, then east again.

Reser sat looking out the window saying nothing. Occasionally, Tagge murmured something into the microphone attached to his headset, but there was no other sound in the car. Just the motor and the tires on the pavement and the occasional thunder of trucks in the oncoming lanes. I rested my head against the back of the seat, closed my eyes, and shut out everything.

It was after five o'clock when we left the freeway and turned straight east on a twisting two-lane highway heading into a range of wooded mountains. The first light of morning was starting to show across the ridgetops but at road level it was still night.

We zigzagged back and forth, climbing steadily into the mountains, trees growing close to the edge of the road on both sides, no business buildings or filling stations, and only an occasional house half-hidden in the woods.

Reser looked at his watch finally and said, "We're due. Where's the turnoff?"

"About half a mile from here," Brookshire said.

"We're all right," Tagge said. "Everybody's right where they're supposed to be."

"Is the highway shut off?" Reser said.

"Tight as a cork. Five miles ahead and five miles behind us. Nothing coming through."

We turned off the road to the right then, went a mile or so through the woods on a gravel road, turned left, and climbed higher through the trees on a hard-packed dirt road. When we stopped in a grassy clearing it was twenty minutes to six, the night was breaking up around us, and a helicopter, painted white with a red cross on either side, sat there waiting, the motor going, the pilot at the controls.

While the rest of us got out of the car, Tagge stayed at the radio. Reser leaned in and said something to him, then turned and headed for the helicopter. "Come on," he said to me, "let's load up."

As we walked he said, "This isn't the chopper we had the other day. This one's smaller and faster. But the doors work the same. So nothing's changed as far as you're concerned. As soon as you're on board, strap yourself in and lock your seat in position. We'll be over the target at exactly six o'clock and we'll lift off five minutes before that. So there's no time to fuck around."

Reser put on the headphones as soon as he was inside the helicopter. He stayed up front with the pilot while I got into my seat back by the doors.

At nine minutes to six, the pilot started the blades and Reser came back to me, handing me the rifle. "It's been checked out fifty times. All you have to do is point it. Once we're over that far ridge up there, your doors will slide open and we'll drop fast. We'll try to time it so he's halfway down the path on his way to the pool. We know he'll be there. He's there like clockwork every morning. But it's tricky. He may be in the water already. Either way, it's up to you to hit him. Don't miss."

He went back to his seat and put the headphones on again. I could see him talking to the pilot but I couldn't hear what they said over the sound of the engines. Suddenly, then, Reser's voice got louder, he shouted something at the pilot, waved his hand in the direction where we'd left Tagge, and we lifted off.

I sat there, warm and loose, the rifle across my knees, my eyes on my watch. Some sense memory in my muscles and my nerves told me it was Vietnam all over again. Stumbling through the early-morning dark, gulping coffee to get awake, climbing into a gun-ship, then low-level hedgehopping over hard terrain, a rifle in your hands, straining to see, eager for a target, programed to kill anything that moved.

This wasn't the same of course. Even strung-out and drugged, I knew that. But one thing made it seem the same. I'd had no choice then and I had no choice now.

We climbed quickly, angling up and speeding forward to top the high ridge and the timber. As we came over the highest trees, out of the dark of the canyon, I saw the sun for the first time, edging up in the east. And, down below, the white house in the compound in the clearing and the bright blue square of the swimming pool down the rise from the house.

As soon as we cleared the downslope, we started to drop, a sharp angle toward the house. The door in front of me slid open and the cold mountain air hit me in the face. The next minutes seemed to pass in a count of ten.

We were at a thousand feet, dropping fast, when I saw him start down the path toward the pool. I brought the rifle up and got him in my sights, watched him grow as we moved closer and closer, a lean, rugged man with white hair and a white mustache, striding down the path in a blue-and-white striped robe, a perfect target.

He heard the engine and looked up at us, waved one hand, and kept coming, walking easy, accustomed to helicopters coming and going. Or maybe the big red cross on the side of the fuselage threw him off. Whatever the reasons, he sensed no threat. He kept walking straight ahead toward the pool.

He was more than two thirds of the way down the path when we leveled off and hovered at two hundred feet. When he looked up then he saw me, I could see his expression change in the sights, he saw the rifle, and it all came clear to him. He turned and started back up the path and I sighted on the center of his back.

Then he did a smart thing suddenly. He only had

178

one move open to him and he made it. His instinct told him that his back was a perfect target going straight up that path toward the house. He dived for the grass, rolled over once, and came up in a half-crouch, running at an angle, back toward the pool again.

I could hear Reser yelling at me from the cockpit and I could feel the fuselage swaying and adjusting as the pilot held it steady for me, but the rifle stayed solid, locked against my shoulder, trained on that blue-and-white target as he zigzagged for the pool, trying to hit the water and stay under it.

As he threw himself forward off the edge in a flat racing dive, his back centered in my sights and I squeezed off three shots.

He was dead when he hit the water, face down and floating, the robe out like wings, a dark red stain spreading around him.

I heard dogs barking then, saw half a dozen of them running toward the pool from all direction, and three men came down the path from the house as the pilot heeled over hard on the controls and we angled up to the left in a steep climb.

Just before the men got out of my sight line, I saw that one of them was carrying a rifle. As the door in front of me slid shut, the first bullet ripped through the fuselage. Then two more.

"Jesus Christ," Reser yelled at the pilot, "get this fucking thing out of range."

The pilot gunned for the top of the ridge, slewing the tail back and forth as he went to make a tough target. A couple more bullets whined through the cabin, but distance was on our side now. We were up at the ridgetop and heading across it when the last shot crashed through from underneath and slammed into the pilot's leg. It hit the artery on the inside of his thigh and blood started to spurt through the hole in his pants leg.

The helicopter lurched under us then and angled off in an uneven twisting float toward the wall of trees at the crown of the ridge.

I got out of my seat and moved forward, pulling my belt out of my pants as I went. I knelt down by the pilot and got the strap around his upper thigh, pulled it as tight as I could. His eyes were clouding over but he was still conscious. When he looked down and saw the blood had stopped, it brought him back a little.

Reser had the headphones on and was clicking away at the radio. He bent over the pilot. "Can you get us down?"

"I'll do my best. I can't guarantee where."

"You're not gonna black out, are you?"

"Not if I can help it." His breath was coming hard. It was a struggle to talk.

"All right. Hang on. You see that strip of road over there? Can you make that?"

"I can try like hell."

The pilot shook his head to clear it and angled the ship off right, toward the road. I held onto the tourniquet around his leg and Reser talked into the microphone. "We're in trouble. The pilot caught a bullet. Can you see us? Good. We can't make the clearing. We're gonna pancake out there on the road. So get the hell out there and pick us up."

He listened, then said, "Forget it. Nobody's coming through there. The compound gates are jammed and the roadblocks won't come down for another ten minutes."

He turned to the pilot. "All right. Listen to me. Just keep your eyes on that strip of concrete. We'll be down in a minute or so. Then we'll get you fixed up. Just freeze those eyes open for another minute and we've got it licked. That's it. Hang in there. Drop us down nice and easy. . . ."

We shot down, steep and sickening, along the slope of the ridge, too fast and too close. But he straightened us out and lifted to a hundred feet above the ground. We floated and dipped and limped a thousand yards across the top of the trees, the skids brushing the branches of the tallest ones, till we came to the road, still gray in the half-light.

He brought us down slowly, listing and lurching to within thirty feet of the pavement. Then his eyes rolled back white in his head, his hands fell away from the controls, and we dropped straight down.

When we hit, my head came down hard on the control panel and I bounced and rolled halfway back to the tail. I crawled forward again to the cockpit, smelling spilled fuel, shaking my head, and trying to think straight.

Reser was pulling himself up, a deep cut on one cheek, smoke was streaming into the cabin, and the pilot was sprawled on his back, blood gushing out of his leg again.

I groped around till I found the belt. I slipped it around his leg and started to tighten it again. But Reser grabbed my shoulder and pulled me away. "Come on, Tucker. Move it."

"Move it, yourself, you son of a bitch. You gonna let this guy bleed to death?"

Reser reached over my shoulder, ripped the belt out of my hands and threw it out of the cockpit on the ground. When I wheeled around I felt the muzzle of a gun pressed against my neck just under my ear.

"If you stay here, you stay dead," he said.

When I turned toward the pilot again, Reser pulled me off balance and shoved me out through the cockpit door to the ground. As I got up on my hands and knees, two cars screeched in and stopped thirty feet away. Brookshire and Tagge and Henemyer got out and ran toward us.

Reser pointed to me and said, "Get him in the car. He wants to be a hero."

They dragged me across the concrete and put me in the back seat of the car. Reser got in beside me, Tagge and Brookshire in the front seat.

Reser rolled down the window and said to Henemyer, "Put a charge in the chopper. It's going up anyway as soon as the flames hit the fuel tank but let's help it along."

As Henemyer ran toward his car, Brookshire made a tight U-turn across the road and headed back toward Los Angeles. We'd gone less than a mile when I heard the explosion behind us.

Tagge turned in his seat and said to Reser, "What do you think?" "I think we're all right," Reser said. "I think we're pretty good."

Two miles down the road we pulled off into an abandoned gravel pit. A blue panel truck was waiting there, a young black man driving it. On the side of the truck it said: "Imperial Dry Clearning."

We got out of our car and into the back of the truck, sitting on cushions between the racks of dresses and suits. Brookshire got in behind the wheel, drove on down the main road for half a mile, then turned right on a rough road through the trees and ridges. We bumped and skidded along for forty-five minutes. When we left that road we were on the freeway, cars speeding past on both sides of us.

Whatever they'd shot into me was wearing off now. The bump on my head was throbbing and I felt sick to my stomach, sick from what I'd seen, and sick from what I'd done. I told myself there was no way I could have avoided it and I knew that was true. Still, some part of me had trouble believing it.

When we got back to the house, Pine came out to meet us in the driveway.

"What's the word from the compound?" Reser said.

Pine looked at me. "What about him?" he said to Tagge.

"Never mind him, for Christ's sake. What's the report?"

"Jay checked in at ten after six. He was dead when they pulled him out of the pool."

"Has there been an announcement yet?"

"No details. They're hedging. Something about an accident in the pool. But everybody knows something's up. The radio's giving a bulletin every five minutes and the television stations got on it full steam half an hour ago. The CBS guy already said there's a rumor he's dead. They can't keep the lid on much longer."

"Let's take a look," Reser said. He started toward the house, Pine alongside him, Tagge and I coming behind.

As soon as we were inside the door I said, "What about my wife?" Pine looked at me as if he didn't see me, turned to Reser, and said, "Down the hall in the billiard room. We've got three television sets and all the radios plugged in."

I stepped in front of Pine as he started to walk away. "Never mind your fucking television sets. Where's my wife?"

"It's all right," Tagge said. "She'll meet you at the airport. Your plane's scheduled to leave—"

"Stop kissing his ass, Marvin," Pine said. He turned

to me. "Don't push your luck, Tucker. You're on shaky ground. If you take my advice, you'll—"

"I don't want your God-damned advice. I want my wife. And I want her now."

"Don't tell *me* what you want," he said. "Or you'll get something you don't want at all."

"Take it easy, Ross," Reser said.

"I don't want to take it easy. This son of a bitch wrecked my hand. Now he's trying to tell me what—"

I reached out, grabbed him by the hair and twisted. Then I pulled him through the doorway to one of the reception rooms just off the hall. I picked up a glass decanter and broke it over the back of a chair.

Still holding him by the hair I spun him around and set him down in a straight chair on the far side of the room. I stood behind him, my shoulders against the wall, pulled his head back with one hand and held the jagged neck of the broken decanter against his throat. Tagge and Reser were standing ten feet in front of us, stiff and silent.

"I'm gonna stay here like this till I see my wife walk in the front door." I pressed the glass against his skin and a thin stream of blood trickled down over his collar. "And every five minutes I'm going to put another slice in his neck. If she's not here in half an hour, I'll cut his throat."

"Jesus Christ," Reser said.

There was a tall clock in the hallway just across from where I was standing. It took them twenty-three minutes to get her there. I didn't want her to see me holding Pine like that, with blood soaking the front of his shirt. But there was no other way to handle it.

As soon as Gaddis brought her through the door, I said to Tagge, "What about our plane?"

Thelma stood there staring at me from across the room.

"It's ready whenever you are," Tagge said.

"Where?"

"Burbank. Out in the valley."

I still had a grip on Pine. "All right. I want to go now. And I want you to drive us," I said to Tagge. "In a regular car. Not that meat wagon with doors that won't open."

Thelma didn't say anything. When I looked at her, she looked away.

Tagge took her out to the car and I followed them, taking Pine with me. Reser and Gaddis and Brookshire stood there watching us.

Thelma got into the back seat. Just before I got in front with Tagge I gave Pine a shove. He sat down hard in a flower bed beside the driveway. I got into the car, rolled down the window, and watched him getting up, touching his throat, staring at the blood on his fingers. He looked at me then, half-disbelief and half-hatred. His lips started to move but no sound came out.

As the car pulled out of the driveway I looked around at Thelma. Her face was pale and her eyes were red as if she'd been crying. And she looked at me as if she'd never seen me before. I turned back to the front and kept my eyes on the road ahead. All along the way, all the way to the airport, I saw flags being lowered to half-mast. And police cars racing by with their sirens screaming.

When we got there, Tagge drove through the parking lot, past the main terminal, and on down to the far end. He found a parking space against the fence, just beyond a long aluminum hangar. Straight ahead, a hundred yards out on the apron, I saw the jet that had brought us up from Costa Rica.

"He's ready," Tagge said.

"The sooner the better," I said.

"It's going to be a long trip on an empty stomach. If I were you I'd get some sandwiches from that wagon over there." He pointed down the drive, where a man in a truck was handing out sandwiches and doughnuts and coffee to a line of workmen moving in and out of the hangar.

"I'll be back in a minute," Thelma said. "I'll get some stuff for us to eat." She got out of the back seat, I handed her some money through the window, and she walked off toward the meal truck.

Tagge and I sat there for a minute without saying anything. Finally, I said, "I want to ask you a question."

"Go ahead. But you may not get an answer."

"I want to know if it's over."

He gave me a long look. Then he took out a cigarette and lit it. Finally, he said, "You want the truth?" I nodded my head and he said, "The truth is I don't know." He took a long drag off his cigarette. "The only kind of operation I ever feel good about is a one-man thing. The more people there are, the more chance there is for a screw-up. The bigger the stink, the more there is to cover up. And the man who worries most is the man who gave the original orders. He always has the most to lose. If he panics, the dominoes start to fall."

"How does that affect me?"

"I'm not sure it does. But it might. Let's put it this way. If I were you and I had a notion to disappear, in Brazil for example, I think maybe I'd do it."

"Without a passport?"

He smiled and said, "That was dirty pool, wasn't it?" He looked toward the lunch wagon. "Here comes your wife." She was walking slowly, balancing three containers of coffee on a package the size of a shoe box. "I'll tell you what I'll do," he said. "I promise you'll have passports by noon tomorrow, delivered to your house."

"One other question," I said. "Why'd you pick me?"

"You fit all the requirements. You were in prison for murder, you're a good shot, and you know how to give injections."

"What's that have to do with it?"

"We had two plans. One was the helicopter thing. The other one was to do it in the hospital. But we couldn't get him to go in."

Tagge walked out to the plane with us, then he went back and stood in front of the hangar to watch us take off. I could see him through the window as the plane taxied to a take-off position. He stood there, shading his eyes with one hand, his hair blowing in the wind.

I glanced over toward the parking lot and saw his car parked against the fence, around the hangar corner from where Tagge was standing, out of his line of vision. There was a man in coveralls by the car, carrying a toolbox in his hand. Just standing there.

I ran up the aisle of the plane and pounded on the

door of the cockpit. "Hold it," I yelled. "Don't take off yet. I have to talk to Tagge again." I pounded on the door and tried to open it. It was locked. I ran back to my seat and looked out the window again.

"What's the matter?" Thelma said. "What are you looking at?"

"Nothing. Go sit on the other side."

"What's the matter with you?"

"Nothing's the matter with me. Just do what I tell you." I felt the plane shudder as the engines got more power. "Go on, damn it. Fasten your seat belt. We're about to take off."

She got up without a word, went up the aisle, and buckled herself into a seat. I pressed my face against the window just as the man in coveralls opened the back door of Tagge's car, put his tool case in the back seat, and strolled away. A car rolled up beside him, he got in, and it turned toward the parking-lot exit.

I ran to the cockpit door again and hammered on it. "Stop it, damn it. I have to get off." The plane started to roll forward. "Turn off your engine, you son of a bitch." Through the door I heard the pilot's voice, muffled, "Sit down, buddy. We're taking off."

I ran back to my seat and looked out the window again. The hangar was slipping behind us. I couldn't see the car. Just before we lifted off I saw Tagge turn and walk toward the parking lot.

As soon as he had altitude the pilot banked and came around, back across the airfield heading south. I moved to the other side of the plane so I could see the hangar and the parking lot. Far down below I saw Tagge. He'd stopped at the fence to watch the plane climb. Now he turned, went into the parking lot, and got into his car. I changed seats quickly so I could still see the car, getting smaller and smaller as we climbed.

Just before the ground disappeared under the cloud cover, I saw a burst of orange and black, flame and smoke. From that distance it looked like the striking of a kitchen match in a dark room.

I sat there looking out the window for a long time. My body felt heavy and solid, attached to the seat. My eyes were dry and hot in their sockets and the skin on my forehead felt shrunken. Finally, two hours after, the pilot's voice on the speaker: "We're over Mexico now." I got up and went forward to where Thelma was sitting.

"You got a sandwich?"

She reached for the box on the floor under her seat. "There's ham and cheese or salami and cheese."

"I'll take the ham and cheese."

She handed it to me, wrapped in wax paper, and I said, "How about you? You're not hungry?"

"I had something before."

I sat beside her and ate the sandwich. Then I went back to the rest room, washed my face and hands, and drank a cup of water. When I sat down beside her again I said, "I'm sorry I yelled at you back there."

"It doesn't matter."

"It's nothing to stay mad about."

"I'm not mad," she said.

"What do you call it then?"

"I'm scared."

"What are you scared of?"

"I don't know."

"There's nothing to be scared of," I said.

"Oh, Roy . . . For God's sake. I'm not two years old. I've got eyes and ears. Do you think I went to sleep for a week, like a fairy tale or something?"

"Well . . . the best thing is to forget it. It's all over now."

"No, it's not. And you *know* it's not."

"It is as far as *I'm* concerned."

"You didn't ask where they were keeping me or if they treated me all right. You didn't say anything. I come back and you're standing there with a piece of glass at somebody's neck, blood all over his shirt, and you don't even say anything about *that*." She turned toward me in the seat. "You think it's better for me if I don't know anything. But it's not. I guarantee you it's not. Nothing could be worse than the things I make up in my head."

"Then don't do it."

"How can I help it? Don't you think I guessed there was something awful going on back there? I could feel her eyes on me, waiting for an answer. But I didn't have one.

She settled straight in her seat again. When I looked at her she was staring out the window.

Finally, I said, "This isn't something to fight about between you and me. I don't keep things to myself because it makes me feel good. I just don't see any reason to rub your nose in it."

"But it won't work that way. That's not the way it works."

"To me, it is. I've been in trouble all my life. I'm used to it. It follows me around. But that's no reason you have to get used to it."

"But I *am* used to it. I *know* you. I *know* what you're like. And it doesn't matter. What matters is you can't be *with* somebody and be by yourself at the same time. I want things to be the way they *are*, no matter *what* they are. But you make me *pretend* all the time."

"I'm not making you pretend anything."

"Yes, you are. You did it before and you're doing it now. Do you think I *believed* that story about somebody getting you out of jail because they thought you got a bad deal and deserved a new trial? I never believed it for a minute. I knew it was a lie but I didn't care. If I could see you and be with you I could pretend to believe anything." She turned toward me again. "Do you think I believed that whole story in Indianapolis? At the trial? Well, I didn't. No more than the jury did. But I pretended to because I knew that was what you wanted. You didn't care what the jury thought as long as *I* thought you were innocent. Isn't that right?"

"I guess so. What's wrong with that? I don't see anything wrong with it."

"I know you don't. That's the trouble. That's what makes me feel funny. I know you want to keep things away from me. You think it's some kind of protection, I guess. But you can't protect me from *you.* I don't *need* that. And I don't *want* it." I could feel her eyes on me. When I turned to look at her she said, "I *know* you killed Riggins. I faced up to that a long time ago. And I *know* there was something rotten going on back there in Los Angeles. Something you were mixed up in. I can swallow that too. What I can't handle is you being two separate people all the time."

I knew she was waiting for me to say something. She looked at me for a long time, a very long time. Then I felt her body turn square in the seat. When I looked at her she was staring out the window again.

We sat there like mutes for the rest of the trip. Finally, just before we landed at Puntarenas she said, "I lied to you before. About not being with a man. It was that friend of Fay and her husband's, the one I said was after me. I didn't want to and I felt terrible

192

about it afterward but I did it anyway. More than once."

I looked at her then but she was still looking out the window. I said, "It doesn't matter. It's all right."

"No, it's not," she said. "Nothing's all right."

As soon as we got to our house outside Juapála, I got in the car and drove back into Puntarenas. I caught Captain Ruiz in the hallway as he was leaving his office for the day.

"What about my passport?" I said. "Can I get it from you now?"

"I wish you could." He took my arm. "Come. Walk with me to my car." We passed the elevators and went down the stairs. "This is a big embarrassment to me. There was some occurrence in the central office in San José. A fire perhaps. And in the confusion, a packet of papers and passports was lost or destroyed."

We came out into the sunshine and walked to his Mercedes. "Fortunately for you, it's no problem. Just a visit to the U.S. consul here in Puntarenas. They contact Washington, and a duplicate passport will be issued to you at once. Ask them to call my office if there's any question about the loss." He slid in under the wheel of his car. "A simple note to Washington. That's all you need."

I stood there on the curb watching him drive away. Then I walked to the consul's office and reported the loss of my passport. I knew when I did it, it was hopeless. But I had to try. Five days later, I had a letter from the consul. I put it in my pocket and read it later on the beach.

Dear Mr. Waldron:

Re your lost passport, No. 1147261: A confusing

reply to our letter to Washington. A Mr. Harry Waldron of Norman, Oklahoma, same passport number as above, reported his passport stolen six months ago. A new passport with a new number was then issued to him. Harry Waldron, as you know, is a common name. This undoubtedly is the reason for the error. We will query Washington again and let you know their answer.

I tore the note into a handful of tiny pieces as I walked along the edge of the water. Then I tossed them in the air like confetti and watched the onshore breeze scatter them through the trees at the back of the beach. In some angular, perverse way I felt relieved. I didn't have to struggle any more. I didn't have to choose. There weren't any choices left.

63

They're closing the ring on me now. Everything on schedule. Ten days ago they sent me a clipping from a newspaper in Alberta. The story said an escaped convict named Roy Tucker had been shot to death by the police. "Resisting arrest" they called it.

Two days later, Reser dropped in on us. He stayed for an hour or so. He had a drink, strolled around the house looking everything over, then left about four-thirty for the drive to San José. Had to catch the nine-o'clock flight to Miami, he said.

Early the next morning, Thelma walked into the village to the vegetable market. On her way home, two hundred yards down the hill from our house, a car skidded across the road, slammed her against a wall, and kept on going. Two men working at the roadside saw the accident but they couldn't describe the car.

They called me as soon as they brought her to the hospital, but she was dead when I got there. Two days later, I buried her on the hill at the back of the house.

Next time I went to the bank in Puntarenas, they told me there was no money in my account. The man who had arranged the deposit in the first place, they said, had drawn the money out. That afternoon, before I went home, I bought a rifle and a box of shells.

The next day, late in the morning, a car pulled into the driveway. Pine and Brookshire got out. When they came around the side of the house and up the stairs to the sundeck I shot them. I put them back in their car, drove it two miles down the coast to the sea cliffs, released the brake, and rolled it over. It hit the water, sucked under, and stayed under.

I walked home by another road. When I got there, the tires on my car were slashed and the wires on the motor were torn loose. I went down to the village then and spent all the money I had left for food and cartridges.

That evening, I sat down at the kitchen table and started writing out everything that had happened since that first day in Ditcher's office. I put it all down, as much as I could remember, and mailed it off to Applegate. Maybe he'll know what to do with it. Or maybe he won't do anything. Either way it can't help me. Not now. All I can do is sit here. And wait to see who shows up next.

About the Author

ADAM KENNEDY has been a professional painter, actor, and screenwriter. A native of Indiana, he has lived in Paris and New York and is currently living in Beverly Hills. Mr. Kennedy's earlier novels include *The Killing Season* and *Maggie D.*

More Big Bestsellers from SIGNET